THE SAVIOUR'S EMPIRE

by
PD Stewart

a World of Melarandra Novel

ISBN 978-1544730486

First Edition Printing

FIC00900 Fiction/Fantasy/General

For More Information Visit PD Stewart's Official Website at:
www.melarandra.com

World of Melarandra Series

Children of the Sun and Moon
Cavern of the Heavens
Shard of the Fallen Goddess
The Saviour's Empire
The Staff of Mordenren

Stories of Melarandra

Malena - A Novella

Order of Maget Trilogy

Creation

I dedicate this book to my cats.

Thank you Ninja, Oliver, and the late Alley. Without your help, I may not have needed to rush, or push so hard at the end, to get this out. I feel the hair on my laptop keyboard will never come out.

PROLOGUE

Aremeth stood in stunned silence. The sight before him, tore at his heart. Every fibre of his being wished to unleash a terrible scream in anguish, but he held his tongue. Those who did this may still be about. Aremeth's eyes darted from side to side as he walked, checking every dark recess. The same sight greeted him. All the livestock lay slaughtered in their pens, and every man, woman, and child were missing. No blood, no signs of fighting, nothing showed the villagers had fought back. The idea worried him.

They were Jacenites. Referred to as Sawa from outsiders. Horse masters, expert fighters, and followers of the wandering god known as Jacen. The simple fact that not one sword was raised to defend his home confused him. Aremeth moved with careful steps, making certain not to miss a thing. When he arrived at the corral, he was not surprised to see all the horses gone. Taken along with his people. Many coveted what this village had, but none had ever attacked with success. Their horses were a special breed, given to them by their god. Nothing frightened them, nor could anyone outside of this village speak to them. Aremeth wondered if that is why all the villagers were gone.

Continuing to walk, his steps were no longer careful. It was clear now that this attack had happened a few days ago, and no one had stayed behind. After examining all areas of the village, Aremeth made his way to the worship house. Here he found the door smashed open, and the scent of decay. Only one person lived within, Korigen, keeper of the holy position as head of the clan. Walking in, Aremeth's heart fell, and his soul felt a crushing blow he felt would never heal. Tears came, and he allowed them to fall. Tied to a post, clearly beaten, and quite dead, was Korigen. Dark hair clung to bloody skin on his face which was barely recognizable. Parts of his flesh were cut away, and the sight caused Aremeth to drop to his knees and scream with rage and anguish.

"I will find those who did this, old friend," he hissed, making certain to embed the sight in his mind. "I don't care if I have to fight the Saviour's entire army in order to bring your soul peace, I will do it." Aremeth stood, kissed his hand, and placed it on Korigen's forehead. "I give my vow."

After saying a silent prayer to Jacen, Aremeth went out and headed to his home. In a secret hiding place, he found his father's sword. Most of the food was rotten, so Aremeth gathered up what dried meat he could find, filled his waterskin, and headed south. It had become clear only one group could have pulled this off. Over the last year, this Saviour person had been attacking all the villages along the shores of the Myran Ocean, taking those they could, and forcing them to become part of her army. It was about time he introduced himself to the land's new ruler.

CHAPTER ONE

Leaning against the railing, looking at the sunrise glistening off the sea, Arket Tzam marvelled at what lay before him. A soft breeze came off the light blue-green water, and the smell of fresh, salty air wafted up to the balcony. The breeze felt good on his bald head, which he rubbed absently. Outside the ramparts, the army marched. Training each day for what lay ahead. Almost six months had elapsed since he was brought to this place, and Arket was still shocked with all which had happened. Below, the city was beginning to wake, and although he and Brin ruled with a heavy hand, it was with much more compassion than it had been with the once-gods.

Arket turned his eyes into the bedchamber, and to his wife, his salvation. Brin's black hair could be seen draped over her pillow. If she hadn't saved him that day in Jijitsa… Arket let the thought pass. He was strong, but she had proven to be far stronger. At first Arket fought the idea of being led by a female, but it only took one day to see why she was ruler of these lands. Brin had bested two gods and ruled a city almost as large as his lands had been. All here worshipped her, and if Arket wanted to survive, he would have to join with her. Brin's proposition of marriage unnerved him, but in the end, Arket went along with it. Now, he relished in the power she possessed, and in his own way, truly loved her.

Arket's gaze travelled back to the sea, then to the city below, as he walked along the balcony, listening. Soon the hall would be full of worshippers, as it always was on the third day. This day all would come to bask in the glory that was the Saviour. The empress and her emperor. The populace wasn't aware, but their constant devotions fed the two rulers. The chanting and love which flowed from the people, gave the two an unusual strength.

Bringing his thoughts back to the fateful day, Arket reflected on the memory. Mostly to the strange light which had almost destroyed him. Hope was what Brin had called it. Something as simple as hope nearly ended his life. Hope had moved through the Temple City but had a different effect than it had in the past. The city dwellers knew the two once-gods were no more, they had sensed the change. To them, the Saviour had proven who she truly was, and hope flowed through the city, as it never had before. Instead of the people realising they deserved more, they became devoted to Brin in a manner which could never be broken. Arket made his way back to the open door and moved into the room. Brin would be waking soon, and they had much to do before the devotion began.

On the third day, the entire city would come to the hall. Today was no different. Not one person dared to miss this day of worship. This day was the only time the city dwellers could show their gratitude to the Saviour. Worship only went for an hour. Brin would say a few words, and the hall would erupt in prayer. All she and Arket had to do was listen, and nod approvingly. Today, however, Brin had a treat in store. When all had taken their seats, a hush ran through the room. Arket always wondered how it was so many people could induce such a quiet.

Brin moved forward, her eyes scanning the crowd. "My people, usually I stand here and say a few words of kindness. Words to express how much I love you all and enjoy being your Saviour. Today, however, I am changing this," Brin paused and looked to as many faces as she could. Most showed confusion. "Today, I bring you tidings. I have come to a decision regarding these lands." Another pause, although this time it was more for dramatic effect than to see their responses. "I have decided to rename the South Lands. From this day forward, they will be known as Kaijitsa Mur: The Saviour's Empire."

The silence lasted for merely a breath before a chant of 'long live the Saviour' rolled through the room. This was followed by shouts and cheers of joy. The sound was deafening, and although it didn't last more than a few minutes, Arket had wondered if the entire temple was going to collapse. Not long after the cheers died down, the prayers began. The two took to their thrones and listened.

A bell rang out, announcing the worship hour had passed. Many would stay and continue to pray to their Saviour, but Brin and Arket always left. There was only so much whining Brin could take, and some days she found it difficult to maintain her smile. Truth be told, she would have preferred them to fear her. Arket pointed out to her many times how it was more beneficial to their rule, having the people want to do her bidding. Much more was being achieved by a blind following than he had ever attained by brute force. Brin reluctantly agreed.

Back in their rooms, which was the sole spot in the castle they could enjoy peace and tranquillity, the two were seated on the balcony, sipping wine. Brin knew Arket wished to bring something up but wasn't certain how. He was preoccupied and rubbing his head often. Something which was very out of character for the strong man.

"Beloved," he began, and Brin sipped her wine waiting for him to continue. "Do you think it wise to move against the lands to the north? You have troops spread out across the desert, ships traversing the sea to the south, and creatures roaming about to protect us. We could easily take less protected areas to start, instead of a full out war. Could you not settle for small pieces of land?"

Holding her goblet tight, Brin stared at Arket, and in an instant, he regretted his words. Brin's face had gone dark, her blue eyes becoming cold, and flashing a dangerous gaze upon him. For a moment, Arket wondered if he was long for this world.

"I will settle for nothing less than the destruction of the Central Lands. Every living being will either bow to me or die in agony." Brin's lips curled into a sneer as she growled the words. "And I look forward to putting each of my family members head on a pike."

Arket sat in stunned silence. He knew of Brin's hatred towards her kin. In her mind, they had forsaken her. Allowing her to live with the Order, instead of coming and bringing her home. It was their fault she was stranded in these lands. Arket had never heard her speak with such venom. There was nothing he could say that would calm her at this time, so instead he poured them each more wine, sat back, and kept his gaze out over the sea, making a mental note to never again question her motives.

Late that evening, when Arket had already retired, Brin went to her study. In this land a study didn't exist. Once-gods did not need such places, so Brin had an area converted to become one. It was a place she could go to and get away from everything. Only a small window graced the room, which she enjoyed. It allowed her to forget where she was for a moment.

This night she was there to open the secret wall compartment she created. Inside sat the figurines containing the once-gods. Dark magic surrounded the items, and it always drew Brin in. The powerful magic the two possessed always intoxicated her. Deep down she knew that kind of power would never be hers, however, Brin still coveted it. Perhaps one day the gods would grant her the gift of unwavering magic. Until then, she would keep practicing so that her body would be able to recover after. Brin knew there was a good chance magic would be used quite a bit in the coming war, and she needed to be ready for it.

Closing the door, Brin went back to her chambers. There was still much planning to do, and she needed everything to go off perfectly.

CHAPTER TWO

Morning came, and it was a quiet time the empress and emperor appreciated. A slight mist clung to the edges of the city. From their balcony, Brin and Arket gazed down at the city below. A fog had rolled in, and was now receding, leaving behind the mist. With the sun just beginning to move above the horizon, the city looked as if it was ruled by the dead. The sight caused Brin to smile. Their subjects wouldn't notice, for the mist was usually gone by the time the city was moving about, but this was a time of day that she and Arket enjoyed.

The sun crept higher into the sky, and the slight red it gave off was absorbed by the fading mist. It was strange to see, as it appeared to resemble a cloud of blood, slowly leaving the city. Arket always took the mornings like this as a good omen. Somewhere, blood was being spilled. Blood of their enemies. Brin was of the same frame of mind. Perhaps some scouts had ventured into their land and met some of the creatures which guarded the sands around the city. Brin's smile turned into a dark grin, and she relished in the idea that her creatures had taken victims. Both their hearts were dark, and minds were on the destruction of their foes. It was always an arousing experience, and it wasn't long before they were back in their bedchamber.

The sun flowed through the window, signalling the time to awaken and greet the commanders. Brin was usually present at all meetings, but today wished to venture outside the city wall, and see how the newly acquired assets were doing. Arket, followed by Boroten, moved towards the war hall. Most palaces this size would have a ballroom for gala events, and other such nonsense. There were no nobility, not in the sense Brin was raised with, in the Temple City, so such things were not necessary. Instead, the room which would have been used this way became their headquarters. Here there were many tables, each one covered with parchment. Ideas for attacks, where, when, and maps strewn about. It was an organized mess, and only their generals, whose names they never recalled, the Elite Guard, Brin, and Arket, were allowed to enter. Not even a servant was seen inside.

Arket made his way to the head of the table and sat down. Many notes from the generals on what was occurring sat in front of him. Most were basic reports on how the soldiers were coming along. Some were of the lazzards, and their unusual customs. Lazzards were unusual lizard like creatures, with the intelligence of a human. Months ago, they had come to Brin, offering their services. She had no idea why they had come but accepted the offer. They loved the sand and heat and were perfect for their army. The soldiers training near the lazzards always felt unnerved. Strange noises came from the lazzard camp, almost every night, making it difficult for most to fall asleep. Arket had no idea what the unusual creatures were doing, and never asked. Brin had brought them in, so she dealt with all issues pertaining to the lazzards. One parchment caught his attention.

The lands to the north were indeed sending scouts, and they were coming further in than they should be able to. Magic wards set up were being triggered, and the idea bothered the emperor. Arket wouldn't bring the problem up to Brin. Her confidence in her creatures was all encompassing. Not for a minute would she think the enemy was wandering so far into their realm. Handing off orders, Arket went back to reading the reports. It was clear everyone was coming along perfectly and would be ready for an attack at any time. Arket sat back and stroked his chin. Yes, the soldiers were ready, but was Brin?

Brin made her way outside through a door in the back of the palace. Only magic could open it, her magic, so she never worried about anyone getting inside. This back area was where the captives were held. People who refused to join her army or follow her rule. It resembled a large pen. Small dwellings lined the outer edge, and a wall of stakes, filled with nails which were poisoned, kept the people inside. These current people bothered Brin. They all had the same dark hair, and most with dark eyes. It was as if you were looking into the same soul. The Sawa were also giving her more trouble than she had thought they would. Dedicated to their god, they refused to give their tribe its own name, preferring to be called Jacenites. Sawa was the name given to them by others. The attack on their village had been executed by the lazzards. Not a drop of blood had been spilled, save their leader. The lazzards had insisted on making an example of one, to ensure the Sawa followed without trouble.

Glares greeted her as she walked along the fencing. All eyes were on her, but Brin didn't care. Some prisoners were being whipped, and not a sound came from their lips. For hours, she roamed about the outside of the fence. Nothing out of the ordinary was happening, so she moved towards the training soldiers. Keeping her distance, and cloak hood drawn tight, she observed the sword play. The men were scarcely clothed and dripped with sweat. The sight excited Brin, for it was clear to her, the soldiers were almost ready to go to war. The sun was blazing in the sky, and they continued to fight until their strength was gone. Much time passed, and Brin was impressed by what she saw. Heading back to the Sawa pen, Brin noticed they were staring to the south. The setting sun brought a slight breeze, which kicked up some sand. Raising their arms, and chanting, sand blowing into their faces, the Sawa chanted in prayer. Shaking her head at the odd villagers, Brin turned and headed back to the door. For some reason, she had the urge to wander about the city.

Hood drawn, to keep the last bits of sun out of her face, Brin moved onto the streets. Most of her people would be home now. The night always brought something dangerous out in the past, so it was their custom to stay indoors once the sun went down. The cooling air felt wonderful on her face, and she inhaled the night air. A call came to her ears. One which held a voice she didn't recognize but knew it all the same. Turning her head about, Brin felt the direction the call had come, and moved towards it. Each step causing her to wonder what was in store for her this night.

Gazing into the darkness, Brin scowled. Something had called her to the edge of the city, and it was bothering her. The waves crashed softly against the rocks down from where she stood. The moon was only a sliver and didn't give off much light. Brin wasn't scared, for as far as she was concerned, nothing could harm her, but she was intrigued. A shuffle in the shadows caused her to tense in anticipation. It was clear the person hidden within wanted her to know they were there, so she waited.

"Are you going to speak or am I here for entertainment only?" yelled Brin into the shadows.

A chuckle came back. "Most would be afraid of what lay within the shadows. I had heard you were a strong witch, but when I sent the silent call, I was amazed at the strength of the wards placed around this city."

The figure moved, and Brin was slightly shocked to see a man standing before her. "Who are you?"

"My name is Fox. I am a Shadow of Ruineh," he replied with a slight bow.

Confusion crossed Brin's face. "And what is a Shadow of Ruineh?"

Again, Fox chuckled. "I forgot, you're from the Central Lands, and have most likely never been taught of Ruineh; the God of Assassins."

For a moment, Brin felt the need to call her magic up, but hesitated. Clearly, this man could have killed her already if that was his goal. "What brings you here?" She queried, intrigued more by his presence.

Fox moved closer, and sat down on a large boulder. "The leader of my order has learned of many changes happening with the world. I was sent to scout and see if you were going to be a threat. Also, to see if you were going to need our services."

Brin laughed, and it was cold. "I have no need for assassins. My goal is to humiliate, and conquer, those who have wronged me. A quick death is too good for them."

Fox turned his gaze up. "Perhaps then, you might need spies? My order is many, milady. Trade has already begun between your old home, and the Realm of Lungast. It would be quite easy to have people slip in."

Brin paced, then stopped and looked back at Fox. "Actually, that would be useful. Could you get someone into each royal household? To know the plans of those who would move against me would be worth quite a lot."

Fox grinned, but there was no warmth behind it. "It shall be done."

The man stood, bowed once again, and then disappeared into the shadows. Brin stared at the spot he left for some time before leaving. Fox hadn't made a sound. There were rocks, gravel and other bits of things scattered about the area, and not a single noise had reached her ears. Fox could be trusted as long as she was paying well. Should a better offer arise, she knew her life could be in danger. By the time she was back in the palace, any negative thoughts were gone. Soon, she would have information on the preparations her father, and the other kingdom, were making. Soon, the lands would belong to her.

CHAPTER THREE

Using the thick brush as cover, Aremeth crouched, staring at the strange man across the river. On many occasions during the last few months, unusual boot prints could be found along the river's edge. Once, they had crossed the bridge, and come close to the village, but never ventured in. Scouts were sent out, and it was determined the man was no threat. It was more likely he was curious as to his neighbours. The tracks had moved south to a lusher land, and it was here the man made his home. Not all accepted that a giant man was not a foe, but their way was not to incite a conflict if it wasn't necessary.

Aremeth was awed by the man. He was huge, with blonde hair, and it was clear he was quite comfortable living alone in the wilderness. Aremeth was average for his people, standing at six feet. This man towered over him. Where Aremeth's people were all dark haired and eyed, this man's blonde hair was an off white which reminded Aremeth of what an old man might grow. The man may be aged, Aremeth was not able to tell, however, he was still quite agile and able. Having built himself a small shack, nestled in a clearing. This was one of the only areas lush with vegetation. The rest was either thin trees, or sand. Movement brought Aremeth back to his gazing, and he noticed the man had filled his water buckets and was moving back towards his home.

"You can sit there and watch or help me carry these back. Choice is yours," shouted the man.

Aremeth smiled. Of course, he had known Aremeth was there. Moving from his hiding spot, Aremeth stood on the bank across from the man. "My name is Aremeth. What makes you think I'm not here to harm you?"

"Names Firadon Dey. If you meant me harm, you would have done it months ago," was the reply.

The river at this spot wasn't very deep, so Aremeth waded across to stand next to Firadon. "You aren't from these parts," he commented.

Firadon handed him a bucket. "Nope. Far north, in an area you've probably never heard of."

"What brought you to this land?" asked Aremeth.

Firadon began walking and motioned the man to follow. "I don't like to stay too long in one place. Makes it easier for enemies to find you. Thought going south would give me a fresh start, in a land where no one

knows me."
"You have much in common with my people. We were once roamers. Wandering the land, making camp where it was best at different times of the year. Only in the past century have we settled in one spot. Other tribes still wander the lands, but our god wished one to stay stationary. We obliged," said Aremeth.
Firadon stopped and looked at the man. "I thought from your dwellings, that you were not ones to stay in one place, but then you didn't leave, so I wondered if I had been wrong. Good to know I still have my smarts about me."
Aremeth let out a laugh. "How are you finding this area? It was once full of game, but not so much of late. I think the new empress, known as the Saviour, is responsible."
Firadon continued walking. "Yes, many men, and odd creatures have been about the area. Not sure what they are up to, but it didn't feel good."

Silence followed until the two made it to Firadon's dwelling. "May I ask why you're going south?"
Aremeth put down the bucket. "My entire village has been taken. Most likely to train horses for the army. I was out on patrol, checking on the dragons, when it happened."
Firadon put his bucket down, and offered Aremeth a cup. Both men scooped up some of the water. "A large caravan was moving across the sands some three days back. Perhaps it carried your people. It certainly had your horses. I must say, they are impressive beasts."
Aremeth laughed again. "Spent some time with them, have you? They are only dangerous if they're given a command."
"Is it your plan to go and infiltrate the Temple City? I hear the emperor and empress have the best protection. What do you wish to accomplish?" Firadon hadn't meant for it to come out so bluntly, but he was never very good at beating around the bush.
"I hope to scout the city, and perhaps find my people," Aremeth responded, his voice cold.
Firadon scooped another cup, and drank deep. "Well, I think you will probably be needing some help. I was once a fairly good tracker. Maybe I can help you follow the tracks to where they took your people."
Aremeth nodded. "I think I could use a companion on this trek. I'm not sure what to expect."
Firadon chuckled. "I've been in a few battles and can handle many

situations. Don't worry, Aremeth my new friend, we will find your people."

Aremeth smiled, scooped some water, and raised his glass to Firadon. "To our adventure."

Taking the buckets the two filled the waterskins they had, leaving some out for them to drink. They spent the rest of the day securing Firadon's home and packing supplies, leaving out enough for them to have supper. With the heat Firadon was getting used to eating dried meat, cheese, and bread. The nights could get cool, which allowed him to whip up a stew from time to time. Tonight, they were dining on the latter.

There was no telling what the trek was going to hold, and it was most likely that they would be dining when they were able to. After eating, they discussed their next move. Both decided that leaving at dawn was their best course of action. A good night's sleep never harmed anyone.

CHAPTER FOUR

The King's Own finally sat moored at the main dock in Keenley. The trek had taken much longer than anticipated. Many storms hit them as they travelled north, forcing the ship to take cover on islands, sometimes for days. The fires which had ravaged the dock a year earlier were fixed. In fact, the harbour looked like a booming business area, and the idea piqued the interest of Gillock and Eric.

Standing by herself was Vernia. Her white hair whipping in the wind, yet she barely noticed. Vernia's blue eyes were locked on the buildings before them. From the moment the city had come into view, dread had crawled into her heart. She was the last of the Order. Any punishment the king wanted to exact would be on her, and he was right to do so. Fingers entwining with hers, and a reassuring squeeze, brought her back to the ship. Vernia turned and was surprised to see the one beside her was Eric.

Eric's green eyes held hers for a moment. Then he leaned towards her. "Your past actions were done on the belief you were doing something good for the Central Lands," he said, his voice low. "Do not think more on it. I will be speaking with my parents on the matter, and so will your father."

Vernia drew a deep breath, and Eric could feel the dread which lay within it. Her gaze returned to the city. "I'm the last of the Order, Eric. It's the right of the king to want to punish me for the dark deeds they performed."

The sound of horses, and a drawn carriage, came to their ears. Moments later, a carriage rolled towards the dock, surrounded by guards.

"It would appear your parents have decided to investigate the strange ship moored in the harbour," remarked Gillock, coming to stand beside Eric. "Although I must say that there seems to be more ships here than I remember from the past."

Eric agreed. "You and I should disembark first," he stated. "Once they see us, things should be fine."

Eric gave Vernia's hand a final squeeze, and moved along with Gillock, to the gangplank.

Captain Goram stood to the side, watching the carriage and soldiers move in. "You make sure and tell them we are all good folk on here."

Eric smiled. The captain's words had been harsh, but the twinkle in his eye gave him away. “You will all be welcomed, of that I have no doubt.”

Gillock and Eric walked down the gangplank, stopping on the dock. Although he was the crown prince, there was a chance the guards had no idea. Gillock shifted his blue robe around his gangly body, as Eric stood tall. The carriage door opened out came King Jeremy, closely followed by Queen Elizanne. It took only a moment for Elizanne to realise it was Eric and Gillock on the dock. Before the guards could react, she was running towards her son. Jeremy stood stunned, and once he saw Eric, shook his head, and began making his way towards the ship.

Eric, upon seeing his mother break into a run, moved to meet her. “Hello mother,” he said, scooping her up into his arms.

Elizanne felt as if her heart would burst. “My dear, you have grown much,” she exclaimed with a giggle.

“This is truly undignified,” said Jeremy, coming up behind the two.

Eric let go of his mother, feeling a fool. “My apologies, your highness. It is only that I missed her,” stammered Eric, with a low bow.

When he stood, Jeremy was shaking his head once again. “Can you spare a hug for me?” he asked.

Eric laughed and hugged his father tight. A loud cough came to their ears, and they all turned to see Gillock standing with his hands on his hips.

“If you three are done making fools of yourself, there are a few people on board who would like to have a bath, and a good meal,” he grumbled.

Elizanne laughed at the wizard. “Looks like you could use a hug as well,” she stated, and before Gillock could reply, Elizanne had her arms around him. “I have missed your grumpy face,” she remarked.

Gillock hugged Elizanne tight. “I have missed you as well.”

Jeremy noticed the anxious faces on board and turned to his son. “Will you vouch for all on board?” he asked.

“Yes. Every one of them is a good soul,” Eric replied.

Jeremy turned towards the ship. “You are all welcome in Keenley. When you are ready, carriages await to take you to the castle. Rooms are prepared for you.”

Jeremy was going to continue, but two women had moved onto the gangplank and were coming towards him. One was a young girl and judging by her unusual honey coloured and dark streaked hair, Jeremy assumed it was Kaitlyn. The other was Vernia. Jeremy once again turned to Eric. “Vernia?” he queried.

Gillock noticed a dark look cross Jeremy’s face. “She is my daughter,

Jeremy. Both Eric and I will vouch for her," stated Gillock.

A strange ripple moved through the crowd gathered on the dock. The breeze picked up and it swirled around Kaitlyn and Vernia. A soft glance from Gillock calmed the strange occurrence down, but it didn't escape Elizanne. The ripple, and wind, had the feel of a frightened rabbit, and Elizanne's gaze fell to Vernia.

"Your daughter," exclaimed Elizanne, turning her blue eyes on the old wizard. "I had no idea."

Gillock gave a slight smile, one that spoke volumes to the queen. "No one did highness. It was a private matter."

Elizanne turned to face Vernia. The woman's white hair was well known in Keenley. "You should probably keep from sight, my dear. Many within the city hold no love for the Order. Even wandering the castle could prove dangerous."

Elizanne's kindness was often discussed, yet Vernia found herself amazed at her words. They were not stated to comfort now yet give way to future punishment. It was to reassure. Vernia allowed a weak smile and nodded. "I'm aware, my queen. Should you feel it necessary, I will not fight if you choose to place me in the dungeon."

"Absolutely not!" shouted Eric, moving to stand beside Vernia.

Jeremy was stunned by his son's outburst, and looked at the faces before him. It was clear to Jeremy that everyone would stand behind Vernia. "No, Vernia, you will not need to be placed in the dungeon. Your old room has not been disturbed. By the time we reach the castle, it will be cleaned and ready for you. I will have to place a guard outside, though, and insist you have one with you when you are not in the company of Gillock." A quick nod to a guard, and the man was off back to the castle, to give the king's order.

Vernia bowed to Jeremy. "Thank you, highness. It's more than I deserve."

Jeremy turned his attention to the rest of those now gathered on the dock. Eric introduced the captain and crew. Goram informed Jeremy that he wished to have a look over his ship before coming to the castle. Jeremy agreed and stated two carriages would be sent when they were ready. Through the introductions, Elizanne couldn't keep her eyes off one of the men. His hair matched Vernia's, and it was clear he was military. The man's gaze never left the other young woman.

"You have the gait of a soldier," remarked Elizanne when they came before him.

Max smiled and bowed. "And you have an uncanny ability. Your eyes never left me from the moment you saw my hair matched Vernia's."

Elizanne let out a laugh. "I apologize. Do you have a name?"

The young woman moved over to where they were, taking up a stance beside him. "His name is Maxwell Naeda, highness. He is the general of my father's army."

Elizanne eyed the young woman with great interest. "Your father's army? I am going to assume you are Princess Kaitlyn Malore." The words were spoken with an intriguing regard. It didn't escape Kaitlyn when Elizanne pronounced her title. Although the princess couldn't figure what it meant, something was behind those words.

"I am," replied Kaitlyn, giving a slight curtsy.

Eric came up, and took Kaitlyn's hand. "Mother, you knew who she was?"

Elizanne gave her son an odd look. "We have been dealing with Traybidon for some time now. Roads have been built, and trade is developing. However, this is not something to discuss now. It can wait."

Again, Elizanne's words appeared to have more meaning behind them. A moment of silence followed until Gillock's stomach got the better of him.

"Let's get to the castle, I'm famished," declared Gillock, who grasped his daughter's hand and headed to a carriage.

Eric laughed, and Jeremy shook his head, motioning to the waiting carriages.

Kaitlyn turned her attention back to Elizanne. "It is an honour to finally meet you."

Elizanne reached out her hand, and Kaitlyn happily took it. "The pleasure is ours. I would like it if you two joined us."

"Of course," replied Kaitlyn, expecting the invitation.

Eric escorted Kaitlyn to the carriage and helped her in, all with his parents watching closely. Something was going on, and he hoped it would be dealt with during the evening meal.

The ride was eventful. Many people lined the streets to try and catch a glimpse of these newcomers. By the time they arrived at the castle, word had spread that Prince Eric had returned. A buzz went about the city, for the arrival of the crown prince had many implications. As luck would have it, the carriage carrying Gillock, and Vernia went unnoticed. For now, Vernia being back within the city was still a secret. Max rode with them and eyed Vernia closely. On their entire adventure, not once did she show this kind of fear.

Upon exiting their carriages, all waited until the king and queen arrived.

"As I stated, rooms are ready for you all," announced Jeremy. "Servants are here to escort you. All but you Vernia. Your father will take you to your quarters."

With a relieved sigh, Vernia nodded and moved off with her father.

"Eric, you do not know this castle at all, so I have assigned a page to show you about until you get your bearings." Jeremy moved and patted his son on the back, then turned his attention to Kaitlyn. "You are a royal guest, so your rooms are just one floor down from ours. As with Eric, I have assigned a page to cater to your needs, although I am certain you and my son will wander about together."

Eric stared at his father in awe. This was not the man he knew. He seemed happier, and more certain of himself. Perhaps moving back to the proper home of the royal family had helped bring this about. Jeremy had always been a great man, but now he was more so.

"Now go, freshen up. The day is growing late, so once you are ready, please make your way down to the dininghall. Much needs to be discussed," stated Jeremy. A sparkle in his green eyes, a happy step in his walk, followed with Jeremy taking his wife's arm, escorting her inside. All the while leaving Eric to wonder what was going on.

Gillock sat on the edge of his bed, staring intently at his hands. Magic coursed through his body, and it reminded him of days gone. So much power flowed through him, and he wondered if it was for the better. Glancing up, he looked at the door which had formed in the wall before him. Standing, Gillock moved into his secret study. A room from another age. All about were things from his past. He glanced at the many scrying devices which were ruined and paid them no heed. He was a wizard of old and didn't need such things. Magic users now require a mirror or water to scry. This wasn't how it was done in his day.

Moving about he looked at the many artifacts and his eyes fell on a particular item. Gillock didn't open the box, he knew what was inside. A Rubsidian Candle, another relic from old days, and a very powerful form of magic. Gillock knew if his eyes fell on the candle, he would want to use it, and it wasn't time yet. He moved over to a bookshelf, and again something caught his eye. This item, he pulled from the shelf. With a sigh, his fingers lightly brushed across the cover, and many memories came flooding back. His diary. The documentation of the early days when he first joined the wizard order.

Gillock moved over to his desk, and sat down, laying the book in front of him. One entry in particular, mattered the most to him, and Gillock felt the need to, once again, be drawn into the world of old. It only took seconds to find the day, but he hesitated to read it. With a deep breath, he dove in, remembering the day well.

Day 114 of the Moon calendar

Gillock Rampor

Today is a great day, and a terrible one. Draxin has become a War Wizard. For the last fifteen years, Draxin has been following every lead and tale he has heard about war wizards. It has been a life quest, and a few months ago, he told me he knew where the final piece was hidden. The last bit of magic needed to bring War Wizards back into the world. I was excited to hear he was almost at the end of his quest, but I also worried. War Wizards disappeared from record, and none of the teachers are willing to explain why. All we are taught is that they were a failed experiment, and it was one never be repeated. Draxin had a life quest that was forbidden by our order to pursue, yet he did. I flew with him to find what he needed. A strange stone only found deep to the west, in a cave that sat within the side of a mountain called the Fallen Giant. The mountain is aptly named. It looks like a giant fell over and was napping. The area was home to strange creatures, but we never went close enough to look. Keeping high, for the cave was at the top, I never saw what they were, only that our presence irritated them. On the other hand, perhaps they had never seen a dragon before. Draxin's dragon was a brownish red, unusual colouring, but was a great camouflage. Within the cave, he found the stone. Dark red, and pulsating, the stone made my stomach grow tight. Draxin snatched the stone, threw it in his sack, and flew us back to the school. No one was the wiser. I hadn't seen him since that day, and now as I look into his eyes, I know my friend is gone.

The wizard masters are not certain how to proceed. Draxin is a danger, but also an asset. I learned this information because I was hiding in the headmaster's study. I also learned something that I will never forget. The reason why War Wizards no longer exist. If a War Wizard is required to use their full power, they are consumed by it, and die. Draxin has been made aware of this and doesn't appear to be bothered. His goal; to bring more War Wizards into being. The masters forbid it and have said only through the bloodline can he be allowed. No other students are to endure the change that he did. Draxin has agreed and plans to create new wizards will begin. Draxin has not taken a bride, and so the masters are going to allow him to use magic to entice women from the surrounding villages. The thought makes me ill, and I wonder just how far the masters are willing to go.

They were livid when Draxin presented himself, yet now are willing to let him use women to create a bloodline. It's days like these that make me wonder if coming here to learn was a good thing.

Gillock put down the diary. Not long after this entry, unrest began in the ranks. A few decades later, Kinsley was beginning his plan to take over. Kinsley was the one who convinced the other masters that War Wizards needed to return. The common humans were beginning to detest magic users and needed to be taught to respect those superior to them. If the masters only saw what Gillock did, perhaps the war never would have occurred.

With a sigh, Gillock left his study, and with a wave of his hand, the door was again hidden. A knock made him realise the evening meal was going to be served soon. Pushing down his worry for Eric, Gillock made his way to the dininghall. This was a different time, and perhaps Eric won't ever need to use his full power.

CHAPTER FIVE

The dininghall held only those who had arrived, as well as the king, queen, General Chenkit, and General Traug. Eric was happy to see that Olrond had indeed forsaken the Order and worked for his father in the fight against Duke Dubar. It impressed Eric to see so many were on his father's side during that time of conflict.

Off to the side sat the crew from the King's Own. Goram was speaking with Jeremy, and it appeared to be a heavy conversation. Vernia sat with Kaitlyn, and it was here Gillock went to seat himself. A soft hum filled the room as small conversations were being held. The servants began bringing in food, and Jeremy motioned for all to take their seats. Pages showed the guests their places, and a hush came over the assembled group.

"Before we begin, I want you all to know, this evening meal is also going to be one of many discussions," began Jeremy, his voice showing the importance of what he was saying. "We have made new alliances, but there is also talk of war. Do not be alarmed, all will be explained tonight. For now, please feast."

As is custom, the king and queen were served, and after they took their first bites, everyone else joined in. Gillock noticed the odd looks on the faces of Jeremy and Elizanne, along with the side glances to Eric and Kaitlyn, and knew what part of tonight was going to bring.

Eric took a few bites of his meal, then eyed his parents. "Father, how does the Central Lands fare? I have been away for so long I feel out of touch."

Jeremy felt his son's curiosity. It was as if his magic was pressing all about in anticipation of the answer. "We have acquired a new land. Jijitsa, now called Malajah, is a part of our kingdom. The elves have helped it become a workable area. Your Uncle Jessup rules there."

Eric sat back. "Uncle?"

Elizanne placed her hand on Jeremy's. Both had forgotten that Eric, after failing to complete the quest, went on to fulfil the prophecy, and was not aware of the spell which had been hiding Jessup for nearly two decades. "Yes, Eric. My brother. You knew him as Korben, but in truth he was Jessup, hidden by a magic spell placed on him by monks from the temple of Allorethna."

Stunned silence followed, and a strange look crossed Eric's face. "I get the feeling there is a lot I am going to be hearing this night."

Jeremy eyes scanned the faces around the table. Most were strangers, but there was one thing which could be announced in their presence. "There is something, and it is the most important at this time," began Jeremy, his voice taking on the tone of the king. "Brin has declared war on these lands. She has forsaken her right to rule. You all are witness to this announcement." Anxious eyes fell on Jeremy, and he turned to his son. "Eric, you are the next in line to be king."

Eric's reaction went from shock to acceptance in the blink of an eye. Kaitlyn's hand fell onto his and gave him a reassuring squeeze. Eric's eyes darted about the table, taking stock in the reactions shown before him, and then back to his parents. "I accept this privilege bestowed upon me, and hope to be the ruler the Central Lands need once your time has ended."

Jeremy was intrigued by this new son seated before him. Koral had thought Eric would argue his position. It was clear to Jeremy the adventures Eric had gone on over the past year had changed him. Before him, sat a young man of seventeen, whose confidence was apparent, and Jeremy knew Eric would make a great ruler.

"To bring the conversation back to Jessup, he is getting married in the fall. To a woman who is from the new land," announced Elizanne. "It will take place in the new keep, where he lives."

The conversation continued about the wedding, the new land, how Koral was doing, all the while Gillock's gaze never left Jeremy. The wizard knew more diplomatic discussions were going to be had. Ones which also needed witness, and he wondered when Jeremy was going to bring up the obvious one.

As the plates were removed, sweets were brought out, and the conversation changed as Gillock knew it would.

"Kaitlyn, I want you to know that I sent a messenger out as soon as we arrived back at the castle to inform your parents where you are," stated Jeremy.

Kaitlyn took a sip of wine, and placed her goblet down, turning her eyes to him. "I appreciate that, highness. They are probably worried."

Jeremy leaned forward, placing his hands together, never taking his gaze off Kaitlyn. "Your father and I have been in discussion for some time now. We felt it would be prudent to both kingdoms to form a sort of partnership." Jeremy paused and reached for his goblet. A long drink, and a soft sigh, followed before he continued. "It is our plan to have you and Eric

wed, in hopes to link our families."
Eric, who had himself taken some wine, choked on it. The shock he had felt about being named next in line for the throne, was trumped by this information. However, it wasn't because he was against it. He and Kaitlyn had discussed the idea on their way back, and he had proposed. Eric turned to Kaitlyn, who smiled and nodded. Understanding she was approving the next step, Eric stood. "Father, mother, and all present. On the last full moon, I proposed to Kaitlyn Malore, and she said yes. At the time, I believed I was merely a prince, and she only a princess. Now, having been declared the next in line for the throne, I am not certain how to proceed."
Elizanne smiled at her husband, and took his hand, turning her eyes to Eric. "My son, the proper way to do things would be to ask your king for his approval, then the object of your affections father. Seeing as this discussion has already been had, and King Tusta is in agreement with the decision, you do not have to do anything. As of this moment, you and Kaitlyn are betrothed.

Goram and Mena looked at each other, then Goram stood, raising his glass of wine. "May I be the first to say, congratulations. Hope I'm invited to the wedding." A long drink, and laughter from Mena, followed.
Eric smiled at Goram. "I would not dream of beginning a new adventure without you there to be a witness," he remarked with a chuckle.

More congratulations, and wine, went about the room. No plans would be made that night, but merriment would be had. The conversation turned to the changes in the land, the elves, and the building of watchtowers along Death's Boundary.
Jeremy turned his attention back to Eric. "I wish to discuss all that is going in regard to Brin, and her army, but not until tomorrow."
This piqued the interest of Max. "Sire, would you mind if I sat in on the discussions? I would like to learn what your thoughts are. Perhaps I could offer assistance. Or at the very least, I could be a presence from Lungast."
"King Tusta has yet to send a representative to be a part of our military discussions. I am certain he would approve of his own general taking counsel with us," said Jeremy.

The night continued on, with Eric telling the tale of his adventure. Goram piped up to keep the story on track, and to make it sound more interesting. When Eric got to the end, and spoke of the goblins, a silence filled the room. Eric's voice cracked, and a tear rolled down his cheek as he spoke of their final moments. "I hope to be as strong and brave as they were."

Jeremy sipped his wine, running the tale through his head. "Hope may have been brought back to the southern area, but it appears to have enhanced Brin's forces. I know the stronger evil no longer rules, but Brin is gaining in numbers. Her city, from what I am told, is enormous. The only scouts to return were the ones I sent in a small fishing vessel," said Jeremy. "But enough of this now. It is getting late, and I am certain you would all like a good night's rest."

A murmur went through the room as all agreed. The merriment, and the idea of sleeping in a soft bed, made all from the King's Own tired. Goram and Mena agreed to stay in the castle, but the crew insisted on staying at an inn within sight of the ship. No one had seen a vessel such as this, and they worried about thieves. Jeremy approved the decision, and had three guards posted on the dock, to help ease the mind of the captain.

The sound of soft drops hitting the window woke Eric. The sky was dark, and rain was rolling through. Moving towards the window, Eric looked out at the rain. It wasn't strong, only a soft summer rain watering gardens and cleaning the city. Although the sky was dark, it was no longer night. The sun hid behind the clouds, but still offered some light. He went over to the door and opened it. No servants moved through the hallway, so he knew it was early. Eric, now awake, decided to bathe, and wait to hear the morning meal was being served.

Eric wasn't the only one awake at the early hour. Gillock had not yet slept. Instead, he had been sifting through his journals, taking in all the memories, and worrying. Before he knew it, a servant was letting him know the morning meal was waiting. Splashing some cold water on his face, Gillock then changed into an old robe, to give the appearance that he had not been up all night.

The meal was simple and set up as a buffet so all those in the castle could float through when they wished. Eggs, breads, morning pastries, and many varieties of fruit filled the tables set up. Eric filled his plate, and sat down to eat, relishing in each bite.

"I remember always eating these at the Festival of the Moon," Eric muttered to himself.

"Is that a day of significance?" asked a voice.

Eric tilted his head up to see Max coming to sit down beside him. "Yes, of sorts. Once it was to celebrate the spring solstice, but that is also the day of my birth."

“I remember you used to eat the wataki fruit until you got sick,” stated his mother, coming over to sit as well. Behind her came a servant to inquire as to what she would like to eat. Elizanne rolled her eyes and told the young woman what she wanted. The look made Eric laugh.

“You do not seem to like being waited on,” he stated with a chortle.

“I am not allowed to do anything. It is beyond frustrating,” Elizanne answered.

Max glanced at the two. “That’s how it is back in Traybidon. Both the king and queen don’t like it themselves.”

A plate was placed before the queen, but instead of eating, she looked at Max. “The more I speak with them, the more I see just how alike we are.”

Max gave Elizanne a smile. “I’ve noticed the similarities.” He placed a few grapes in his mouth and sat back. “How is it that you can send messages so quickly? My apologies, but I was roaming this morning and heard a page say you had received a response from King Tusta.”

“A wizard, from your realm, asked the elves to speak with a breed of eagle. It is my understanding they agreed to be messengers between the kingdoms,” remarked Elizanne. “We also have set up a few new stops between here and Lungast so that soldiers can ride without stopping.”

“You are mentioned in the communication,” said Jeremy, coming up behind them. “King Tusta agrees that you should take counsel with me. He has also stated that the King’s Own and its crew are to remain here for a time. However, they will be heading back to Traybidon within a few days, by carriage. Travel back via the sea would take months. The ship will remain here, until King Tusta wishes it returned.”

Eric scooped his last forkful and looked at his father. “Have you informed Captain Goram?”

“Yes,” said Jeremy, taking a seat opposite Eric. “He is not happy but understands. From what I was told, a new ship has been commissioned for the royal family.”

Eric smirked at the thought. “It will have to be some ship to get Goram to leave the King’s Own.”

Jeremy waved off the servant wishing to bring him food, settling for tea. “When you are all finished, please meet me in my private study.”

Elizanne watched her husband leave the dininghall and turned her attention to Eric. “We sent a message to your sister. I expect she will be arriving within a few days.”

The news brought a smile to Eric. He noticed Max had finished his meal,

and so did his mother. “Guess it is time to go meet with the others.”
Elizanne stood. “Yes. There is much you need to hear.”
The ominous tone his mother had made Eric wonder, and strange thoughts plagued his mind the entire walk to his father’s private study.

Two guards stood outside the study door, making Eric wonder even more about what he was going to hear. Inside, there were only three people. General Traug, Gillock and Jeremy. He, Elizanne and Max sat down, and waited for the meeting to begin.

Jeremy looked at his son, and Max. “I spoke last night of the new watchtowers being built along Death’s Boundary. What I did not state, was the fact that I have also sent many scouts and soldiers into the boundary. I know the area is home to strange creatures, all which are hungry. Gillock has informed me that when the war happened, somehow magic was thrown into that area. There were always creatures within. Experiments, designed to protect the lands from whatever lay south. The surge of wizard magic during the war made it change. Not one of the men who entered ever came back out. A week ago, when the builders working on the watchtower nearest Dreadwood Forest woke, strange footprints were seen all about the area. Every day since, each tower has reported the same thing. No one was harmed, and nothing was ruined, but the footprints were immense.”

Eric glanced at his father, then to Gillock. “Do you know what it is?”
Gillock cleared his throat. “My wizard masters altered orcs and trolls to become mindless killing machines and threw them into the boundary. There weren’t many, perhaps a couple of dozen, but they were designed to live long, and do nothing but kill. I believe one of these creatures has become brave since magic changed and is venturing out of its home.”
Eric listened to Gillock, and for some reason, felt he wasn’t speaking the entire truth. Something lay within his words, Eric just didn’t know what.
“I recall the stories of these things,” remarked Elizanne. “I always thought they were tales told to keep children from venturing too close to that area.”
Gillock’s black eyes looked into Elizanne’s. “They fell into legend, as do most things that aren’t seen,” he said, his voice going quiet.

Jeremy’s face was hard, not giving away a single emotion in regard to the defences. His green eyes had their usual deep stare, and he made certain to make contact with each person present. “General Chenkit left this morning to go oversee the towers. They are almost complete, and I have already sent a garrison of soldiers to patrol. What I need is a plan to move through the boundary and have the ability to scout the far side. It is my plan to set up a force there as a first line of defence."

"Has this area never been mapped?" asked Max.

Eric jumped out of his chair and looked down at Max. "The maps! The ones Painish gave us. Perhaps they can be of use."

Eric whipped open the door and ordered one of the pages waiting to find Captain Goram and get all of the maps he possessed. Shutting the door once again, he took his seat, and looked at his confused father. "The goddess gave us many maps. Most showed us how to get to the island of Drakendir, but some were of the lands. They might be old, but perhaps you can use them to at least have an idea of what you are up against."

Elizanne hid her smile and looked at her husband. He maintained his military look, but for a brief moment, his eyes had softened, showing pride for his son. "I have suggested we look through the library of Zanth as well," stated Elizanne.

The mention of the library grabbed Gillock's attention. "The library!" he exclaimed.

"Koral brought it from the dwarven city, and it now rests where the Wizard's School once stood," said Elizanne softly.

Gillock's eyes flashed with excitement. "I will happily go to the library and see what I can find."

Jeremy nodded. "Then you are tasked with finding information on the world to the south," he declared.

A knock caused Eric to again leave his seat. He whipped open the door, grabbed the maps from a startled page, and slammed it close. "I know something in here will help," he said, placing the maps on a table set up to the side.

Jeremy allowed his mouth to show a slight grin. Getting up, he moved to stand beside his son. "I am certain something will present itself," he said, patting his son on the back, and looking at the maps. For the first time in many months, King Jeremy felt like they might actually stand a chance in this war.

CHAPTER SIX

Sitting at the edge of a deep pond, Koral sat, focusing her attention on the deep blue water before her. A small waterfall fed the pool, causing a soft current to flow by her. Within, dryads danced and played. Koral didn't notice any of it. The water had her full concentration, and it wasn't long before a ball of liquid floated above the pond. Slowly, Koral moved the water over to some wildflowers, releasing it in as a sprinkle.

"You are getting good at that trick," commented Darly from across the pond. With four quick leaps, using some rocks protruding from the water, Darly landed next to Koral.

Koral looked up to her friend, remembering their first meeting. Koral had thought Darly's brown hair and eyes were boring for an elf. Now that Koral was an elf herself, Darly's eyes appeared to sparkle, and her hair had a glow, giving her an ethereal look. "Hard to believe it has been over a year since I learned that spell," remarked Koral softly. "It once drained me, now I barely notice." Her gaze moved to Darly, "You have been watching me for some time."

Darly sat herself down next to Koral. "You are not a human anymore. Many things have changed, and I do not suppose it will end soon. As for watching, you come here a lot. I see you sneaking off from the castle and slinking through the forest to this spot."

Koral leaned her head back and laughed loud. "Slinking and sneaking? You make it sound as if I am a burglar trying to hide from the guards."

Darly joined in the laugh. "Well, it is close. You do try and make yourself invisible."

Koral threw a rock into the pond, startling the dryads. "So much is happening. This forest, the new city, I am not quite sure how I fit into it all."

Darly stared intently at her friend. "Your purpose will show itself in time, highness. You just need to be patient."

Koral thought on the words and kept her gaze on the water. "I have the feeling you did not come out here just to talk. Is there something else?"

Darly placed her hand on Koral's arm. "As a matter of fact, yes. Eric has returned to Keenley. I thought you may want to go for a wander back that way and see him."

"You bet I do," exclaimed Koral, jumping up from her spot, and grabbing

Darly's arm in the process, dragging the woman behind.
Darly let out another laugh as she followed the excited princess back to the city.

Glavlin stared at the letter sent from his brother. The news wasn't unexpected but did appear to be sudden. A commotion outside the window drew his attention. Moving from his desk, he saw Koral and Darly coming towards the castle. For the first time in many days, Koral was smiling. The sight brought joy to Glavlin, and he realised how little he had seen of Koral over the last few weeks. There were no pressing matters requiring his attention today, so he left his study, and went to greet the two women.

Light laughter and voices came to Glavlin's ears as he moved out into the courtyard. Whatever the two were discussing, was something of importance. The elf king moved around a bush, where he found the two conversing.

"May I ask what has you both in such a mood?" Glavlin asked, grinning.

Koral moved to him, and pulled him into an embrace. "Eric has returned, along with his new companions. I was hoping we might be able to make a trip to Keenley."

Glavlin stepped back, keeping his hands on Koral's hips. "Well, nothing major is going on within the city, except for trying to decide a name. I think we could make the trip. Would be nice to see my father. Might be your father needs some new eyes on the issues from the south?"

Koral's eyes glittered with excitement. "Shall we pack and leave as soon as we can?"

Glavlin laughed. "I will speak to Auroram and let him know what our plan is. How about we leave at dawn?"

Darly turned her head to the sky and noticed that the day was waning. "The king is right, Koral. Night is fast approaching, and there are things which need to be done first."

Although Koral was upset with the delay, she understood Glavlin needed to inform his head Protector, and leave someone in charge while he was away. "That would be fine. I will head to my room now and begin packing."

With a slight kiss on the cheek, Koral ran off towards her room, leaving Darly and Glavlin behind.

Once out of sight, Glavlin and Darly began slowly walking towards their rooms. "When are you going to ask her?"

Glavlin kept his eyes ahead and shook his head. "Koral is still confused about many things, Darly. I am not certain if marriage right now would be a good idea."

Darly chuckled and patted him on the back. "Your highness, with all due respect, you can ask her, but not have the event for a time. Better yet, perhaps you should share a room. We are not like the humans. There is no protocol which states you cannot bed together before you wed. Maybe that is what she needs right now."

Glavlin eyed Darly, but the more he thought about it, the more he knew Darly was right. "You have a way of getting ideas into my head," he remarked, again shaking his head.

"So what is your plan then?" asked Darly.

Glavlin stared down the hall to where Koral's room was. "I am going to speak to her now. We can make it formal once we return."

Another pat on the back, and Darly was off to her room. This was something Glavlin needed to do alone.

Koral looked about her room and plunked down on the bed. Eric back from his adventure. She was now an elf, with unusual abilities and knowledge. It was all so strange to her. They were only seventeen, and already lived more than most would in their entire lifetime. A soft knock on her door brought her out of the daydream, and she got up to open it. Koral had thought it would be Darly and was surprised to see it was Glavlin.

"What can I do for you?" asked Koral.

Glavlin looked into her eyes, and Koral noticed an odd twinkle in his violet eyes. "May I come in and speak to you about something?"

Koral moved from the doorway and waved him over to a seating area. They both took a chair, and Koral waited to hear what Glavlin had to say.

"Koral, you and I are developing into something," he began, never taking his eyes off her. "I believe it is time to move our relationship along. When we come back from this trip, I would like you to move into my rooms with me. Make it a more formal joining."

Koral was genuinely shocked. "Are you certain this is what you want?" she stammered.

Glavlin took her hands in his and leaned close. "I feel that you and I will be together until the end of our days. This is a first step towards that."

Before she could respond, Glavlin's lips were pressed against hers, and she allowed them to stay for a time before leaning back.

"Yes, Glavlin, I will be happy to move my things into your rooms," she responded, her words sounding breathless, and full of emotion. Glavlin kissed her again, and then stood. "I still need to speak with Auroram. I will see you at dawn."

Koral walked him to the door and shut it softly behind him. She had wondered what life in this city had in store for her, and it appeared she was going to find out. With a new spring in her step, Koral went about finding the few things she would need for the trip to Keenley.

Hearing the door close, Glavlin moved off to his chambers. "Am I to assume you will have a guest staying in your rooms now?" asked Auroram, coming up behind Glavlin.

"Where have you been?" asked Glavlin, glancing over his shoulder.

Auroram smiled. "Watching all, as usual. I know you received word from your brother, and that a message came in stating Eric was back in Keenley. I knew it was only a matter of time before you would be heading out."

Nothing ever got past Auroram, a thought which amused the elf king, and Glavlin shook his head. "Yes. We are going to Keenley. As for my brother, he is now married."

Auroram stared ahead. "Ah, court life in Almberson. Probably pressured into it from the council."

"Yes, he was, and it is understandable. War coming from all sides. They want to make certain the bloodline stays true," replied Glavlin.

"Darly will be travelling as your guard?" asked Auroram, although his tone made it clear it wasn't a choice.

"Of course. I do not think she would let Koral out of her sight," stated Glavlin.

"I know that leaves me with running the city," said Auroram, feigning exasperation. "Be sure to say hello to your father. I hope he is faring well."

Glavlin said he would and entered his room to pack.

Dawn arrived with rain, but it wouldn't dampen Koral's mood. She had saddled her horse and was singing to herself the entire time. Darly couldn't help but giggle at it all. Koral was headed to visit her brother, and her relationship with Glavlin had moved to the next level. Nothing could bring her down on this day

"Are we going to rush, or can we take our time and enjoy the scenery?" asked Darly

Koral stared at the woman. "Can we not do both?" she asked, playfully.

Darly squinted, and pointed her finger at Koral. "Normal travel takes over a week. So how about we do it in three days."

“I think that is an excellent idea,” commented Glavlin, bringing his horse up to theirs. “We can ride fast to the border of our lands, then proceed at a somewhat normal pace. This way we can see how the lands are faring.”

Koral smiled at Glavlin. “Sounds perfect. Shall we get going then?”

With a jump, she was on her horse and headed out of the city, leaving a laughing Darly, and stunned Glavlin behind.

The first day was spent in the rain. The moist ground did not hinder the elven steeds. In no time, they were passed their border, and the pace slowed. The forest was quiet, and the falling rain bouncing off the leaves on the trees was soothing. Only a few wagons, and a handful on lone riders, passed them by. They made camp in a small glade and enjoyed a night of talk. When they turned in, they all laid awake for a time, listening to the hum of the forest.

The next day was still gloomy, but the rain had moved off. For the first half of the day, they saw few travellers. When night came, and they made camp, the reason why became clear. Knowing something was about, Darly and Glavlin moved into the brush for cover. Koral set a fire and took a seat beside it to cook supper. The moment she sat down, two trolls came lumbering in. Koral assumed they were scouts since they didn’t attack at first. It could have also been because Koral was alone, and the trolls were certain there had been others only moments earlier. Koral continued to show no fear and stirred the pot over the fire. Unnerved by the elf’s calm demeanour, the trolls looked into the shadows.

In an instant Darly and Glavlin flew in, attacking the trolls and striking them down before the beasts knew what was happening.

“I wonder why they were so far south?” questioned Darly, glancing at the dead bodies.

“Perhaps they can give us an answer to that,” replied Glavlin. He proceeded to pat down the two and found nothing.

“They may have been drawn to the mountain,” offered Koral, moving to join the two. “It could be they wanted a tribe to be further south.”

A dark look crossed Glavlin’s face. “If they are already trying to scout new territory, we could be in for some trouble from the north.”

“I don’t think that’s a worry, King Glavlin,” said a voice. Payton moved into the light to find three swords pointed at his chest.

Once noticing who had spoken, Koral sheathed her sword. “Payton, what brings you here?” she queried.

“Those trolls. They weren’t scouts, they were rogues,” he stated. “A few weeks back they left the mountains, and it was clear by how they looked it was forced upon them. They were beaten up pretty good."

Three more men came out of the woods, and Glavlin motioned for them all to sit. "Klayhern fares well still?"

Payton and his men sat, and accepted the food Koral had prepared, and some ale. "We have to send regular patrols out, but so far, no instances. Seems as if the trolls want to keep to their own area right now."

"That is good news," said Koral. "Has my father appointed anyone to take over Klayhern yet?"

Payton raised his eyes. "You remember Lord Markus Tetery? He has been promoted to baron, and now controls Klayhern all the way to Sprague."

Koral thought back and remembered the lord. He was quiet, and usually kept to himself at festivals and other events. "Do you approve?"

The new general shrugged and nodded. "Yes. He is a good enough man, and now has a wife and son. So far, they have done a good job."

Silence came as they all ate their fill. Once done, Payton and his men stood. "We will take our leave. Need to head back and report that the trolls have been dealt with." He ended his sentence with a wink to the elves.

Glavlin smiled. "Good travels."

The men said their thanks and disappeared into the night. No one wanted to sleep, but all three knew they must. Tomorrow, they should be at their destination.

Midday arrived, and so did the gates of Keenley. Although Koral wanted to rush all the way to the castle, they always made certain to stop at the Star Dancer Inn. When they rode through the gates, Koral saw the glances and knew word would be taken to the castle about her arrival. Wasting no time, they arrived at the inn, and made their way inside. As always, it was full, and the smell of food assailed their senses. Taking a table in the middle of the room, all three ordered. Miles was tending the bar, and when the server pointed out the table, hollered at the three and brought them ales.

"What brings ye to the city?" he asked, taking a seat.

"Eric is back," replied Koral.

Miles shook his head. "Ah. A strange ship be in the harbour. Guessing he came in on it."

The talk turned to the inn, how well it was doing, how their old acquaintances were faring, and other small talk. More people began to pour in, and Miles had to excuse himself to serve them. The three elves finished their meal and left to head to the castle. Waiting outside was a carriage and guards. Koral smiled and got in without a word. One of the guards took the reins of the horses and informed the three that their horses would be placed in the royal stable.

As they rolled along, Koral's excitement grew. It had been a very long time since she had seen her brother. Much had happened, and more was still to come. With a soft sigh, Koral glanced out the window, watching the city roll past.

Glomain elf eyes stared hard at the darkness. He knew eyes stared back, ones belonging to the many creatures hiding within. Some, however, were quite intelligent, and watched his every move. For an hour he stood, not moving, on the far side of Evan's River. Most of the eyes had grown bored and moved off. However, two sets remained. One hiding high in the trees, the other in the forest below. Glomain walked to the bridge further down and crossed. His intent clear. He was going to stand on the very edge of the Dreadwood Forest and see if something would appear. As he neared, Glomain could feel the evil. It had been muted when he was across the river. Here, it was so strong it actually filled his heart with dread. "Now I see why the locals named this forest Dreadwood," he remarked to himself.

Glomain got to within a hundred feet and stopped. The forest breathed death and fear and was familiar to the elf. Glomain wasn't certain what had taken residence in the forest, but it was one with a dark soul. Quickly he turned and broke into a run. King Jeremy wanted a report on the forest, and Glomain was certain the news he was bringing was not what the king was hoping to hear.

CHAPTER SEVEN

The night was humid, and a storm threatened to make land. Lightning flashed over the sea, casting a brilliant light which allowed Brin to make out the clouds. It was large, and she knew they were in for a night of heavy rain. The area was a desert, hot and dry, but it had been created. Heavy rains caused the areas close to the Temple City to become muddy and quite treacherous. Brin had learned, in her early days within the city, this was the reason behind the strange building style, and the need for the enormous temple itself. Usually, when a storm was pressing in on the city, the temple would push the clouds around. Yes, many lives had been lost outside the walls, but the city itself rarely felt the full wrath of a storm. Arket had helped her add in a sewer system, which help divert water entering the city streets. Construction outside the walls occurred with the same principle in mind. Divert water to prevent mud from building up, and perhaps, destroying her military significantly.

A large area outside was where her army lay. Some could not be near others, for fear of an internal disagreement. Many were forced into her army, but now served willingly. Hope had helped make that possible. Beyond where the men lived, was her pride and joy. Creatures which had come to her call. Strange beings, whose footing on sand was amazing. They could run full out, and not falter. Arket had said one of the creatures were kin to minotaur's. Trentataur's, as they were called, walked like minotaur's, with horned heads but that is where the similarities ended. Their faces resembled a small moose. Their bodies were hard and covered in a hide which was cream coloured to reflect the sun away. Brin's favourite, however, were the snake-men.

Lazzards. They walked on two legs, had two arms, longer than a human's and not a single hair on their bodies. Their skin was scaly, their teeth sharp, and tails to help them balance while running. It was also an effective weapon. Lazzards had a speech all their own, but also spoke the common tongue of the lands. An oddity they refused to explain. Although they were few in numbers, they were vicious fighters.

A thunderclap followed by a lightning flash, signalled the storm's arrival. Brin moved from the balcony and back into the hallway. Her steps were slow, as she listened to the storm raging outside. The sound was invigorating. Brin wasn't headed to her rooms, but instead made her way to the war hall.

Inside, Arket sat, pouring over their campaign ideas. He was not at all happy with delays, and it annoyed her. Brin knew this fight would span many months. To rush would bring failure. However, she did see his point. They should have moved towards the Central Lands by now. Summer was waning, and Brin had thought at the very least, they should have drawn the forces of the Central Lands into theirs. Perhaps it was why she kept delaying.

Arket looked up from the map when Brin entered, but only briefly. He was alone, which Brin had expected. "Have you any ideas?" she asked, approaching the large table.

Arket sat down, shaking his head. "We have no idea what they are planning. I know our friend has stated that King Jeremy is still uncertain how to proceed, but they should have an idea by now."

Brin ran her eyes over the map and saw what she always did. "I am sending a squadron of Trentataur's across the river and into the forest. Their goal is to move into Death's Boundary and attack any human or elf they see."

"Is the order already given?" he questioned, and his voice had a hint of annoyance.

The tone bothered Brin, but she let it pass. "No. I wanted to let you know first. I will order them to leave once the storm quiets down."

The statement appeared to appease Arket, for he didn't offer any argument. Brin gave her husband a smile and moved out the side door. As she suspected, the generals were waiting outside, hoping for orders. All stood to attention when the door opened, and when Brin gave the order, they were gone without a word.

The storm raged for a better part of the day. When evening was approaching, the rain slowed. Not long after, a light dust cloud could be seen moving towards the north. The two rulers were seated in their usual spot on their balcony, and the sight brought a slight smile to both of their faces. After enjoying the cool, moist air for a few hours, a thought came to the emperor.

"How are they going to get across the river?" asked Arket.

"We are going to help them," replied Brin.

A strange look flashed across Arket's face, yet he smiled. "When do we leave?"

Brin's blue eyes sparkled with anticipation. "They travel with great speed, enhanced by magic. I assume they will arrive by sunset tomorrow, so we will leave shortly. I wish to be there long before they arrive."

A chuckle came from Arket when he realised what his wife was up to. "Another way to show our dominance. Arriving first."

Brin didn't reply, instead she stood and glanced down at the city below. Yes, they dominated, and it didn't hurt to reaffirm why they were the rulers of these lands, but something wasn't right. Or better put, something wasn't right with her. She felt distant, and it was a strange feeling. When she thought on it, it grew worse, so Brin quickly pushed the feeling aside. "We best be off. We really are not certain what we will find at the river's edge," she stated, moving into the room.

Arket was not far behind.

A chant and a flash of light brought them to the rock cropping near the river. The two moved with careful steps, listening to all around. No sounds came to their ears, but the odd feeling passed over Brin again. Silently they walked along the river's edge, when out of the blue, Brin collapsed to the ground. Arket was only two steps behind and caught her as she fell.

"Beloved, what ails you?" his concern evident in his voice.

Brin sat on the ground and realised what was bothering her. She clasped his hand and pulled him down beside her. "Only now did I realise why I have been out of sorts of late. I am with child."

Arket pulled her in close. He was centuries old and had fathered many children. Killing each one. Finally, the words the gods had spoken to him so long ago were coming to pass. He was having a child with another magical being. "This news is wonderful!"

He pulled away and saw the look on Brin's face. It didn't show happiness. "Wonderful," she said softly. "I wanted to be at the front of this war. Now, I must hide until the child is born."

Arket held her again. "Yes, that is true. We do not want our child to come to harm."

Brin sobbed quietly, then composed herself. Dawn was a few hours off, and she wanted to scout the entire area. No sounds had greeted them, but that didn't mean there wasn't anyone watching them.

The two wandered in separate directions along the river's edge. It was clear no one hid in the forest beyond, but something about the area bothered them both. An off feeling had crept into their bodies, causing each to be on edge. This was why they went in different directions, to see if they could find the cause of their trepidation. Brin, already annoyed with the recent revelation, was becoming more irritated by the feeling.

Arriving at a part of the river, which was far wider than the rest, and curved slightly south, Brin noticed the sensation became stronger. Rapids sprung out at the turn, and dangerous water flowed towards the east. Brin knew the Sea of Arran wasn't far off, and assumed the river switched to flow downwards into the sea. Pushing herself through the bushes lining the shore, and onto some rocks in the water, Brin sat down and stared at the river rushing by. Her eyes darted about. Something was here and watching her.

Bubbling and churning, the river's song began to relax Brin. Twinkling on the water drew her attention, and she watched it for a time. The soothing sounds and lights were beginning to make her feel drowsy, and an evil smirk crossed Brin's lips. Had her mind not been on the revelation of being pregnant, Brin would have fallen trap to the dryadshee. Brin thought on the creature, recalling the tales. They were creatures who would call to you through water and light, beckoning you into their depths.

Brin was no longer entranced by the beauty before her. Instead, she waited. The creature was patient, but so was she. The sun slowly crept into the sky, and the water down from her changed colour, revealing the dryadshee. Brin let her eyes dart about the water, as if looking for something. Out of the corner of her eye, she saw the dryadshee rise up from the river. Taking a deep breath, Brin chanted a spell. It was a simple one, designed to trap fairy creatures, and one she hoped would hold the creature. The dryadshee moved closer to Brin, and once it sensed the magic, was caught. Slowly Brin turned to face the creature. Unable to move, the dryadshee eyed Brin with eyes which showed death.

"How is it you have captured me, mortal?" it hissed.

Brin's eyes ran over the dryadshee. A wisp of a creature, it was hard to imagine how dangerous she was. Of course, that is how they were able to easily capture prey. Blue-green hair and skin, allowed it to hide in water easily. A beautiful face, obviously female, scowled at Brin, but the eyes were what Brin was focused on. They were black, and their stare made Brin feel uneasy.

"Is this your territory?" asked Brin, hoping her voice didn't betray her feelings.

The fairy creature eyed Brin, and relaxed slightly. "This had been my home for many centuries. It has been a long time since anyone has graced

this area."
Brin let out a chuckle. "Back then, tales of you would have been spread far. In my time, this area was hidden from the people. I think you should know humans and elves will be passing through soon."
Shifting in the water, the dryadshee appeared annoyed with the news. "And what reason would they have to come this way?"
Brin stood and looked at the dryadshee. "I have threatened the area north of here with war. I expect them to push through Death's Boundary into this forest as a counter measure. The desert side is mine, and it is well guarded. They will most likely try many areas to cross the river, and attack."
The dryadshee shifted again, as if contemplating her next move. Brin was certain her spell was holding fast, but this was her first encounter with a fairy creature, so there was no guarantee.
"I will allow you and your mate to leave this area. However, should you ever come this way again, your spell will not work. That particular version is only temporary. If you feel the need to test me, you will die." To accentuate her point, the dryadshee glided towards Brin, gave a dark smile, and then disappeared below the water.

The sound of approaching hooves came to Brin's ears. All along Brin was under an enchantment. Hours had flown by, yet the fairy creature had allowed her to live. With barely a thought, Brin began running towards the sound. The trentataur's came into sight, the expected dust cloud surrounding them. At the sight of Brin, they stopped. Moments later, Arket came up behind Brin.

"Why you come?" growled one, pulling itself to its full height, which was well over eight feet.
Brin smiled to herself. They were amazing warrior's but didn't have a grasp of her language yet. "You will need assistance getting across the river. Once there, head north and you will find a great rock area. Here, you are to stay. Nothing within is stronger than you are. Take it as your own and stop our enemies from passing through."
The leader nodded and motioned the rest to the river's edge.

Brin began to chant, and Arket joined in. The river churned, as if fighting the spell, but the two wizards won out. The water hardened to resemble stone.
"Move now!" shouted Brin.
There was no hesitation, and within a moment, the beasts were across. The two released the spell, and the river once again flowed free. Brin couldn't

shake the feeling that the river was angered by the magic. An odd sensation, and one that stuck in her mind for many days following.

Back and forth, Brin paced. With the announcement of an heir, the city rejoiced and celebrated. Brin, however, did not feel like participating in revelry. More than three weeks had passed, and there was still no sign of the enemy. Brin had taken to going to the river daily to check. Each time leaving in an angry cloud. Rain once again threatened the city, which made Brin's mood grow even darker. It wasn't until a visit from the midwife, did she calm. After being told to relax, or lose the child, Brin's demeanour softened. The last thing she wanted was to be the cause of harm to her unborn child.

Fox sat on the balcony floor, leaning against the railing. He watched Brin stomp about the room, and listened intently when the midwife came, and practically scolded the empress. Stroking his chin, he contemplated this new development. A baby might change how this war was going to be fought. The Lady of Shadows, the name the leader of his order went by, was very intrigued by this new area suddenly becoming accessible. Then war was spoken of, and she became enthralled. War was always good for their business. Fox wondered how this latest development would make her feel.

Standing, Fox drew his cloak tight about his body, and stepped into the shadows. Within a breath, he was outside the city, emerging from a shadow cast by the wall. He glanced back towards the palace, sitting far in the distance, and smiled. One day, he may be tasked to remove the royalty in this land. For now, he used the cloak's ability to spy. Fox turned away from the wall and headed out to the desert. It was time to head back home and report this news.

CHAPTER EIGHT

Eric stood, sword held out front, balancing on one leg. It was a favourite stretch of his, and one he was still attempting to master. The night was cool, and although he could be using the practice arena, he preferred the east courtyard. The proximity to the sea always helped his concentration. Soft sounds of waves crashing against the outer wall helped him focus. Eric's mind needed the calm sounds of the sea, for it was on more than stretching these days. The odd surge of power he had experienced weighed heavy on his mind. It had been intoxicating, and terrifying. Continuing his movements, he lowered one leg, then shifted to raise the other. A soft breeze blew through, causing him to lose his balance. Annoyed, he began again.

"It wasn't so long ago that you and I would play hide and seek in the northern woods," said a voice.

Eric faltered at the sound of his sister's voice and collapsed to the ground. Koral couldn't help but laugh, and she moved to her brother's side, offering a hand up. Eric took it, laughing along with her. When he stood, Koral grabbed him in a hug.

"I do not know if I can ever get used to that musical laugh, you now have," he said, motioning to a bench off to the side.

Koral sat down, and looked at her brother. "I am not certain I can ever get used to the idea that we are only seventeen. Feels like it has been years since we started our quest."

Eric sat beside her, nodding. "I know how you feel. Moreover, you are right. Two years ago, we were playing games, and trying out small spells in the forest. Now look at us."

Koral sighed, and her eyes turned to the castle. "So many things have changed and are going to keep changing. An uncle we did not know about, now getting married. I live in the forest with elves and have never felt more comfortable. New areas are under the control of father, and next in line for the crown is you. Not the life I thought we would have at this point."

Eric put his arm around Koral and pulled her tight. "I am also getting married. Most think it is to align our kingdom and Lungast, but Kaitlyn and I had planned it before we knew what was going to happen."

Koral turned her head to Eric. "Married? You? What happened to being a great hero?" Koral's tone was joking, but it wasn't far off.

"Again, a thought from a previous life," Eric said with a shrug.

Movement on the terrace caught their eye as Elizanne and Kaitlyn moved out into the fresh air. The sight brought a smile to Eric's lips. The two siblings stood and walked over to their mother.

"Is something amiss?" asked Koral.

Elizanne smiled. "No, my dear. I am just here to inform you that your father will be holding meetings every day until he moves against the south, and he wishes for you to be in attendance."

When Koral had arrived at the castle, Glavlin and Darly had gone to find Jeremy, so this news was expected.

"We are also out here to enjoy the afternoon air with some wine and sweets," remarked Elizanne, pointing out an area already set up. "You both are welcome to join us."

Eric kissed his mother on the cheek as she moved to sit. "I must freshen up, mother, but will be back to join you soon."

With a wink to Kaitlyn, which caused her to blush, Eric went inside.

Koral smiled at Kaitlyn and took a seat across from her. "I hear congratulations are in order," said Koral, taking a drink from her wine glass.

"Thank you, Koral. Although we have no idea when it is going to happen," Kaitlyn replied.

"Planning a wedding between two kingdoms is already proving to be quite the ordeal," said Elizanne with a smile. "I have no worries though. Everything will come together when it is meant to."

Koral looked at her mother, then back to Kaitlyn. "Honestly, I am more interested in hearing the tale of your adventure."

At the mention of the quest, Kaitlyn perked up. "Oh, what an adventure it was. I thought being hidden away and on the run with Garelin was interesting. This last quest certainly showed me the strange ways of this world."

A sip of wine, and Kaitlyn went about telling her tale. Part way through, Eric returned, and added his own information. When Koral heard about the goblins, tears came to her eyes, and she allowed them to flow freely down her cheeks.

"They were the last true worshippers of Nelvlick," stated Gillock, coming up to the table. "However, I believe the god lives. So many on our trip learned of this good god. Perhaps some have begun to follow him."

Koral stood and hugged the old man tight. Taking a step back, Koral noticed the strange look on his face. “Is there something wrong?” she asked, sitting down.

Gillock took a seat next to Elizanne, and looked at Koral. “I'm happy you're here. Tomorrow, I plan to tell King Jeremy that it's time for us to move into Death's Boundary. We have sat on the defensive for long enough. It's about time we find out what we are up against.”

Confused, Koral stared at Gillock. “What does that have to do with me?”

“We are elves,” replied Darly, joining those seated. “Gillock has made it clear that humans alone cannot enter the boundary. There are too many creatures unknown to them.”

A servant refilled the wine glasses, and Koral grasped it tight. “That makes sense. We do have heightened abilities. Will you be joining us?” she asked Gillock.

Gillock placed his glass on the table and gave Koral a strange look. “Yes. I'm hoping to be able to help eliminate some of the dangers lurking in the boundary.”

A door opened, and Glavlin and Jeremy joined the group outside. Jeremy sat down next to Elizanne, a look of exhaustion on his face.

“You look quite tired father,” stated Koral.

Jeremy sat back, and looked at his daughter. His eyes then moved to Eric, and he realised how much his children had grown over the last year. “I am, Koral. This war business is out of my league. Lucky for me, I have amazing advisors, and generals willing to follow my lead.”

A silence enveloped them, and all which could be heard was the waves crashing against the outer wall.

“A storm is brewing,” said Mena, walking up to those seated from the garden area. “I'm happy we are on land for this one.”

“Aye,” hollered Goram, running up to join his wife. “By the looks of the sky out over the sea, this storm is a ship sinker.”

“Those clouds are really dark,” commented Max, who had joined the group as well.

“Boy, you've never seen what clouds like that look like from underneath. Now that's a sight!” declared Goram.

Before anyone could ask about it, Goram had taken a seat, and begun to tell tales of being on the ocean in his youth. Within half an hour, tension and thoughts of war were replaced by laughter and merriment. With everyone enjoying their time outside, Jeremy arranged for a small dinnere to be served on the terrace. Goram regaled them well into the evening with tales of his travels, and stories he had been told as a child. When all retired for the night, Jeremy had renewed hope. All felt better than they had in weeks. All but Gillock. Instead of going to bed, he headed to the library of Zanth. He needed to be reminded what awaited them in the boundary.

Two weeks went by, and the day came. The elves, Eric, and Gillock stood facing the passage they had decided would be the best place to enter. Soldiers lined behind them, with General Chenkit and General Traug out in front. Behind the soldiers, Jeremy and Glomain sat. Neither wanted to be left behind, but both knew they couldn't risk going through until the way was made clear. It was King Jeremy's hope to be through by the end of summer and have a camp in place on the far side to deter any attack coming this way. The impending battles were foremost in Jeremy's mind, but so was the marriage of his brother-in-law. With all the dark times, which appeared to lay before them, celebrating was necessary to keep spirits high.

Dawn appeared a few hours prior, and clouds had rolled in, much to their happiness. No shadows to play tricks on their eyes. Sounds, however, were another story. Strange whispers were coming from the boundary.

"Wisps," remarked a soldier, and no one scoffed at the idea. No one was certain what they were going to find.

A shout from Glavlin to the generals, and the five moved into the opening. The soldiers were to wait half an hour before following unless they heard the sounds of fighting.

With cautious steps, the small group wound their way down the trail. Small branches moved off in different directions, but Glavlin, who was in the lead, kept them on the main trail. Gillock brought up the rear, and although those in front of him had their eyes darting in all directions, his gaze kept forward. Glavlin was right to keep to this trail. After his reading in the library last night, Gillock was certain most of the unusual creatures the wizards had placed within had died out. Now, moving through, he had a sense of trepidation. He didn't sense the dark creatures created, but there was something. An hour passed, and the feeling didn't leave, but they also hadn't been attacked. Behind them, the elves could hear the soft footfalls of the army, slowly coming up.

Another hour went by, and the footfalls turned into echoes. The soldiers wore their armour, and even though they were moving slowly, the boundary was causing the shifting armour to echo down the trail. The noise caused Gillock to shake his head. Whatever stealth they began with, was lost to them. A hand signal from Glavlin, and they all dropped into a crouch. Above, shadows shifted, and a large cat came into view. No one moved, but Glavlin knew the group had been spotted a while back. The cat, which looked larger than a horse, most likely had come to find out what was causing all the noise. The animal leap from ledge to ledge until it landed, behind Gillock. When on all fours, the cat was as tall as the wizard was. It hadn't taken on a menacing stance; instead, it paced back and forth across the opening, eyeing the five.

Gillock watched the cat closely, trying to recall what type it was. On one pass, it was all black, but when it shifted to turn, you could see stripes across the fur. The elves had come to stand beside Gillock, with Eric keeping his eyes to the front of the trail in case this was a trap. The cat stopped its pacing, and sat down, eyes on the elves and Gillock.

"You are a strange animal," said Darly, cocking her head at the cat. The cat turned its eyes to her and moved his head in imitation.

"You're a mountain, moor cat," stated Gillock, and the cat nodded its head, causing all to gasp.

Koral took a step forward. "The noise coming from behind is our army coming through. We do not wish you any harm, and it would be best if you stayed hidden when they passed. Humans tend to attack what they do not understand."

The cat again cocked its head and nodded. With a great leap, it ran back up to the ledge, and into the shadows.

"Too bad not all creatures in here are as friendly," remarked Gillock, shaking his head.

Glavlin motioned them to continue. "We were lucky it wasn't hungry."

Another half an hour passed, and still nothing attacked. "We are being tested," stated Darly softly.

Gillock agreed. "Something is watching us and waiting. Perhaps they wish to see how long it will take until we let our defences down."

Glavlin glanced about. "Yes, that would be a good tactic."

A strange sensation passed down the trail. Something magic, but nothing like they had ever felt before.

"I wonder what caused that?" questioned Koral.

The trepidation Gillock had felt earlier became stronger. "Something sent out that magic. A thing as I have not felt for centuries, but I can't place what it was."

With Gillock stating he was unsure as to what was going on, the other four became worried. “What should we do?” asked Eric.

A breeze began to move through the rocks, stirring up the dust.

“Run!” shouted Glavlin, and no one hesitated.

Moments after they moved, a large rock came rolling down to their location. The dust had made it hard for them to see, but Glavlin was in the lead and his elf eyes had no trouble, yet. The elves could out distance the humans, but instead kept their pace slow. When a large space was before them, Glavlin had them halt.

“There is a great place for an attack,” Glavlin stated, and no one disagreed.

Darly looked about, and pointed to the right side. “We have no choice,” she said pointing.

Through a small passage, there were trees.

Glavlin sighed hard. “We will move, but with great caution. We do not know what is waiting for us.”

A soft hum was heard as the wind whispered through the rocks. It was also the only sound which reached their ears. Eyes forward, and senses heightened, they awaited the inevitable attack.

CHAPTER NINE

Daylight waned as the sun moved behind the small mountain range running through the land. The old man finished setting his camp and started a fire. Within half an hour, the smell of cooking food wafted through the trees. Glancing about, he knew all was ready. Soon he would have visitors, and it was only polite to have supper ready for them.

"This heat is going to be the end of me," growled Firadon, causing Aremeth to chuckle.

"So you keep saying. Then night comes, and cooler air brings you back to yourself," remarked Aremeth.

Firadon shook his head, and continued down the trail. They had been travelling for weeks, trying to find a place they could cross the desert. Once they hit the edge of the forest, all which lay before them was sand. The tracks they were following were wiped away by the winds which ran across the desert. Not knowing which way to go, they moved back into the tree line. When the sun began to set, they moved back to the desert, to see if something could be found. Each day, all that greeted them was never-ending sand. There was also the strange heat. Firadon noticed it slightly back where he had made his home. Out here, it was difficult for him to tolerate. It was as if the moment the sun was in the sky, the sand heated up, giving off an intense heat.

After a time, the trees became thicker, and the small mountain range, known as Torkra, could be seen in the distance.

"Our travels have taken us farther south than I would have thought," stated Aremeth.

Firadon glanced about. "How long has your tribe stayed in one spot?"

"A few centuries now," replied Aremeth. "I admit I travel more north than south, but with our path moving as it had, I didn't figure we would be this far off course. That is not the only thing bothering me. We haven't come across a single camp. At this time of year, most of the other tribes are stationary. Strong winds come up off the desert and travel is very dangerous."

Firadon let out a gruff sound. "You can say that again. I don't think any of our food doesn't have sand in it."

The comment caused Aremeth to laugh. "Well, night will soon be upon us.

Best to keep moving and hope we find a place to make camp."

Aremeth moved passed Firadon, patting the large man on the back. They had become fast friends, as tends to happen when you travel with a stranger, and only have each other to depend on. The sun began to set, and the scent of food, cooking, came through the trees.

"Perhaps a tribe still exists," said Aremeth, hopeful.

Moving towards the scent, the two weren't quite certain what it was they came upon. What they found, was a camp set up, and a lone elderly male sitting by a fire, cooking up strips of meat and vegetables. Cautiously, they moved to the edge of his camp, watching. Both listened to hear if there were others hidden about, but the crackling fire, and sizzling meat made it difficult.

"You can gawk at me from the bushes until the fire goes down, or you can come enjoy the food," hollered the old man.

Immediately Aremeth stood, moving to stand behind the fire. "It wasn't our intent to insult you. It's just we haven't come across any people, so we were worried this was a trap."

The man stood, and both men knew this was no ordinary old man. Even though his stature was smaller than Firadon, the northman knew he would not be a match for this old one. His entire body appeared to be muscle, and a deep intelligence hid behind his dark eyes.

"I may look old to your eyes, Aremeth, but I have no need for others to do anything for me," stated the man.

Aremeth smiled, and nodded. "May we join your fire and take of your food?"

The old man returned the smile. "My fire and food are yours to have as long as you need."

Firadon glanced between the two and knew something was going on that he wasn't aware of. Not truly caring, the big man plunked his pack down, and sat himself on the ground a distance away from the fire.

"Kind of strange place to make a camp, isn't it?" questioned Firadon.

The old man produced some wine and offered it to both. "This is where I need to be," he replied.

Aremeth, who had been staring quite oddly at the old man, took the glass timidly, and sipped it. Firadon found it strange and waited patiently for things to reveal themselves. For a time, they sat in silence, staring into the fire as if in a silent contemplation.

“You are Jacen,” came out of Aremeth’s mouth in a jumble of words.
The old man stoked the fire and turned his eyes to Aremeth. “Yes, my son, I am.”
Firadon sat with his mouth hanging open. Before him was a man with weathered skin, dark hair pulled back, and eyes which showed many feelings. He was also a god. “Jacen. As in the wandering god?”
“I am he, Firadon Dey. To answer your next question, I am here to turn your quest back to the north,” remarked Jacen.
Aremeth, although still awed at the presence of his god, became upset. “But the villagers lie to the east. I can’t abandon them.”
Jacen sipped at his wine, staring into the fire. “There are no tribes in this land. I sent them all across the strait, down into the old country, and they will remain there until I find these lands are again safe. Your village was the last, and sadly, it is too late for them. You are needed north. A young prince, of Firadon’s acquaintance, is heading on a quest. For him to succeed, both of you need to join him.”
Firadon spit out his wine and coughed deep. “Eric’s going on another quest you say. Last one I joined him on was quite an ordeal.”
Jacen smiled at the man. “He just returned from one which had him out on the sea for a great length of time. He is most likely not excited about this, but it must be done.”
Firadon watched as the old man’s smile faded, and a look of sadness took its place. “Far be it for me to go against a god, but I don’t suppose you can give more information on this?” queried Firadon.
A wistful look came to Jacen’s eyes. “I am sorry, but I can only see parts. Know that you must abandon this path you are on, and help Eric complete his task.”

Aremeth had grown silent listening to the two. His heart broke at the idea of leaving his people behind, but he knew that Jacen only appeared when the need was dire. There was no choice but to go north as he asked and help this friend of Firadon’s. Their conversation ended, and Jacen left the fire. Aremeth watched as he left, and noticed the god had a sadness to his steps. Growing weary, he moved over to his pack. Using it as a pillow, he fell asleep.

Firadon watched as his companion fell asleep and began to feel drowsy himself. His thoughts wandered to Eric, and this new quest. Well over a year had passed since he left Eric that day in the cavern, yet the northman found himself thinking about the young prince. Often wondering how Eric was faring. This new quest piqued his interest, although Firadon was curious as to why he was needed for this quest. With a smile, he recalled saving Eric from the goblins, and in turn becoming the prince's guide. Shaking his head, the northman joined his companion in rest, hoping the morning would shed more light on this strange turn of events.

Jacen stood in the shadows and watched as his sleeping spell took hold of the two. A good meal, and nights rest, was all he could offer the two. The quest they were joining was not going to be a pleasant one, but Jacen knew the two were needed to help make it succeed. Turning his eyes to the east, Jacen allowed a tear to fall. Soon, Aremeth's tribe would find him, and he needed to be ready.

CHAPTER TEN

Within seconds the group moving through the boundary were under attack. Strange two-legged creatures, their faces resembling a moose, came at them from the rocks. Each one moving with grace across the uneven terrain. Their hooves had no issues gripping the moving stones. Gillock threw a spell at them, barely slowing the creatures down. Once magic was shown, the creatures changed their target. Instead of attempting to strike them all down, their focus moved to one.

"They appear to be focused on Gillock," shouted Glavlin. "We must defend him!"

Swords slashed all about at the beasts, but to no avail. Even a hit from an elven blade did little damage to the torso of the strange creature. Gillock threw different spells at them, drawing their ire. This is why they altered their attack to take out the wizard. Their master had told them to focus on those who used magic. At the moment, Gillock was only the one.

Once Koral and Eric heard Glavlin's statement, both changed from using swords, to using magic. Koral's, being that of the earth, was useless. She called upon roots to grab at their legs, but the area itself was magic, and it took much out of her to pull up one from the ground. Eric, set his sword aflame. His blade, being blessed by Nalmala, was lit with a deep orange glow. As with other encounters, it gave the enemy pause. When one attacked, and his sword cut it clean through, the others backed off. Eric could feel the magic surging through him, demanding to be released. With angry cries for blood, Eric moved to engage more of the odd beasts.

More sword clashes echoed, then shouts as the rest of the army moved into the area, taking on the unusual creatures. Max was in the lead, and with his sword drawn, he went after the first beast who crossed his path. The fight lasted another half an hour before all the creatures were destroyed, and a fourth of the army was either injured or dead.

"I suggest we push on into the forest and see if we can find a suitable campsite," stated Darly.

Koral looked at the opening, and to the trees beyond. "Hopefully there are no more surprises."

"Those creatures were an attempt to slow us down," remarked Gillock. "It won't be long before the army of the south is coming at us. We must go now."

The harshness of the old wizard's tone shocked them, but no one said anything. Gillock's robe was torn in many places and stained with blood. It wasn't clear how much of it was his. Without waiting for anyone to agree with him, Gillock headed towards the opening. Eric glanced at his companions, and with a shrug, moved to follow.

Gillock's hard steps echoed within the small opening, but he didn't care. The creatures which had attacked them were trentataurs. Beings created centuries ago to protect the wizards. They were bred to kill, and they weren't the only things created to do so in that age. Some had been locked away in the Void, others tossed to the south, and blocked from returning to the Central Lands. Gillock didn't know if they had attacked him because they remembered what the wizards had done, or if his magic alone had drawn their attention, but it didn't matter. He should have sensed them, and more men wouldn't be lying in the dirt, dead. The forest opened up before him, and he paused. Magic was present, but it was hard to tell if it was hostile. There was no stopping now so on ahead he walked.

Their steps were cautious, eyes checking every shadowy place. The trees were different from what they were used to, older, but not as thick. Upon entering, all three elves felt the strangeness.

"This place is old, wild, and unusual," remarked Glavlin.

One tree caught Koral's eye. Walking over, Koral placed her hand on it. Closing her eyes, she tried to listen to it. "They are curious about us," she said, taking her hand away. "They know us to be elves, but none has been in their midst for centuries."

Gillock went and stood beside Koral. "When the wizards cut off this land, no one was able to come through. The forest is old, and something is off about it. Be cautious."

"There is a large clearing to the right," said Darly, coming up to them. "I am going to scout about the forest to the west."

"I will go inform the army," stated Eric, moving back towards the rocks.

"Guess that leaves us to move to the river and see if the army is already camped out there," said Glavlin to Gillock and Koral.

The first thing they noticed when moving through the forest was the heat. It was cool on the north side, but here, a warm temperature was held in the trees. It was unusual, but not unexpected. After all this side of Death's Boundary was mostly desert, and an unnatural desert at that.

They moved cautiously through the trees until the river came into view. It was clear scouts had paced along the river's edge. Many sets of

footprints could be seen by elven eyes, and not all were human.
"Unusual creatures have patrolled that side of the river," remarked Gillock, concern evident in his voice.
"There are many strange creatures in this desert. I am not at all surprised that Brin had taken them into her army," stated Koral, her tone taking on a darkness, as it did whenever Brin was mentioned.
Glavlin scanned the area across and saw no movement. "There is no one over there now. This is the best time to set up camp, and watches."

Moving back into the forest, a strange call came to Koral. It was weak but felt dangerous. Glancing at her companions, it was clear to Koral the call was only heard by her. They continued walking, and Koral never heard it again. Her eyes glanced east. Something dark lurked in that direction, and she wondered if it was a trap set by her sister. Pushing the dark thoughts down, Koral continued to follow the others to the camp site. They didn't have much time to set up before she and the others were having to leave. Making certain the ones in charge were ready for anything was more important than a strange call.

Night came, and everything was set. Most of the army was spread out through the forest area, with scouts even further down to ensure no attacks came from the sides. The area across was the best spot for an army to sit. Many rocks for cover, and for archers to hide behind and launch volleys into their forest. The elves helped with the king's archers, ensuring they were hidden well, and could escape if needed. When morning arrived, Jeremy left, with the elves and Gillock in tow. Only Glomain remained to help. Max wish to remain but was asked to be present at the wedding. With Kaitlyn attending, Max understood why they wanted him there. None of them wanted to leave, but all knew how important it was to the Central Lands to be in attendance. All they could do was hope that when the battle was fully engaged, they would be back to stand with the men.

Vernia sat on the wall edge, looking out over the sea. It was a peaceful place to contemplate life, and she had many thoughts on her mind. Foremost being the fact that she and Max were the last of the true bloodline, of the followers of Painish.

"That is not a safe place to sit," came the voice of Elizanne.
Vernia turned and got down. "No, but it is the best view, and I like to sit and watch."
Elizanne smiled and came to stand beside the young woman. "And to think

on these unusual events of late?" questioned Elizanne. When no response came, she added. "It is nice to see you out of your room."

Vernia gave her a slight smile. "It's rather stuffy in there, so I came out to get some fresh air."

"You usually do it when the sun is down," stated Elizanne.

The young woman blushed. "Yes, I do tend to slink about the castle. I guess it's because I know it so well."

"I often forget you were stationed here," said Elizanne.

"I never wanted to leave the Tower. I felt safe there. Once I came here, that all changed. I enjoyed everyone avoiding me or cowering as I approached. It made me feel powerful, and I realised that I had nothing to fear. No one was a match for my abilities here."

Seeing the guard's eyes shift as they made their way passed the two women made Elizanne wonder. "How does it feel to walk around here now?"

Vernia took a deep breath and thought about it. "People still fear me, and I no longer enjoy that."

"It will take time for everyone to get used to the idea that you are no longer a threat to them," stated Elizanne.

Vernia stared out, and said nothing for many moments. "I don't think they will ever accept me."

Elizanne placed her hand on Vernia's arm. "That is a possibility, however, I wish you to know that Jeremy and I accept you."

Silence followed the remark, and the two stared out over the water together. They stayed there, enjoying each other's silence and company, until a guard came running up.

"Highness, I don't wish to intrude, but there has been an incident in the city."

"What kind of incident?" asked Elizanne, worried.

"A small child has been found dead," stated the guard, his voice quivering. "Not just dead, highness. Something more terrible than that."

"Take me to the body," demanded the queen, and her tone made it clear the guard was not to ignore her. Vernia tagged along, keeping quiet.

The carriage rode hard down the city streets. All persons were ordered home, and those who didn't have a home moved to the sewers, hoping them safer than the streets above. They arrived at the scene, and the wails of a destroyed mother could be heard. Elizanne burst from the carriage, and immediately moved over to where the woman, Marly, was.

Her husband, Elman, was on his knees beside his wife, tears falling freely. Laying before them was a blanket with a shrivelled body on it.

Elizanne's heart broke at the sight, and she knelt down across from them. "I am so sorry for this," she said softly.

The two lifted their heads and were stunned to see the queen. "Majesty..," began Elman, but Elizanne lifted her hand to stop him.

"As queen, I am responsible for keeping the streets safe, especially for children. It is my duty to be here."

Eyes red and face wet from the tears, Marly reached across. Elizanne took her hand and kept her eyes on Marly's. "You don't know how much that means," she said through sobs.

Elizanne squeezed Marly's hand tight and nodded. "You may take your child home at any time, and if there is anything you require, please let me know." Another squeeze and Elizanne stood, moving back to the carriage.

Vernia stayed back but made certain to have a clear view of the body. It was beyond anything she had seen before, as if the child had every last bit of fluid in his body taken. Vernia was well versed in ways to kill, but this was something she was certain no mortal could achieve. The idea frightened her. Glancing about, for a moment she thought something in the shadows across the street was watching. A dark chill moved through her body, and she was positive something unnatural caused this child's death. When Elizanne made her way back to the carriage, she followed closely behind. Vernia knew the ride back to the castle was going to be an interesting one.

Kaitlyn woke and knew something was amiss. The usual bustling castle felt muted. Throwing on her robe, Kaitlyn opened her door, and ordered breakfast. The page gave a bow and left. As she shut the door, Kailyn noted that the page hadn't smiled, as he always did.

An open window allowed a soft, warm wind to blow in. When her breakfast arrived, she was dressed and took in on the small balcony outside her room. Her balcony overlooked the main garden, and the scent of a dozen varieties of flowers blooming wafted up to her. Once done, she noticed something else coming up to her balcony. The sound of marching guards. Standing, and looking about, she noted more guards on the outer wall. Something was going on, and although she had been given no warning, Kaitlyn worried what it could mean.

Hours later, Kaitlyn was summoned by the queen. In the room, sat

Vernia, and both appeared to have slept little. When they explained the events of the previous night, Kaitlyn understood the addition of more guards.

“What can I do to help?” inquired Kaitlyn.

Elizanne took her hand. “Right now, there is nothing any of us can do. This deed was done by something unnatural. All we can do is wait for Gillock, and hope he knows what to do.”

Kaitlyn looked to the faces of the two. “They are on their way. It is almost time for the wedding. I agree with telling Gillock, but perhaps it should be kept from those at Hope’s Light Keep for now. I know it sounds awful to say, but the new area is having issues. They need to believe this joining is going to improve the situation.”

Elizanne stared hard at the young woman. “For someone so young, you are well versed in dealing with unusual situations.”

Kaitlyn bowed her head to the queen. “I have led an unusual life.”

Elizanne nodded her understanding and waved the princess off. She was right. The wedding would go on, merriment and joy would be had by those in the new realm. Talk of dark creatures would have to wait.

CHAPTER ELEVEN

The sun slowly rose in the sky, causing the treetops to look aflame. Koral walked along the seashore, taking it all in. Since coming to Hope's Light Keep in preparation for her uncle's wedding, she had enjoyed sunrise walks along the shore. The waters drew her attention. Merfolk had taken to scouting the waters, most likely watching the new fishing boats. Although they kept themselves hidden, her elf eyes had no problem finding them in the water.

As the sun crested, it cast a brilliant glow onto the Keep, and it drew a smile from Koral. It might be a Keep, like many before it formed in a military way. However, the simple additions from the people of the area gave it a beauty that no one had yet been able to describe. The name suited this new place, and the town was blooming in its glow.

Koral's eyes turned again to the Sea of Arran. A breeze had come up causing the sunlight to sparkle off the slight waves, and a calm came over her. With a deep breath, Koral moved away from the shore and headed back to the keep. Soon everyone would be moving about, setting up for the wedding, which would take place in only a few days' time. Koral broke into a jog. She was in charge of ensuring the clearing where the ceremony was to take place was as beautiful as it could be, and she didn't want to disappoint.

Pacing across the terrace, the sunrise was the only beauty Malya could see so far this day. She had only awoke an hour ago, and already letters from outlying towns were flowing in. A small group of people, her people, refused to be under another ruler. Riots had occurred during the initial building of the Keep, causing Jessup to give them a small area of land, free from any outside influence. Now, they were bandits. Attacking caravans, and small villages.

Throwing the papers down, Malya sat hard. Jessup was out in the town, making certain what work was to be done this day could be. A small number of the disgruntled were in the city, causing building problems. Each morning, Jessup would visit the next area to be worked on and check over the materials to ensure they had all which was needed. The constant delay which had plagued them, were now under control. Little needed to be done, and Jessup was pleased.

Standing again, Malya moved to the side of the Keep, and looked down at the fishing vessels in the harbour. A flicker of deep red hair caught her eye, and she spotted Koral, jogging into the forest, most likely to see to the area in which the wedding would occur. Malya allowed herself to relax. The wedding would be perfect.

The guests in the Keep flitted about. Breakfast was served in their rooms, and the day was theirs. Most went out into the city, to view the shops which had popped up. Jeremy and Elizanne took part in a tour, showing the progress. Both observed how Jessup gushed over the entire area. Malya smiled at his enthusiasm and pushed aside the negative feelings she had felt only hours ago.

The next day clouds rolled in, but no one paid it any heed. This was the day before the wedding. A great luncheon was held, a practice that Malya's people once did. The entire city was welcome, and it was the duke's way of involving all in his special day.

Shaking hands, and eating far too much, put a smile on Malya's face. Later in the evening, she was whisked off by Elizanne. Being apart until they were married was a Central Land custom, and Malya looked pleased when Elizanne showed up to take her away. Jessup kissed her cheek and watched as she disappeared down the hall. Closing the door, the duke wondered if he would get any sleep this night.

Morning arrived with more bustle than Jessup thought possible. Eric, Koral, and Gillock ensured all guests were seated properly. Gillock went and took his seat, as the twins moved off to join their respective sides of the wedding party. Max and Kaitlyn were beside Gillock, and the old wizard couldn't wait for the festivities to begin. Far too much time had passed since everyone was able to relax. This would be fleeting, but it was a nice distraction. Moments later, the music began.

Multi-coloured leaves floated softly to the ground. The sight brought a tear to Malya's eye, although today her eyes were always in this state. The sun was shining bright, with only a few wisps of clouds gracing the sky. A light breeze was coming off the Sea of Arran, and it was a welcoming cool for the anxious bride. Taking a deep breath, Malya moved down the path with slow, careful steps. All eyes were on her, and she felt them. Her gaze, however, was on Jessup. She had never seen him in his royal apparel. Normally he was adorned with work clothing, helping the construction along with the others. Today, he was in full dress wear, and the sight made her heart skip. Jessup's brown hair was cut short and brushed back. His blue eyes never moving from Malya as she walked towards him.

Below her feet, Mayla could feel the soft rose petals being tossed by the young girls in front of her. She was barefoot, as was the custom for her people, but that is where it ended. Upon her own insistence, she wanted to be wed in the proper way of the kingdom. Conducting the ceremony was King Jeremy. It was the king's wish to perform at least part of the ceremony based on her culture, showing that both could live in harmony. As such, she agreed to walk barefoot down the path, with only rose petals marking her way.

Another step and Mayla could see the wetness falling from Koral's eyes. It brought a smile to her lips, and she remembered when she had asked Koral to stand up with her. Beside Jessup stood Payton. Once again, Malya's eyes fell on Jessup. He looked nervous, but not in a bad way. More in his usual way of hoping he wouldn't mess anything up. Malya wasn't worried. Even if those who refused rule rioted again, it wouldn't matter. Today was already perfect.

Jeremy looked to the faces before him, and then surveyed those gathered. Elizanne and Koral stood at Malya's side, with Payton and Eric on Jessup's. When all went quiet, he began the ceremony.

"We are all gathered, in this forest glade, to celebrate the joining of two people. This might be a royal ceremony, but it is also a historic one. Never before has the Central Lands witnessed this kind of event. We are all witness to the joining of two hearts, which existed, until now, in very different worlds. There is no precedent set for this kind of ceremony, so I have decided to make it a simple one." Taking a step forward, Jeremy held out his hands. "Please place a hand within mine," he said to each. Malya placed her left, and Jessup, his right. Jeremy grasped them tight and turned the two towards each other. Lifting his hands, Jeremy continued. "These two stand before all, showing that their love for one another knows no borders. So, as I join their hands, the two will become one." Moving their hands, he placed Malya's over Jessup's, and then added his own. "By the powers given to me as king of the Central Lands, and by your witness, I pronounce thee; husband and wife."

Malya leaned in to give a light kiss to Jessup, but he pulled her tight, and kissed her hard. The cheer from those gathered echoed through the forest. Laughter, along with tears of joy followed the two as they walked away from the glade.

Payton escorted Koral, with Elizanne taking her son's arm. The four followed the newlyweds, with Jeremy right behind. Tears flowed, and a joy filled the wooded area. Koral's heart had soared when she saw Malya walking down the aisle. Never had she seen someone so striking. The white gown looked beautiful against her darker skin. Tied up in her hair were roses, and the sight was breathtaking. Thinking about it now, the tears came. She was happy for her new friend.

Glavlin watched as Koral walked by and marvelled at her beauty. While all eyes were focused on the bride, his wouldn't leave Koral. Once the precession was complete, and everyone was socializing, Glavlin walked up to Koral, and pulled her in close. "You are beautiful today," he whispered.

Koral tilted her head up at him. "This day is beautiful, I only became a part of it."

The two stood in their embrace, until they noticed things had gone quiet. Glancing about, they noticed the stares. Some eyes were on them, some at the forest. Birds flitted in unison, and the trees creaked an unusual sound which had a relaxing effect on those present. Koral and Glavlin looked to each other and laughed. This new forest was their creation, so it was responding to the joy the two were exuding. With a shake of her head, Koral wiped her tears, and moved away from Glavlin. A feast awaited.

It wasn't long before the ballroom was filled with guests wishing to give thanks to the new couple. Food and drink filled all areas, and people feasted. Malya beamed, and Jessup had a grin from ear to ear, which made Elizanne's heart ache with joy. It was a wondrous day.

Jeremy made his rounds, but his heart was not into celebration. He was happy for Jessup and Malya however a fight was on their doorstep. Tonight, was a distraction, and Jeremy was happy everyone was enjoying it. There was no telling what the days ahead would bring.

CHAPTER TWELVE

Clouds filled the sky, hiding the setting sun. Although no storm had hit yet, it had been days since the sun had graced them with its heat. The unusual cool was welcome in the palace. There was no hiding her condition anymore, so Brin had taken to wearing light gowns which hugged her growing belly. Brin absently rubbed her stomach as she thought about the recent weather.

Only a week earlier, she had remarked on how difficult it was becoming to handle the heat. The next day, clouds rolled in. The humidity didn't jump up, nor did any rain come. Only light clouds cooling off the surrounding area. At first, the inhabitants had thought it a bad omen. This is when Arket suggested they begin to again mingle with the common folk.

Their first trek, they had ridden in a carriage. Since then, they walked. The city is vast, and impossible to traverse in a day, so the people took to meeting them in the central courtyard. Each day, surrounded by guards, the rulers walked amongst the people. When the announcement of her pregnancy reached all corners of the city, gifts began to flow in. Everyone was excited at the birth of an heir. It proved to the populace even more how much their rulers were like them. Brin couldn't understand their devotion but gave each person a smile upon passing. This small gesture usually brought a glow to the person's face. These peasants belonged to her, and inside she felt sorry for them. Blind following usually leads to a devastating end. Her own experience was proof of that.

A light wind blew up to where she stood on the balcony. Brin took in a deep breath, and began pacing around the entire area, surveying all. The harbour was lined with ships, all manned and ready should an attack come by sea. The spy in her father's house had given detailed descriptions of the vessels being built just south of Keenley, and they were ready for them.

Walking along the balcony, Brin arrived at the south side. Below, she could hear the grunts of her army practicing. The number was vast, and Brin couldn't wait to use them. Another half an hour, and she came to the north area of the balcony, and her attention became directed there. Sand as far as the eye could see and guarded by dragonworms. Brin smiled when she thought of what an army would do when they encountered her little pets. Some had grown to five meters long, and all had a mouth with three rows of razor-sharp teeth. Brin wasn't certain if anyone had tried to cross the river into her land yet, but if they had, they were dead.

"Bring your army across the river, father. Come at me head on, and watch your soldiers die," Brin whispered to the wind.

Arket moved out onto the balcony, joining his wife. "I see your gaze falls to the north again. Perhaps we should go and see the river. Scouts have reported noises from the woods beyond."

Brin looked up into Arket's eyes. Their love was not traditional, brought about by a mutual desire, but they did love each other.

Brin absently rubbed her belly again. "In the morning, we shall travel."

Before the sun was up, the rulers were ready. They didn't go by carriage because that would have taken weeks. Instead, they moved with magic. Both had been to the river's edge many times and knew a perfect spot to arrive. A few large boulders concealed them from prying eyes looking that way. Arket was wearing sand coloured clothing, and Brin matched. She also had a hood, thrown over her dark hair. Each peeked out from either side of the boulder, hoping to catch a glimpse of their enemy.

"The scouts were right. Something is happening in those woods," whispered Arket.

Pulling back, Brin moved to stand beside him. "My magic was never strong within that forest," she growled.

Arket turned to face her. "We knew it was unlikely we would be able to attack them with magic alone. The trentataur's slowed them, but it is clear they no longer threaten the army's advance. Perhaps it is time you moved the lazzards to the area."

Brin moved her gaze from the forest edge. "The dragonworms will keep this side of the river safe. The lazzards will guard the area near the city."

Arket didn't agree with her plan but understood why she felt this way. Her condition was making her slightly paranoid, and so he kept his views to himself.

When battle was engaged, the lazzards would move against the enemy, regardless of where they attacked. The smell of blood attracted them, and once they began an attack, they wouldn't stop until either they were dead, or their enemy was.

"Let us head back, and take a look at the current plans," suggested Arket.

Brin gave him a slight smirk. "Fine. We can go to your planning room. I think it is time the army began to make its way to this spot."

A giant grin moved onto Arket's face. He had been wanting to attack for months and was happy to hear that his wife finally agreed. With a few words, they were back on their balcony. Both changed into their normal royal attire and headed down to the planning room.

"When do you want me to give the order, your highness?" asked the general.

"Now," replied Arket. "I want them all moving by sunset."

A wave to a page, and the written orders were out. Two hours later, the sound of an army gathering its things could be heard echoing throughout the city. Wagons carrying weapons, clothing, and food were loaded. Each surrounded by armed men on horseback. When the area began to darken, the army moved out. In the lead were more armed men. Next were the wagons, followed by the rest of the army, on foot. Arket stood on the wall, watching them leave.

"Are you certain it is wise for us to stay behind?" asked Brin.

Arket put his arm around Brin. "Once they are set up, and send word things are safe, we will move. I do not want the enemy to think you are weak, because of your condition. They may take advantage of you if they see us riding up with the army."

Brin thought on his words, and realised he was right. With a heavy sigh, she watched as the last of the men were lost from view. "Were the horsemasters taken care of?"

Arket stiffened. "Changru and his men are dealing with them as we speak. All will be dead shortly."

Brin's face broke into a cruel grin. "They are the first to fall to us and will be a warning to anyone who attempts to attack us."

True to his words, the kidnapped village was slaughtered, their bodies laid out for all to see who approached from the south. Although they thought the people were killed down to the last child, they were wrong. Many of the adults had made their children hide with the horses. The noble beasts would not make a sound, so they would be safe from what they knew was inevitable. When the deed was done, the horses, which had refused their new masters, and were to be killed as well. The animals heard a call from Jacen and moved towards the huddled children. Kneeling down, the children understood, and each took to a horse. Throwing themselves into a battle rage, they broke from their pens, and ran towards the west, leaving a stunned enemy in their wake.

A mist clung to the ground, and wove itself through the trees.

Jacen glanced at his guests beside the fire. The two men through the trees had fallen asleep quickly. To mortal eyes, the mist was heavy, but not unusual in the early morning hours. To Jacen, it was something more. Within he could see the faces of those murdered. None had died a warrior's death, for their enemy was weak and wouldn't even attempt a fight. They had died due to magic weakening them, allowing the enemy to slaughter them easily. Months earlier, he had ordered all the other tribes to the south, across the strait, and into the old lands. All but these. They were the only tribe he had asked to remain in one place, becoming more than the rest. His plan for a better people had worked for a time. Now, it was over. A dozen children and Aremeth were all who remained.

Jacen focused on the faces and allowed himself to join them. It was his responsibility to guide them to their new journey. The spell he cast on Aremeth, and Firadon would wear off soon. By then, the horses and the children would arrive at the village, and Aremeth would go onto the quest Jacen had given him. Hopefully, all would go as planned, and the tribes of the wandering god would begin again.

CHAPTER THIRTEEN

Six weeks after the army left the city, the river was in sight. Travel had been slow due to the heat. The clouds which kept the city cool only reached a few hours away, making them need to travel at night. By the time the sun was setting, Brin and Arket were there, walking through the camp, and showing the men they were there to fight along with them. Some were wary due to Brin's condition, but they were quickly put in their place. It was clear to the majority that if their rulers were willing to risk their unborn child to fight alongside them, they were confident of a glorious win. The talk came to both their ears and was ignored. Brin would not be on the front line, nor would Arket. They were there to counter any magic attacks, and to give support.

Scouts watched the forest across the river. Long before the army had set up camp, a silence enveloped the forest. The birds no longer chirped, and the sounds of people became quiet.

"How long has it been this way?" asked Brin.

"A little over a week, highness," replied a scout, who served at this post for over a month.

Brin cast her eyes to the trees, attempting to see what lay beyond. When her eyes revealed nothing, she changed to magic. Sending out feeler spells, she tried to determine who was across, and why the forest appeared so forbidding. She touched the minds of a few soldiers, then the spell was blocked. The burning pain only lasted a moment, but it was enough to bring on a headache. A scowl crossed Brin's face, and her eyes narrowed.

"An army is hiding in there, one containing elves. I have been blocked from seeing into their minds, but perhaps I can draw them out."

The scout shifted, and it was clear he felt uneasy.

"Is there something else?" Brin asked.

With a gulp, the scout stared down at Brin's feet. "Majesty, the first who arrived set up rafts along the river to allow the army to cross and attack. When morning came, they were gone. I'm not sure what's on the other side, but something isn't right."

Brin's scowl turned to rage. Her face went red, and her eyes flashed dangerously as she stared across the river.

Moving to stand in front of the men, Brin raised her hand, pointed it at a large tree, and released her magic. The tree, which should have been cut down and lying across the river, still stood. With an odd ripple, the entire area absorbed the magic. A voice, carried on a breeze, came at them. "Your magic will not work here, Brin of the south. Try and send your army across the river and you will watch them be torn apart by arrows."

Brin didn't recognize the man speaking, but by the tone, he was an elf. Most likely the reason why the forest was now concealing the army within. Brin turned and stormed back into her ranks and ordered a volley of arrows to be released at random. Their soldiers won't be able to cross, but she was going to make certain that her enemy didn't try it either.

Glomain watched as Brin stormed off. With soft steps, he ran towards the general's tent. "They have arrived, and I must leave to speak with Gillock. I will also inform the king the army has set up. I am certain he will arrive as quickly as he can."

Olrond nodded to the elf. "You would go much faster than a courier. Leave, and may you arrive with speed."

Glomain threw a light pack over his shoulder and was off running. Olrond glanced at Ender, and both turned their gaze towards the south. The enemy had arrived.

Their tent was filled with pillows, yet Brin felt uncomfortable. She went from sitting, to pacing, and back again. Nothing could ease her mind, and it was affecting her body. Each day which passed was giving the enemy time to plan. They had sent men into the water, only to watch them be struck down by arrows. Although it was clear most of the archers were human, at least one had the abilities of an elf. Moving further down in different directions didn't help either. The enemy had the shoreline well protected.

The battle raged, arrows flew from both sides, and Brin along with Arket still tried spells to see if they could weaken the forest. For a time, it appeared to be working, then one day they woke, and the forest across was strengthened. It became clear to the rulers that more elves had arrived. Their suspicions were clarified a few days later. As the sun rose, standing across the river was Koral, along with her father. Neither appeared to be worried about being hit by an arrow, but Brin sent a volley at them anyway. Before they even came close, the arrows were knocked from the sky. With satisfied looks, the two moved back into the forest. Brin's anger could no longer be contained, and all of the archers who failed, were struck dead where they stood. Arket moved to calm his wife and forced her back to their tent.

"They are taunting me!" she screeched, and not for the first time. Arket didn't disagree with her assessment. The two presenting themselves as they had, made it clear they wanted Brin to know they were there. "Beloved, please sit down. You need to be careful."

Brin glared at Arket, but knew he was right. If she continued to rant, there was a chance she could harm the baby. Dropping onto the soft pillows, Brin lay back, and closed her eyes. "We must come up with something," she stated, her voice now calm.

Taking her hand, Arket kissed it. "There is much magic in the forest. I fear the only way we will harm them at all is to take some of it away from them."

Sitting up, Brin poured herself a glass of water, and tried to remain calm. "With Koral's new abilities, my mother, and Gillock on their side, there is little hope of that."

Frustration was evident in her voice, yet she stayed calm. Arket thought she was finally relaxing, but her face went white, and she fell back onto the pillows. "What is wrong?" he asked, moving to her side.

Fear in her eyes, Brin slowed her breathing down. "I do not know."

Not wanting to wait a moment, Arket took Brin into his arms, and chanted the spell to return them to the castle. Once in their room, he ordered a midwife be brought to assess his wife. It felt like forever, but the midwife came, and looked at Brin.

"Highness, you have overworked yourself. The baby, and you, are fine. You need to relax, and try not to move around too much," she stated to Brin.

Arket promised to make certain his wife would relax more and participate less. Annoyed, and extremely frustrated, Brin drank some tea, and remained quiet. This fight was not going her way, and she needed to discover a way to change that.

CHAPTER FOURTEEN

The wedding was a welcome distraction. Giving everyone the chance to relax, even if it was only for a moment. The ride back to Keenley started out full of chatter, but after a day, reality set back in. They had learned the enemy had finally arrived, and that the fight wasn't going anywhere. Even with the guidance of General Naeda, who had fought against the elves, and was knowledgeable in the art of war, they couldn't come up with a plan which would see them take the upper hand.

Glomain spoke with the trees, as such creating a protective barrier which prevented most of the spells cast from getting through, but it wasn't enough. Each side wasn't gaining any ground, and Jeremy knew it could lead them to a dangerous frame of mind. Fighting is one thing, but when it appears you aren't gaining any ground, the men could become complacent. Knowing now was the time, Jeremy sent out orders he would be returning to the fight within a week.

In the days following, Gillock spent more time at the library, and was growing more concerned. It was clear to everyone that something was bothering the wizard. He had taken counsel with Glomain on a few occasions, and both looked quite agitated. Days passed, and finally the worries Gillock was feeling needed to be addressed. With quill and parchment, he wrote out instructions. Later that night, Gillock delivered them. A soft rap and a scraping as a piece of parchment was pushed under the door is all each received. "Follow this map. It will take you to a room, and to a meeting you must attend" was scratched along the top. The map was instructions. Turn left and open the third door on the right.

Now, here they were, gathered in a strange room, even Jeremy had no idea existed. It was slightly larger than his audience study and furnished more lavishly. Four small, overstuffed couches created a seating area, with chairs thrown in to add to it. It was obvious this was created for the group to sit down in, so they had. No one said much, most just looked about trying to figure out why they were here.

Jeremy looked to the faces in the room. All were those to whom he took counsel with on the current matters. It was clear this meeting was to be in secret, and when Gillock moved through a hidden opening, Jeremy wondered what it could be about.

"I see you are all comfortable," remarked Gillock, glancing about.

"Good. What I need to discuss with you all is of the utmost importance." He was about to continue but stopped. Everyone wondered why, but none would ask. Instead, they all sat silent, waiting for him to state why they were here. Pacing back and forth, Gillock appeared to be trying to gather his thoughts.

"I don't know where to begin, so I will jump about. Please bear with me and keep your inquiries until I have finished." He moved to a large chair, and plunked himself down, wiping his brow with a kerchief. "When the twins returned magic, and the Void came down, it wasn't just Malena and the Wizard's School that were brought back into this world. There were other beings banished to that place, ones from the days of old, when the Wizard Order first came into being." Gillock paused, looking down at his hands. "The worst of the creatures were dreadwraiths. They are denizens of Ruineh. When the Shadows of Ruineh were created, they were led by many priests. Their devotion to their dark god went beyond just prayer. They wanted to be his ultimate weapon. Ruineh seized the opportunity and granted them their wish. Each endured a brutal ritual, turning them into beings that live in the shadows. They absorb the life-force of all living things to grow stronger."

Jeremy stood. "Those children found drained," he stammered. "It was the work of those creatures?"

Gillock nodded. "I'm afraid so. When I heard about them, I knew immediately what it was. They start with children, then as they grow, take on bigger creatures. Eventually, they become so powerful that almost nothing can kill them."

Jeremy sat back down, shaking his head. "How many?"

Gillock looked up at the king, his dark eyes showing fear. "Four. We destroyed the others, but four were locked away in the Void. They were locked away, so that they could be studied. War broke out not long after, and they faded into legend."

"How do you kill a dreadwraith?" asked Koral, her voice low.

Gillock turned his gaze to her, then to Eric. "The easiest way is by using ragnafire. It's a spell only a War Wizard can perform, and it requires special stones to achieve."

Eric's face dropped, and horror crossed his face. "If they know this, then all of you are in danger."

Gillock's dark eyes never left Eric, and a hard look crossed his haggard face. "Yes. They know I exist and will most likely come after me. If they sense your power, Eric, they will destroy the entire castle to find you." Softening his look, he sat back in his seat, again wiping his brow. "Only one is within the city. I have taken counsel with Glomain and feel another has made a home in the Dreadwood Forest. I assume the other two ventured to the home of the Shadows of Ruineh, to present themselves to the head of their guild."

Elizanne observed Gillock. Her eyes never left the old wizard, and what she saw was fear. Something about this, and what Eric was going to have to do, bothered him immensely. The mere thought made Elizanne anxious. After many moments of silence, Gillock continued. "Eric, you must go on yet another quest. To a place, no one from this realm has been to in many centuries. It's a venture that will span many months. Dragonback was the quickest way. Sadly, they have left us, so we must make this trip on our own, and I'm afraid I have no idea exactly what is waiting."

Dread filled Elizanne. Another quest, and again, a dangerous one. "Where must he go?" she asked, her voice cracking.

Jeremy reached out and took his wife's hands. They were cold, and she appeared to have a slight shiver. Fear was taking over her heart.

"Deep in the heart of the Unforgiving Wilderness, is a mountain range. It's called the Fallen Giant. In it, there are many riches. A hoard from a dragon long gone, and one which holds many wizard items. Here, there are stones. Small in nature, they somewhat resemble a ruby. They are blessed with the fire of dragons, and in the hands of a War Wizard, can wreak havoc on creatures who exist in shadows."

The moment the Fallen Giant Mountain was mentioned, Koral went rigid. Bringing herself to stand, all talk stopped, and eyes focused on her. Slowly she blinked her eyes, and a moment later, they went pure white.

"You risk much, wizard. You know what was banished to those lands, what still exists to this day; hatred." Although Koral's mouth was moving, two other voices spoke with her. It was clear, the two wizards existing within her were the ones doing this.

Gillock stood abruptly. "You banished your kin. Yes, you had good reason, but the manner it was done was beyond what was necessary. Raising the shoreline to become a cliff, creating the wall, and the maelstrom which sits at the entrance to the river. All more than what was needed to keep them at bay."

Magic crackled in the room, but Gillock held his ground.
"We sent them away, for all they thought of was dominance and war. The Therin are our creation, but we did not place the evil in their hearts. They worship dark magic, and they are coming. You go to the mountain, and find the gems you so desperately need, and when you return, hell will be on your heels. Be warned, all of you. Death is coming."

Colour returned to Koral's eyes, and she collapsed to the ground. Glavlin moved beside her, but she was strong enough to move back to her chair. With a deep breath, she glared at Gillock. "The river is two dragon tips wide. The humans are nothing more than slaves. Almost all who live there have lives ruled by hate. Dominating each other is the goal. And the mountain," she hissed, "that mountain, is full of darkness. And not only due to the Therin. Old magic dwells there. " Her voice had taken on such a tone it gave all goosebumps.

Gillock fell back into his chair and placed his hands over his face. Sighing, he lowered them and looked at Koral. "This trip is full of dangers but let me make myself clear. The darkness that we are certain to face is nothing compared to the dreadwraith."
Koral's face softened. "I was shown them as well. Four indeed now roam the lands," she whispered. "You will need much from those mountains to keep them at bay."
"Not so," remarked Glomain. "The stones will accentuate the spell Eric can cast, but there is also something more. The staff of Mordenren."
Gillock stared at the elf. "The staff," he exclaimed. "Yes. If Eric could create one, we should be able to banish the dreadwraith from the lands. And perhaps, even keep the Therin in check."

Silence settled in the room. Each person unsure as to how to take it all. Gillock saw their faces and understood their fears.
"So another quest. I am guessing we must leave immediately?" asked Eric.
Gillock nodded. "I'm afraid so."
Jeremy stood and made certain to look at them both. "I do not want to see you go, but if it will help things then you must. I will be heading back to the front tomorrow, so all I can say is I wish you a safe journey."
Eric stood and embraced his father. "I understand and wish I could be there to help." Turning to Gillock he asked, "Who is coming with us?"
Clearing his throat, Gillock looked to those in the room. "Max and Kaitlyn. We need to keep this quiet and small. To have any more could arouse unwanted attention."

Kaitlyn stood, taking Eric's hand. "My father will help us any way he can."
With a heavy sigh, Elizanne said, "It is settled."
"I will see to everything, majesties. You worry about that army standing at our doorstep," reassured Gillock.
With a nod, and heavy hearts, Jeremy and Elizanne left the room. Gillock was right, they needed to focus on the fight at hand, not Eric's quest.

The shadows shifted, and her child's mind was filled with possibilities. Could it be a fairy come to take her to a magical land? Or even to grant her a wish? Her steps were not careful or quiet, in the hopes to make whatever was in the alley come into the light, but the shadow didn't move. For a moment, the young girl thought it might be her brother playing a trick but pushed the idea down. He wasn't smart enough to stay quiet this long. She took a step, then another, still no caution to her movements. Her steps had become slow because she was trying to focus on the darkness. A pause, then another few steps. Now, she was close enough. With one quick movement, the dreadwraith scooped up the child. Before she could scream, the small child was caught up in the cloak like body of the creature, and her life force drained. Innocence fed the dreadwraith far better than anything else in the world, and he relished in the meal. The wraith threw the corpse behind some bins, knowing that soon the child would be missed. An evil grin played across the face of the dreadwraith as he glanced up at the castle. His feedings were now daily, and it meant he was growing stronger. Soon, he would be able to take on the wizard of old. Soon, the death of his kind would be avenged.

CHAPTER FIFTEEN

Silence. Once Beluse could think of nothing he would love more than silence. Now that he had it, something about it made him uneasy. Throughout the Keep, people were on edge. They had constant noise from the forest beyond the wall for months, then one day, nothing. The attacks stopped, and the trees no longer moved as if a large force was coming for them. At first, everyone had thought it was due to the snow falling. Perhaps whoever was leading the attack had no idea about the cold. Beluse even hoped, for a time, that their unknown enemy might be from the far south, and snow would deter them. So far, this had been true, but something didn't feel right about the entire situation.

Moving out of his meeting area, Beluse wandered through the Keep, his thoughts dark. Information from the dwarves stated unusual mountain troll activity up north. A thought which he found curious, but it was the events from weeks ago which bothered him. The wizards had been killed, but no one else had been harmed since. Too many questions and no answers. It was beginning to wear on the duke.

Beluse paused when he passed his mother's room. Once spring had allowed travel, she headed to Traybidon to greet her new grandson. Her plan was to be back before it snowed, but things come up as they tend to do, and she had decided to remain. It was lonely without her counsel, but Beluse was happy she wasn't around to witness this new issue. Heading off, he wondered more about how to deal with the low morale.

As Beluse wandered the halls, pages approached with word from all areas of the wall. Still nothing. Wanting nothing more than to have his thoughts, Beluse moved to his private study. It was a place he didn't retreat to often, however, with all the strange things going on, he found himself hiding here more often of late. If he was going to deal with silence, it might as well be there.

Closing the door, Beluse moved to the chair in front of the hearth. A table with a light snack, and a pitcher of ale, waited. Beluse watched the flames dance before him, taking comfort in the heat. Snow, and a strong wind, dominated the winter so far. It was normal for Marlsman Keep to be segregated from the rest of Lungast, but again Beluse was plagued by an uneasy feeling. Everything was occurring as it usually did during the winter, yet it wasn't. In the back of his mind, he knew something was amiss.

Border Wall. A wall which sat in the shadow of an immense Keep, clearly designed to withstand a fight lasting years. A wall with no history. Well, no human history. Most who dwelled in the north had the same theory. It was placed by the gods, which meant mere mortals shouldn't question why it was there. Beluse was of a different thought. It was created for a reason, and a dangerous one at that. No one builds a sixty-foot-high wall spanning from the ocean shore to the base of a mountain range for nothing. Something on the other side of that wall needed to stay where it was. There might not be anything recorded in the human history books, but Beluse firmly believed one of the other races knew why this wall was here. He would never speak of it to anyone, save Eldrina, but deep in his core, he knew it to be true. With a frown, Beluse sat back in his chair. Trying to keep dark thoughts down was becoming difficult, so Beluse closed his eyes, sipped his ale, and let his mind wander to areas far from Marlsman Keep.

Family dominated his thoughts, or more to the point, the idea of someone wanting to overthrow the king, or even he. Beluse knew had no worries. This was Marlsman Keep, a spot no one wanted. It was common for the nobility to send unruly children here for a year. Usually, it straightened them out. As prince's, he, and Tusta were expected to spend a few years, so they would know all areas of Lungast. Eldrina had spent her entire life, before marrying, in the Keep. Her heart always wandered back, and when her father died, Beluse jumped at the chance to take over for his grandfather. No, he had no worries about being overthrown, or killed for his title. Tusta, however, isn't so lucky.

His throne was coveted by most of the nobility. With Kaitlyn marrying a foreign prince, and a son being born, their hopes were dashed. Now, their only chance would be if the royal family died. A shudder ran through Beluse. He didn't envy his brother at all.

The uneasy feeling crept back into his heart and was strong. A thought came to Beluse then, one he knew wouldn't be well received. Grabbing ink and parchment, he wrote to his brother. In the letter, he stated how Eldrina should remain in Traybidon. It also asked if there were any wizards in the area who might wish to come to Marlsman Keep. Beluse knew word had spread of the violent deaths and wouldn't blame anyone for not wanting to come.

A few more letters were written. These ones for the few towns situated near the Keep. In it, he instructed them to leave once spring allowed for it. There was no immediate danger, but a nagging feeling which wouldn't leave Beluse. They may not be at war now, but it was only a matter of time. The silence didn't mean the unknown enemy was retreating, it meant they were planning their attack. Beluse had no proof, but he knew he was not alone in that assumption. Most of the soldiers on the wall felt the same way.

Jax and Minx, his right-hand men, had expressed the sentiment on more than one occasion. Katstraya, head of the archers, had also stated how she felt. An attack was coming, most likely in the spring, and they had better be ready for it.

CHAPTER SIXTEEN

The scream was heard in every corner of the city. No matter what was thrown at the enemy, they were still holding strong. Brin had thought her magic mixed with Arket's would be a match for her family. The thought of being wrong made her feel weak, and the idea disgusted her. It was clear her pregnancy was causing her abilities to be different, and sometimes she felt off, but nothing truly made her feel weak, nothing but the spells being thrown back, or blocked. Brin had no idea how they were stopping the spells and needed answers. When the frustration became unbearable, she walked onto the balcony, tilted her head back, and screamed.

An unearthly sound echoed through the war room, causing Arket to jump to his feet. Pushing all out of his way, he ran all the way to his quarters. Upon entering the rooms, he found them in shambles. Brin's figure stood on the balcony, and he ran to her.

Grasping his wife, Arket pulled her in tight. "What is wrong?" he asked. Brin tilted her head to look in his eyes. "I am sorry if I worried you, my love. The frustration of this war is beginning to wear on me."

Arket took her hand and moved her over to the padded bench. Once seated, he poured her a glass of water, and sat beside her. "We are all annoyed with the current state of this fight. It is clear they have something we do not."

Brin sipped her water and shook her head. "No, this is something I should have seen. It is not what they have that is defeating us. It is where they are. The forest protects them. As long as they elves are there, the forest will help keep them safe."

A though passed through his eyes, and Arket raised an eyebrow. "The elves? Or one in particular?" he questioned.

With a heavy sigh, Brin sat down. "I am not certain if it is only one. The forest is old. It might be many, or it might just be the creature which was once my sister."

Arket sat down beside her and placed his hand on her lap. "You will figure this out. I will head back down and discuss finding a new strategy with the generals. Perhaps the problem is we are over thinking each step. Maybe a simple solution is what is needed."

He stood, and gave Brin a kiss on her forehead, then headed back down to the war room. Once shutting the door, a dark look crossed his face. With all the magic they both possessed, neither had been able to do much damage with their spells. Frustrated and angry, Arket made his way back to the war room.

"Sire, one thing we do know is that winter had settled into their lands. The empress has said as much. Is there a way we can exploit that?" Changru, who usually kept quiet in the talks, decided it was time to add his thoughts to the discussion.

It was clear these generals, although competent, were not used to fighting this kind of battle. For years, they travelled the land, keeping people in line, and even fighting entire villages who tried to be independent. Unusual creatures, now a part of their army, were once hunted for sport by these men. They were intelligent warriors, but when it came to the northern area, more like naive children.

Arket turned to his bodyguard, and back to the map. "Perhaps we have been going about this wrong. Yes, something in the forest across the river is preventing our spells from doing damage. However, what if one was sent behind them? Or even into the river itself?"

The four leaders looked to each other. Magic was not their providence, so they stayed quiet.

Turning once again to face Changru, Arket smiled. "Thank you, old friend. I do not think I could survive long without your counsel."

Although Changru hadn't actually stated anything, his mere presence usually helped the emperor focus. Waving the generals out, Arket sat down with Changru. Something simple was the way to go.

Lying in bed, staring at the ceiling, Brin was finally calm. Absently, she rubbed her belly. Soon, the child would be here. The midwife figured another month at most. The idea excited, and unnerved her, but she was ready for whatever lay ahead. Sitting up, she glanced about her room. A soft breeze was coming through an open window, bringing some of the salty air from the sea. A curtain fluttered, and she stood to pull it aside. A glimmer of sunlight flicked off her mirror, and an idea came to her. Moving over to her bookshelf, she pulled out the false drawer, and the spell book. A year ago, it helped her best the once-gods, and save the man who would be her husband. Perhaps there was something within which could help them now. Brin couldn't recall how many times she read this book cover to cover, yet she could barely remember what was written. Propped up on pillows, Brin sat down on the daybed, and began to flip through the pages once again. Enthralled with what she was reading, as she always was, Brin studied each page carefully, hoping for a solution.

Arket, along with his four bodyguards, went out into the city. He had the need to continue the tours. Brin usually went along with him, but with her condition coming to an end, he felt safer going without her. The idea he had discussed with Changru was foremost on his mind. Such a simple idea, yet it could still give them an advantage. The only issue was how to do it. The plan required lowering the temperature of the river to freeze it long enough to allow the men to rush the other side. Another part was to bring more snow to the far side. The latter was going to be the most difficult one to achieve, and even he, a powerful wizard, wondered if there was a way to do this.

Hours went by as he made his way to every corner. Brin wanted to ensure the people knew that even though they were at war, they still remembered them. Once Brin's condition was obvious, the people understood why both were around the palace, instead of the front lines. Whispers went through the city, but they were ones praising the two for thinking of their child. By the time he arrived back at the palace, his mind was made up. Without hesitating, he made his way to the rooms to tell Brin his idea.

Scanning the page for a second time, Brin felt elated. A spell, a most wondrous spell, and it was perfect. Harnessing the Power of a Storm, it was titled, and as she read over it yet again, she knew. Jumping up with glee she twirled about the room, and a moment later, Arket came in.

"My dear, are you alright?" he asked, an odd look on his face.
Brin smiled and came towards him. "I found a spell, one which looks like it could cause major harm to our enemy. It does require a wait, but I still feel it will work."

For a moment, Arket considered not telling her his idea. The feeling went away, and he asked her to join him on the balcony.

"What is it?" she questioned, wondering if he was bearing bad news.

"I was speaking with Changru, and came up with an idea of my own," he started, taking a seat beside her. "If we could freeze the river, even if just for an hour, we could send a good part of our forces across and engage the enemy properly. No more arrows and spells."

Sitting back, Brin considered his idea. Moments later, a grin spread across her face, and she gripped her husband's hand tight. "If we work our spells together, I think we can bring my father's army to its knees." Moving

inside, Brin grabbed the book, and brought it out to her husband to read.
"Harness a storm?" he asked, confused.
Brin pointed to what it said. "Read it, and you will understand."

Please note: this spell must only be performed by someone strong of will and heart.

Harnessing the Power of a Storm

When a storm is raging about you, there is much power within. If you are focused, you can absorb a part of it, and use it. Storms are connected to the gods; be wary. To gather even a slight amount will give you temporary abilities. You are mortal, so it will not last. Do not depend on it. To cast the spell, you will need a rubsidian candle, a focused mind, and an idea of your goal from this. It must be used as soon as you can, for the longer you wait, the less potent the power will be.

Side note: a woman in labour will be able to steal a little more than the average magik user. However, do this with great caution. The power must be used as soon as it is gathered, or it could destroy you.

Arket read the passage again and understood why his wife was so excited. "If a storm is here when you go into labour, we can freeze the river right after you attack with a spell, eliminating the elf enchantment. The soldiers can move across immediately after, destroying anyone left."
Smiling, Brin nodded at her husband, her eyes flashing with delight. "Yes. Many storms have been about lately. If a large one rolls in, I will have the midwives give me the herb which induces labour. I am far enough along that it will not affect the baby."
Arket stroked his chin in thought. "What about this rubsidian candle required for the spell? I have never heard of it."
Brin's smile faded. "Neither have I, but I wonder if the assassins have."
Shock registered on Arket's face. He didn't like dealing with them, and of late, their intelligence had been useless. "If you feel it wise to converse with them about this, I will raise the flag given us to summon them."
"I am certain this is the only way," Brin replied calmly.

Arket moved over to where they held the flag and raised it high above their rooms. Although the sun was setting, the flag had a magic about it, and it would be seen by those looking for it. Having such an unusual piece of material nearby always unnerved Arket. Brin wasn't disturbed by it. Then again, there wasn't much which worried her.

They took their supper in their rooms, and by the time they were done strange soft footfalls could be heard on the balcony. Yet another thing which bothered Arket. Nothing appeared to be able to stop the Shadows. Brin rose, and Arket followed.

"You have need of me?" hissed a female voice from the shadows. Try as you like, the cloaks the Shadows wore will only allow them to be seen if they wish it. Brin gave up trying to see the face of whomever answered the call.

"Have you ever heard of a rubsidian candle?" inquired Brin.

The woman shifted, and moved into the light, a move which awed Brin and Arket. "Yes. They are from the old days. A wizard tool," she stated, her tone odd. "Why do you seek one?"

Brin sat on a chair near the edge of the balcony and eyed the Shadow. "I need one, and that is all you need to know. Is it possible to get one?"

The woman paced, and it appeared she was anxious about something. "Gillock would have one," she said after many minutes.

Brin let out a heavy sigh. "I had forgotten about him. He was one of the last true wizards. Can your spy in my father's castle find one?"

Although the woman had stopped pacing, her demeanour was still tense. "His room is guarded by magic, but there might be a way. I believe his daughter can enter his rooms. Perhaps she can get it for you."

For a moment, Brin was going to scoff at the Shadow, but a thought hit her. Vernia had travelled with her brother, and the spy had suggested she was close to Gillock. "Vernia," she said aloud, and a cruel smile crossed her lips. Moving inside, Brin went to a small chest on her bureau, and pulled out an item. "Get the spy to give this to Vernia. It does not matter how, but Vernia must wear it." Reaching out, Brin handed the woman a simple silver chain with an opal stone set in silver. The amulet was simple, but beautiful.

"I shall see it is done. I was also told to warn you, your favours have been used. Should you raise the flag again, a price will be attached."

The woman shifted in the darkness, and silence followed. Without a word, the two moved back inside, locking the doors behind them.

Clouds again filled the sky, and the gloomy days were beginning to wear. Elizanne stayed in the castle, seeing to the running of the lands.

Vernia, who had wanted to travel with Max back to Traybidon, stood on the steps, watching the converted carriages pull away. With them traveling quite a distance, the wheels were now sleigh feet. Something was developing between the two, and it scared Vernia. It was nice to have someone who understood the gift, even though hers wasn't as developed. She had also wished to spend more time with her father, but Vernia felt her place was here. With the king off fighting against his own daughter, Vernia wanted to be certain the queen had a friend at her side.

Walking back through the doors, Vernia smiled. Friend of the queen. Not a title Vernia ever felt would be one she wore. Down the halls, she moved, her pace slow as she admired all about her. Vernia again smiled, for although Elizanne had spent her youth in this castle, Vernia had spent many years recently as the official Order representative. Dealing with the nobility daily gave Vernia insight into many things, and this was something Elizanne appreciated.

Servants, who had been on staff since her previous time in residence, still gave her looks. The ones brought in since, saw the relationship Vernia had with the royal family, and treated her as one of them. A guard still accompanied her, but that was more to ease the nerves of the nobility. Vernia had suggested keeping the guard, especially once she learned her father would be leaving to help Eric on this new quest. The last thing Vernia wanted was to give the ones who were against the king something to use.

Her musings brought her to the king's study, now in use by the queen. Inside, some of the advisors sat going over the requests from the townsfolk. Elizanne liked this day. Helping with requests from those who needed it, made her feel as if she were accomplishing something. Vernia remained outside until Elizanne was finished. When the advisors left, Vernia moved in.

"The carriage left," remarked Vernia, taking a seat across from Elizanne.

Elizanne waved at a servant, and two glasses of wine were placed on the desk. "I wish I could have said a proper farewell."

Vernia heard the sadness in the Elizanne's voice. "They understood you're busy and waiting wouldn't have been wise. The sky speaks of a storm."

Sipping her wine, Elizanne eyed Vernia. "I am happy you stayed."

Although Vernia knew, she smiled and raised her glass. "You need someone to guard your back. Oddly enough, I'm the best one for the job."

The remark brought a laugh from Elizanne. "True. A year ago, I would never have thought you and I would ever share a glass of wine, in friendship."

Placing her glass on the desk, Vernia sat back. "I'm happy that life is behind me."

The Order hadn't been mentioned, but Elizanne knew what Vernia was referring to. One day Elizanne hoped Vernia would get past her previous life, but as with all things, it takes time.

A rap on the door frame drew their attention, and a servant asked if they wished to have lunch. Elizanne stated yes and looked to Vernia. "Would you like to take it in the sunroom?"

The sunroom was one of Vernia's favourite places. Somehow, the gardener was able to keep the flowers alive inside, and it reminded her of a beautiful summer day. "I would love that."

With a bow, the servant nodded and left to set things up. Elizanne and Vernia, glasses of wine in hand, made their way to the sunroom.

Their pace was slow, and their discussion focused on the decor. Some things Elizanne loved because it reminded her of her childhood. Other things, she found ugly. Vernia always had a light laugh when Elizanne pointed out the works she didn't like. Almost all were commissioned by Duke Dubar. Once they arrived, the conversation changed to family.

"Must have been hard to learn about Jessup," said Vernia, taking her seat.

Elizanne motioned for the meal to be served, and shrugged. "It was hard hearing he had died. Finding out he was alive was unusual. It is said that twins know things about each other. I observed it with Koral and Eric. When I was told he had died, it did not feel right. To hear he was alive, and always nearby made everything clear. Not once did I ever feel he was gone."

Listening to Elizanne talk about family brought up memories of her own childhood. Not knowing where she fit in. Magic was forbidden, plus her mother had visions. Growing up in a small village had made it easier to hide the abilities. For that, she was thankful.

The meal was light, and it wasn't long before duty called, and Elizanne needed to tend to requests. Vernia excused herself and headed back to her room. It was mid-afternoon, and the weather outside was gloomy. With nothing to do, relaxing in her room sounded wonderful. Opening the door, Vernia went over to the chaise set up near the window.

The sky was grey, and a light rain had begun. Although Vernia didn't want to be out in it, something about the weather always relaxed her. "Having a blanket right now would be wonderful," she thought as she spied one draped over the chair at her vanity. With a sigh, she got up and went over to grab it. As she reached for the blanket, a box on her vanity caught her eye. For a moment, she worried it could be something dangerous, but the delicate writing with her name on it made her curious, so she picked it up and carried it, along with the blanket, back to the chaise.

With the box set down on a side table, Vernia, although curious, was still leery about opening it. Instead of sitting back down, she opened her door and asked the servant to bring her some tea. A few minutes later, a hot pot of tea sat beside the box. Knowing she would have to open it eventually, Vernia picked up the small card sitting on top. What was written within surprised her and brought a smile to her face. It was from Max. A small farewell, and a hope to see her again is all it said. Without a thought, she opened the box to see a beautiful necklace.

Vernia ran her fingers over the setting and marvelled over its simplistic beauty. Sipping her tea, she decided to put it on. Once again, she stood in front of her vanity, this time to marvel at the necklace she put on. Another smile graced her lips, and she went back to her chaise and tea. Sitting down, her eyes went back to the weather outside, but this time something was different. A reflection in the window caught her eye. It looked like Brin, standing out on the balcony, a cruel grin on her face. A moment later, Vernia realised the truth behind the necklace. A dark voice echoed in her mind; you are mine.

Brin stood before the mirror. The second Vernia had touched the necklace, Brin had known. Everything was ready, and she waited until Vernia put it on. It wasn't a long wait. With a grin, Brin stood before the mirror, and entered Vernia's mind. "You are mine," she thought, and then sent the command to enter her father's room and find the rubsidian candle.

Vernia was familiar with every secret passageway in the castle. She was also in tune with all the magic about and had known from the beginning that her father had a room set in the space between times. It wasn't a complicated spell, but it was one only the strongest of wizards could maintain. Using the passageway which started down the hall from her room, she slipped through the castle, and entered her father's room unnoticed. Gillock had placed wards in his room, but the same blood flowed through her veins, and he had not thought his daughter to be a threat. Closing her eyes, and not by choice, Vernia felt where the entrance stood, and sent a spell to enter. The door appeared, and Brin threw her through the door. Vernia hoped her father had placed a spell which allowed him to know the room had been entered.

Once entering, Vernia was in awe. Magical items that hadn't been seen for centuries existed within. The room was spectacular, but Brin was only interested in one thing. It only took a moment to find where one was. Sitting out on a desk, Vernia grabbed the candle, wrapped it in a handkerchief, and left. Instead of heading back to her room, Brin made Vernia grab a cloak from her father's closet, and head outside the castle, out of the city, and into the southern forest.

The rain was cold, but Vernia had no choice but to obey. As she entered the forest, Brin stood before her. The cruel grin hadn't left her face, and Vernia wondered how long she had to live.

"Do not worry Vernia. You are going to be my contingency plan," she said, walking towards Vernia. "If the spell I need this candle for fails, I will use you to win the war."

Vernia's eyes flashed defiance, but her thoughts never wavered. Brin could take her prisoner, but she would never again be used. Elizanne had received a note from Jeremy stating Brin was pregnant, and that could make her more dangerous. It was clear his assessment was accurate. Brin grabbed Vernia's hand, and suddenly they were in a strange room. Out the window, the sun was shining. Heat hit Vernia, and she realised they were in Brin's palace.

"I hope you enjoy this room. I feel a dungeon would be beneath someone of your abilities, but I would not try and escape," stated Brin. Motioning to the window, she continued. "We are quite far up, and there is a spell designed to dampen your abilities."

Without another word, Brin left, candle in hand. When the door closed, Vernia moved to the window. Leaning out slightly, she saw nothing but waves crashing against jagged rocks. Vernia thought it impossible to be as high up as they were but understood the power which once existed here had created most of what was around. Looking about the room, Vernia noticed it wasn't at all like a cell. A comfortable bed sat against one wall, and she even had a bathing chamber. It made her curious to see Brin had created an area with such comfort.

Sitting hard on the bed, Vernia allowed a tear to fall. There was no telling when anyone would know she had disappeared. She also wasn't certain if anyone would believe she hadn't joined Brin of her own accord. The sea voyage with Eric had changed her views drastically, and with one single act, it could all be stolen. Trust was hard to build, and Vernia could only hope Elizanne would know the truth.

Gillock sat up and ran to the window. His secret room had been entered, and not by a stranger. Vernia had gone in, and something was taken. He couldn't tell from here what had been removed, but one thing was clear, Vernia hadn't done it willingly. There was a second magic attached to her. The wizard didn't know what it meant, but he knew it couldn't be good. His companions were in the common room enjoying each other's company. Gillock had wanted to sit in his room and contemplate their quest. At this moment, Gillock was happy he had. Running as fast as he could, Gillock went to the messenger station, and sent off a note. Gillock knew it would arrive within the hour, as he was sending it via eagle, but he also knew it would be too late. The magic attached to Vernia was one he recognized. Brin.

Less than an hour later, Elizanne sat in her study, reading the note from Gillock. In a flash she throw the note to the floor and ran to Vernia's room. Startled guards picked up the chase, even though they had no idea what was going on. As the note stated, Vernia was gone. Elizanne's thoughts went from worry to anger. Turning to the guards, she demanded an eagle to send a message to her husband. Brin had just stepped up her game.

CHAPTER SEVENTEEN

Another barrage of arrows, followed by a spell, hit the forest. As with all the previous attempts, it failed. Jeremy let out the breath he had been holding and moved towards his tent. The magic of the forest, brought about by the elves, was holding, but for how long? Outside his tent stood Koral, her usual youthful appearance looking worn. Without a word, Jeremy pulled back the flap and motioned her inside. A servant brought them tea, which Koral took eagerly.

"Speaking with this forest is wearing on you," said Jeremy, trying to hide his concern.

Koral gave her father a weak smile. "It is taxing, but necessary."

Jeremy sat down, with Koral following suit. The tea was hot and felt good to Koral. The spell was indeed draining her, and it was unusual. Darly and Glavlin were not having the same issue, and Koral couldn't help but wonder if the strange sensation she had felt weeks earlier was the cause. The intense look of concentration was not lost on Jeremy. "You appear to be contemplating something."

Koral brought her attention back to her father. "Weeks ago, when we first arrived here, I felt a strange call. At first, I thought it to be a trap from Brin, but the more I thought about it, I realised the magic felt different. Older, yet familiar."

Jeremy sat back as she went quiet, waiting for her to continue.

Taking another sip of tea, Koral looked at her father. "Something dangerous exists to the east. I do not know what, but the magic in me is reacting."

Jeremy reached for his tea and paused. "Perhaps you should go and seek this magic out," he stated, and Koral could hear the worry in his voice.

With a slight smile, Koral reached and took Jeremy's hand. "Do not worry father, it is not too far off. I will not be gone for more than a few hours. Besides, I will make certain to bring Darly."

Jeremy chuckled and squeezed Koral's hand. "Strangely enough, I do not worry about you as often as I used to."

Silence enveloped the tent as the two enjoyed their tea. When Koral was finished, she gave a quick hug to her father, and left the tent to go and find Darly.

Darly sat on the topmost branch in the tree. The movements of the army across the river were odd. Sometimes they were quite organized, requiring the elves to use more arrows than they should have. Other times, it was as if they purposely sacrificed their men. Glavlin had brought in a dozen elves to assist. Eight were spread out to the west, the other four watching the east. Reports of strange creatures, some moving below the sand, were coming in. Small rafts were being put together by the elves in the west. It was Jeremy's hope to send a few men across to scout around behind and see if they could be caught off guard. With strange creatures roaming about, Darly felt in her heart the men sent wouldn't be seen again. Soft footfalls came to her ears, causing her to glance down. Below stood Koral, and it was clear something was on her mind. With a few jumps, Darly landed beside Koral.

"Something amiss?" Darly questioned.

Koral sighed. "Yes. I need you to come to with me on a little trek. Something to the east of us called to me weeks back. I think it could be the reason why I feel so drained every day."

Darly glanced across the river, then back to Koral. "The enemy appears to be up to something. Let me find Glavlin to report, then we can go."

Koral nodded, and followed Darly as she made her way down the treeline. Not far off they found Glavlin. He, too, resting in a tree, attempting to figure out the enemy's next move. After Darly reported her thoughts, Koral told of their small trek to the east.

"There is an odd magic in that area. That is why I had the four trackers set up there. Nothing has been seen, but perhaps it is a good idea to check it out," he remarked, then took Koral's hand. "If it is something dangerous, try and follow Darly's lead." With a quick kiss on her forehead, Glavlin climbed back up the tree, leaving Koral stunned, and Darly laughing.

Two hours passed, and the elves came upon a pool sitting off the river. It was indeed where the magic was emanating from, and Koral knew she had been right.

"Something hides in the depths," whispered Koral.

Darly nodded her agreement. "It knows we are here. It is waiting for us to move closer."

Koral stood and turned to Darly. "It is me it called to, so I will go out."

"This is most likely a trap, but we have no choice. I will try and watch your back," remarked Darly.

Without another word, Koral moved from the bushes to stand beside the water's edge. A moment later the water began to sparkle. The

light danced about, and Koral could feel herself becoming relaxed.
"So that is how you catch your prey," Koral thought, and played along.
A quick hand signal to Darly let the hiding elf know it was a ploy. Darly could only sit and wait.
A strange song began to flow from the water, making Koral drowsy. It wasn't long before the creature allowed itself to be seen. Instead of an attack, the strange thing rose from the depths, and stared at Koral.
"You are not enthralled, and you are not a true elf," came its voice.
Koral eyed the creature. A memory flashed before her eyes, and she knew what stood before her. "You are Maginlor. Once a forest dryad, changed because you aided an enemy. Despite the tales, you are the only dryadshee in existence."
Maginlor's eyes flashed dangerously, and the water around her began to froth. "All who know that name are long dead. How is it you speak as if you know?"
Although the creature's movements were angry, her voice showed curiosity.
"Within me are the memories, and abilities, of two of the wizards who cast you out. I do not know all, but I do know much," stated Koral, bringing her magic to bear.
With a flick of her hand, the dryadshee had seaweed come out of the water and grasp Koral. The quickness of the movement caught Koral off guard, but instead of easily casting the spell away, she allowed it to hold her.
Water continued to froth, and Maginlor glided across to be before Koral. "I am of the fae. We fairy creatures exist as dark and light. Rarely is there separation. What the wizards did to me was to show their power, not to punish." Maginlor's voice turned into a hiss, and she raised her hand once again, causing the seaweed to tighten on Koral.

Koral closed her eyes, and a smile crossed her lips. When she opened them, the colour had gone, yet her voice remained her own. "You assume much, dark one," Koral hissed. One quick word and the seaweed was wrapped about Maginlor. Koral, moving across the top of the water, put her face right before the dryadshee. "My natural ability allows me to control water. The two wizards give me power to do so much more."
Colour returned to Koral's eyes, and she glared into the black pools before her. "I am going to do what they feared. Banish you to a land beyond their reach."
Chanting, Koral raised her hands to the sky. Slowly she lowered them until

her hands were submerged in the water.

"Only the Earth Mother can do this!" screamed Maginlor as the water began to rise and surround her. The dryadshee's black eyes glared at Koral as the spell took hold. "I will return, false-elf. I will avenge myself upon all elves, starting with your bloodline!" she screeched.

With a final word, Maginlor was dragged down, below the water. The river to the side raged as if it was responding to Koral's spell. Many seconds passed before everything calmed down. Koral, forgetting she was floating above the pool, splashed down into it. Darly had been watching in awe and couldn't help but let out a loud laugh when she saw Koral fall into the water. Dripping wet, but happy she was able to send the creature away, Koral walked out of the pool.

"I no longer feel the creature," remarked Darly as they headed back to the camp.

"I sent her to a pool in a land far away. It was not my intention for it to feel like banishment, but more somewhere she would be with other odd creatures," said Koral sadly.

Darly placed her hand on Koral's shoulder. "Perhaps she will find peace, and her curse upon you will not come to fruition."

Koral gave a weak smile. "Her heart knows only hate. One day, I will have to face her again."

The rest of the walk, they enjoyed the call of the birds, and the whisper of the wind through the treetops. At least something good had come from removing the dryadshee. Birds once again flitted about the trees.

"This is dark news indeed," stated General Traug, handing the note back to the king.

"Do you think Brin intends to turn Vernia to her cause?" asked General Chenkit. Ender, having worked with Vernia for many years, was one of the people who wondered about this change in her. The thought of Vernia joining with the enemy brought fear into his heart.

Jeremy placed the paper on the table and sat down. "I am not certain. Vernia is a powerful wizard, but Brin has shown new abilities herself. If Vernia is tortured, she may turn." Taping the note, Jeremy looked to his general's. "What worries me more is what she took. I was not aware of this magic room of Gillock's. Brin might now have something that could turn this war to her favour."

Commotion outside stopped the discussion and a scout was escorted inside.

With a bow, he accepted the glass of ale handed to him, and sat down. "Four rafts are ready to attempt crossing the river. The elves are ready whenever you are, majesty."

Jeremy sighed. Finally, some good news. A storm had hit, making it difficult for supplies to come to them, and then the report from his wife about Vernia. "Take eight of your fastest men, and head back to the elves immediately. Once night has fallen, I want you to cross."

The scout finished his ale, bowed once again to the king, and left.

Supper fires burned bright as Koral, and Vernia made their way through the camp. The smell of bread and stew was everywhere, making the two realise how long it had been since they last ate. Vernia went to go and report to Glavlin, while Koral moved off towards where her father was certain to be. Waved in, Koral wasn't expecting the mood within.

"Is something wrong?" she asked.

Jeremy looked and waved Koral over to the table and handed her the note. When she was done, Koral sat down. "Vernia stole something, and is now with Brin," she muttered. "This could be what changes this fight."

Jeremy handed her a glass of wine. "We cannot dwell on this. Some of the men will be crossing the river tonight. Hopefully they will come back with information that will help us."

Koral drank her wine and stared at the map which covered the table. Men and creatures were all over the far side of the river. They were able to destroy their rafts and other attempts to cross, but no one was gaining the upper hand. All she could do is hope that the small group going across the river will find something to help.

CHAPTER EIGHTEEN

As the sleigh bounced along the road, Eric's disposition grew darker. Leaving to go on another quest, when a war was being fought, annoyed him. Across from him sat Kaitlyn and Max. Beside him was Gillock. None looked impressed.

"I thought turning this carriage into a sleigh was supposed to make the journey smoother," remarked Gillock, trying to lighten the mood.

Eric eyed Gillock. Since leaving the last inn this morning, the wizard was acting out of character. It was as if Gillock was trying to keep something from them. Kaitlyn speaking turned Eric's mind back to his fiancée.

Kaitlyn, who had been watching out the window, turned to Gillock. "I think it is due to the fact that the ruts from carriage wheels have not been smoothed out yet. It is common in Lungast."

"Did you travel often by sleigh?" asked Eric.

Kaitlyn gave Eric a small smile. "My grandfather lives on the coast and my mother and I used to travel there often in the winter. I love the snow-covered trees," replied Kaitlyn, her tone wistful. "Feels like a lifetime ago."

Max looked at Kaitlyn. "In a few weeks you will be back there, princess. Winter has settled in, and the beauty will have returned. I'm certain you will be able to take a sleigh ride."

Another smile from Kaitlyn didn't help ease the odd sensation which had crept into Eric, and silence once again filled the sleigh.

Another day, and the forest thinned to reveal Evan's River, running not far off from the road. This caught Kaitlyn's attention, as did the building which came into view.

"A temple to Narkomet," she remarked absently.

Gillock, who was sitting on the same side of the carriage, looked out. "I had heard they were building a temple here. The clerics can teach the people of these lands much."

Eric leaned over to catch a glimpse of the structure. "My father hopes the new gods coming into our lands do not cause an uprising. For many decades we only knew of the sisters existence."

Gillock sat back, thinking about Eric's words. "I'm certain some will cause problems. It's their nature. As for an uprising, Jessup is already dealing with one. New gods are not the cause."

It was true, the group in Malajah were upset about a new ruler, not about new gods. Months back, they swore to never follow another ruler, and struck out on their own. They were angry, and causing minor havoc in the area, a perfect setting for a prince to learn how to negotiate. Eric grew annoyed once again. Yet another thing happening in his homeland, and he was leaving.

After many days of travel, the sleigh reached the edge of the Central Lands. A post had been set up to greet travellers, as well as offer provisions if needed. It was also created to keep an eye on the dark forest which lay beyond the river. A small inn sat across the road and was ready to receive the prince and his friends.

It was just past midday. The common room held a few travellers and smelled of stew. Breathing in deep, Eric and his companions took a table near a small hearth. Although they had stayed in inns all the way, this one had a different feel about it. Perhaps the fact that in the morning they would be heading into Lungast, and towards the beginning of a new quest, that made them feel different. Food ordered, and wine served, the four began to relax.

After supper, they talked for a time, and then the group decided to settle in for the night. All except Gillock. It wouldn't be long before Elizanne would reply to his message, and it was making him uneasy. He had no idea what Vernia would have taken from his room. Many things held within could turn the war in Brin's favour, but would she have known that?

Gillock crept down the stairs and took a seat near the window. Staring through the frost, he ordered an ale from the barmaid, and waited. More logs were thrown onto the fire to keep the cold at bay, and a messenger came in the door. No words were spoken as the small piece of parchment exchanged hands. Many seconds passed before Gillock opened the sealed note. Within, his fears were realised. Vernia was gone, and no one knew what that meant. Gillock crumpled up the paper, threw it in the fire, drew his cloak in tight, and went out into the night.

There was no destination planned, Gillock only needed the fresh air to clear his mind. He walked across the road, and towards the river. The cold had yet to freeze the river solid, and the sound of rushing water could be heard. The sound always helped Gillock focus. This night, however, it brought a sense of trepidation. The moment the lights from the inn faded behind him, Gillock sensed the dark creatures in the forest beyond the river. Dreadwood Forest sat across from where he stood. Glomain had spoken to him about what lay within the forest, and Gillock had forgotten. A dreadwraith, and Malik.

Where Draxin had succeeded with his experiment, Malik had failed. His plan had been to take on the features of an orc, wanting the strength and cunning. Instead, the merging broke Malik's mind. A shiver crawled down Gillock's spine, and he headed back towards the inn. A quick glance over his shoulder, he noted the spot. Tomorrow morning, he planned to return, and see if he could ascertain what was truly going on in that forest. The night brought a restless sleep to Gillock. So much was going on at once. This quest needed to stop the dreadwraiths, but it could end poorly.

Reports of strange deaths came to the inn while they were having their late lunch, and Gillock knew the wraith from Keenley had realised he had left the city and was following. All Gillock could hope for was that they would be out over the ocean before it found him.

The group met downstairs for breakfast, which Gillock excused himself from. The moment the door shut behind Gillock, the three companions moved to follow. Max had known the wizard hadn't gone to bed until quite late, and something was bothering him.

"How far back should we stay?" whispered Eric into Max's ear.

Max peeked from out from the shed they were hiding behind. "I don't think he will notice us."

Standing several yards back from the river's edge, Gillock stared across. Something told him to stop, and not go any closer. Time ticked by, and finally there was movement in the forest beyond. Trees cracked as something large pressed passed them, and not long after, Malik came to stand on the side of the river.

"Who is that?" came a voice behind Gillock.

With a sigh, Gillock turned to see his three companions. "That is Malik. He is an orc-mage. A creation which should not exist."

Malik, as if hearing his name, let out a roar. Magic enhanced it, and it froze the four to their core. A whisper from Gillock's lips countered the magic, and they found themselves gasping.

"Do not enter my forest, Gillock of the order," shouted the beast. "To do so would mean instant death."

Another roar, and Malik moved back into the woods. Gillock let out another sigh and shook his head. Motioning to his companions, they all headed back to the inn. The wizard had seen what he had come to see. Now, the focus needed to be on the task ahead. One day, he would have to come and deal with the orc-mage.

No one spoke as they gathered their things. In fact, no conversation was had at all until hours later, when they came to ride beside the new lake which signalled the elf lands.

"I wonder how Garelin is doing," said Kaitlyn, staring out at the lake.

"He is married now, so I'm certain his focus is securing the bloodline," replied Gillock. "It's the elven way," he added when he saw Kaitlyn blush.

A holler from the driver, and the sleigh came to a halt. Eric leaned his head out the window and laughed. "Or he's on a patrol of his lands, and is stopping people travelling," Eric stated, opening the door.

A confused look crossed Kaitlyn's face until an elf poked his head in the open door.

"Your highness, a pleasure to see you again," stated Garelin.

Kaitlyn took his outstretched hand and exited the carriage. A female elf stood off to the side, observing what was going on. When the four companions stood outside the carriage, Garelin introduced her.

"My friends, this is Alyarra. She is my wife," he said, and the pride was obvious in his voice.

All knew the marriage had been forced on Garelin and were elated to see it was one he was happy with.

"She is a tracker, like myself. Which helps when I want to run off and see how the borders are faring," Garelin added with a chuckle.

Alyarra rolled her eyes at her husband. Turning her head towards the travellers, she pointed west. "Two days travel down the road, there will be an unusual sign. Here, if we elves allow, a road will appear. Just down it, is a lodge, designed to help weary travellers, or the ones we wish to help. You are welcome to spend the night there. The next stop is at the Town of Two Rivers."

Eric smiled at Alyarra. "Thank you for allowing us to stay there. It is quite a ride to Two Rivers. Being able to spend the night somewhere outside of this sleigh will be welcome."

Garelin patted Eric's shoulder. "There are stops set up to exchange horses as well. That was an agreement made between the elves, King Tusta, and King Jeremy. We do not wish to see horses pushed to near death to get past our lands."

"That is most gracious of you," remarked Kaitlyn.

"It was more for the horses than people, princess," Garelin replied with a wink. "However, it has been beneficial to us. News we would not normally hear comes to our ears now."

Alyarra coughed, interrupting Garelin. "We must be finishing our patrol."

Garelin smiled at his wife. "Yes, you are right. My friends, we will meet you at the inn. It has been a long time, and I wish to catch up."

"Your company is most welcome," said Max, shaking Garelin's hand.

"Until then," said Garelin, then he and his wife turned and ran towards the lake.

As they were told, after travelling for a little over two days, a strange road appeared. Although the drivers were wary, the horses didn't waste a moment before heading down the road. About fifteen more minutes of travel, and they arrived at a beautiful lodge. The entire thing appeared to be a large tree, moulded to look like a lodge. Smoke rose from the chimney, and the smell of fresh bread wafted at them. Without hesitating, the four exited and went inside.

"Welcome," said a musical voice, and a young elf woman moved out from behind the bar area to greet them. "King Garelin said to expect you. He and his queen are just freshening up in their room. If you will follow me, I will show you to yours."

Everyone followed silently. Each not wanting to break the spell the lodge was casting on them. Not once since the trip had started did they feel at ease with their travels. This day, they were more relaxed than they thought possible.

Each one was given a separate room, and upon entering, were in awe. A large bed, with a private bathing area, lay within. All the rooms were bright, with a feeling of home. Across from the bed was a hearth, already lit, filling the room with warmth. After a long warm bath, each made their way to the common area. Garelin and Alyarra were waiting, as was a feast. It was just before the lunch hour, and the scent of the food caused Eric's stomach to growl. This brought a giggle from the innkeeper, as she brought wine to go with the meal.

Each ate far more than they had expected too, including the elf king and queen. The hearth was large, and the fire burned strong. Heat, wine, and food had them all feeling drowsy. At the suggestion of Garelin, all retired for a nap. After two days in a carriage, it didn't take long for the companions to fall asleep.

A soft rap on each door brought them all awake, and they were told it would be an hour until supper was ready. The tired, achy bodies now felt rejuvenated, and Gillock wondered if perhaps something had been added to the wine or food. Coming down the stairs, the hearth still burned bright. Garelin and Alyarra still sat in the same spots around a table. The companions all wondered if they had left.

"How are you feeling?" asked Alyarra.

Kaitlyn took a seat across from Alyarra. "Better than I have felt since leaving Keenley," she replied.

Seating himself, Gillock poured himself a glass of water, and looked to Garelin. "How do you lands fair?" he asked.

Leaning on the table, Garelin eyed Gillock. "Many things are occurring, Gillock. Although our lands are safe, the dwarves have been in constant skirmishes with trolls. We also have word things are changing at Marlsman Keep, and no one is certain what it means."

A round of ales were placed on the table, something Eric thought odd for an elven lodge to have, but he accepted and drank deep. "I am certain you have received word on the fight my father is facing right now. Has he even asked for assistance?" asked Eric.

Garelin turned his eyes to the prince. "He has not yet asked for help. My father, however, has. Should the war in your land takes a turn we will offer aid. For now, I have some elves helping the dwarves."

Alyarra took a sip of her ale and glanced to the faces before her. "Regardless of the dwarven fight, the wedding of Grund and Drundle is going to occur in the summer."

This news brought a smile to Eric's face. "That is excellent news."

Gillock laughed in his gruff manner, and slapped Eric on the back. "Too bad we won't be invited. Dwarves rarely allow outsiders to attend a bonding ceremony."

Eric slumped slightly but knew they wouldn't be attending. "It is not like we will be in a position to attend anyway," he remarked.

The comment caught Garelin's attention. "We knew you were heading this way, but even my father was reluctant to explain why."

Gillock looked to his three companions, then about the room. "Eric and I will be heading into the Unforgiving Wilderness sometime within the next month. For now, we are on a trip to Traybidon to bring the princess home to see her family."

At the mention of the Unforgiving Wilderness, Garelin stiffened. Gillock knew Glomain was aware of what was sent over, and upon seeing this reaction, figured it was passed to Garelin. "Where will you be headed?" asked Garelin, his voice quiet.

"Fallen Giant Mountain. To find the horde of Karabine and reclaim some of the wizard treasures stolen so long ago," replied Gillock.

Garelin's eyes moved to his hands, which were clutching his glass tight. "The Therin exist in the shadow of that mountain," he began, almost in a growl. With a deep breath to calm himself, Garelin continued. "It is the belief of the council that the reason strange things are happening at the Border Wall and Keep is due to the Therin. It is possible they are on the move."

Max, who had been very interested in this conversation, grew anxious. "What does this mean to the realm?"

Garelin turned his eyes to Max, but it was Alyarra who answered. "They are a plague, knowing only hate. Should they enter these lands, they will slaughter every elf, and enslave all others."

Kaitlyn gasped. "Can they be stopped?"

The fear in Kaitlyn's voice was clear, and it created sadness in Garelin. "Princess, know this. The Therin's goal is to eradicate all life they cannot control. Their end goal, however, will be to kill the elves."

A dark silence fell upon those seated at the table. Many questions had come into each mind, and the answers would only be found when the quest had begun. After many moments of quiet, Garelin once again spoke. "I would like two elves to accompany you. They are excellent scouts and would also be able to ascertain if the Therin are indeed on the move, and a concern."

Without a thought, Eric agreed. The number of people going was small but having elves would be a bonus to them. Although a date had yet to be decided, Garelin informed them to just send word, and the elves would be waiting for them at their ship.

Night fell, and their minds were heavy with fears. Although a soft mattress made them comfortable, dark thoughts plagued each one well into the night. When dawn came, the hearts of each companion still carried worry. It wasn't until the sleigh began to move that a glimmer of hope sprang. The sky was grey and threatened more snow, but a break in the clouds allowed a soft beam of light. It illuminated the lodge as they moved away, and that simple deed made the heavy worry lighten.

Days after the humans left the elven lands, a creature far darker entered. Its urge to feed strong, the wraith moved through the shadows. The moment it entered the lands, the elves knew. Scouts were sent to destroy the foul creature. When none returned, Garelin ordered everyone to bar themselves inside until further notice. The creature moved about the city, and when no victims could be found, howled in anger. Elf scouts, hiding in the trees far above the creature, watched as it sniffed, and turned to the north. With another howl, it ran off, heading towards the human city of Traybidon.

Malik sensed the dreadwraith's passage. It was the youngest of those banished into the Void and was determined to end the wizards. The one within his forest was the oldest, and quite content with hiding in the darkness, feeding off those stupid enough to attempt to enter. Moving back towards his fortress, he thought about what was in store for him. Clearly, the wizard was up to something. Malik thought his rebuilding of the fortress would have garnered attention, but it was clear other issues had people occupied.

CHAPTER NINETEEN

Night fell, and not a cloud was in the sky. Moonlight glittered off the water before him. Firadon stared across the river, taking in the sight. The ferry wouldn't arrive until morning, so this night he and Aremeth were going to relax on this side of the Talbainy River. A small inn now sat on the river's edge, welcoming those who dared travel. With a shake of his head, Firadon moved to sit by the fire. Soldiers patrolled this side of the river and kept a fire going constantly. Although the Drapen Wood was no longer a threat it was clear King Tusta wanted a military presence.

Firadon, wanting to travel as quick as they could, took the route which brought him to the southlands. Aremeth had no familiarity with the area and followed Firadon's lead. Wandering the woods was not as difficult as Firadon thought it might be. The forest had snow, but not enough to hinder their efforts.

Moving into the area, Firadon noted that although there were a few changes, things were still the same. Goblins and gnomes remained in Lurkman Forest, and the ogres who had answered the dark call of Malena now dwelled back on the Plains of Jade. Things were a normal chaos, yet calm existed. Firadon shook his head once again, marvelling at the changes enacted by Eric and Koral. Returning magic to the world appeared to have done wonders to this once dangerous forest.

"How far is it to this place we need to go?" questioned Aremeth. He was huddled under furs, sitting as close to the fire as he could get. Firadon smiled. "In the morning we will take the ferry. After we supply in Two Rivers, we will head west. About another few days travel by carriage, and we will be in Hucksley."

Aremeth shivered and drew the furs about him tighter. "I never believed such a cold could exist."

Firadon patted his friend on the shoulder. "Come, let's go inside the inn. The temperature will be much warmer inside."

Aremeth managed to nod before throwing off the furs and practically running for the front door of the inn. Firadon let out a loud laugh and followed his friend inside.

A large hearth sat to the right of the door, and Aremeth made his way over. They were the only guests this night, and the southman was quite pleased about it. Sitting at a table near the raging fire, Aremeth began to warm up. Firadon joined him and ordered two hot beverages. When they arrived, Aremeth eyed it with curiosity.

“It has the scent of apples,” he remarked.

“It’s called apple cider. Will take the edge off, and warm you some,” replied Firadon. He didn’t feel it necessary to state it also had whiskey in it.

Taking a small drink, Aremeth smiled. “Now this is something I hope we can get at any time on this journey.”

Giving a smile to his friend, Firadon drank his cider. Within the hour, the two were in their rooms, with Aremeth finally feeling warm.

Although they ate breakfast while it was still dark, the sun was well in the sky when the ferry came across. Supplies were unloaded, and once the two paid their fare, it began its trek back. Travel was slow going, as the river was partially frozen. Small chunks of ice bounced off the ferry, but the driver paid them no mind. Aremeth, however, was quite unnerved.

When they docked, and were off into the town, Aremeth finally relaxed. Many weeks had passed since they left Jacen and headed north. Now, it was beginning to feel as if the end was in sight. He followed Firadon about the town, and was in awe at the many stores, and things available to buy. Aremeth had traded with people in Winetown, but it was not a bustling town. Two Rivers was one large marketplace, with many wonders to behold. Strange timekeeping devices caught his attention, along with the scent of a bakery. Aremeth’s stomach grumbled as he took in the smells, and Firadon made certain their path went to the bakery.

Packs full with supplies, Firadon took them to a carriage house, and booked them one. The northman didn’t want to hesitate any longer, so he paid extra to have it leave within half an hour, promising the driver that he, and Aremeth, had enough supplies to get them to Hucksley. The owner informed them they would have to switch out horses, otherwise, they were free to move as quickly as the roads allowed to Hucksley. Firadon knew it would be necessary to exchange horses and shook hands in agreement. Once the sleigh began to move, Firadon sat back, and closed the curtain. The less he saw of the dismal countryside the better.

Silence woke the two. The sleigh was no longer moving, and no sounds could be heard outside. With careful movements, Firadon pulled the curtain facing the front of the sleigh back slightly. There was no sign of the driver.

“What do you think is going on?” asked Aremeth, his voice low.

Firadon closed the curtain, and shifted towards the door. “No idea, but it probably isn’t good.”

Taking a deep breath, Firadon swung the door open hard, and dove out, rolling along the ground. No arrows were fired, and no swords were pointed at him as he stood. Aremeth, who had followed Firadon’s lead and dove in the opposite direction, made his way to the front of the sleigh. The horses, and driver, were indeed gone.

“I get the feeling this is a robbery set up,” stated Firadon, glancing into the woods. Darkness greeted is eyes, and the big man frowned. Moving back to the open door, Firadon grabbed his pack, and tossed Aremeth his. “We better get moving. No idea how far away we are from any town, and this reeks of a setup.”

Aremeth shouldered his pack and agreed with Firadon’s statement. “The quicker we get moving the better.”

The two headed off at a steady pace. After a time, they heard shouts echoing down the road. Angry sounds came to their ears, and Firadon smiled. “Good thing we didn’t drink too much from that waterskin the driver gave us,” he remarked.

“Apparently he and his friends figured we were easy prey,” responded Aremeth with a chuckle.

“Let’s speed up. I think I see lights through those trees. We might be closer to a village than we thought,” stated Firadon.

Changing their pace to a run, the two made their way down the road with ease. Luckily for them, the road was well travelled, and the snow was packed down. They were also lucky to find a town come into view not long after they began their run.

Lamp lights were beginning to fade, and it was clear dawn wasn’t too far off. Not wanting to waste any time, Firadon and Aremeth made their way to a trading post. A man greeted them, and although leery of strangers showing up on foot at dawn, sold them two horses with tack. By the time the sun was in the sky, they were on their way, hoping the would-be robbers had forgotten them.

CHAPTER TWENTY

After a long and weary ride, the gates of Traybidon came into view. Since leaving the elven lodge, the four had much on their minds. So many questions, and few answers, plagued them all. The sight of the city walls brought a glimmer of hope to Kaitlyn. Home, although she wasn't certain it would feel that way anymore. Her brother, someone who dominated her dreams of late, was most likely walking by now. Dominic was a stranger and would probably stay a stranger. Once Eric was done with this quest, they would wed, and her trips to Traybidon would be rare. The idea saddened her, but this path gave her a purpose in life. One far greater than what she would have believed.

The carriage slowed as it approached the gate. When it came to a halt, Max jumped out to speak with the guards. It wasn't long before they were moving again, and when voices were heard outside, Kaitlyn opened the curtain. It was almost midday, and even though snow blanketed the ground, people were about. Eric watched as she closed her eyes and breathed deep. A smile crossed her face and it made Eric smile along with her. Kaitlyn turned back into the carriage, her eyes sparkling.

"Happy to be back?" asked Eric.

Kaitlyn shook her head yes. Too many emotions were running through her, making her wonder if she spoke, how her voice would sound. Eric reached out and took her gloved hand. Bringing it to his lips, he kissed it softly. Wetness came to her eyes, and she turned them back to the streets.

Travel to the castle wasn't long, but after being on the road for what felt like forever, the group couldn't wait to arrive. The door was opened by a footman, and behind him stood Max and Luc.

"How did you beat us?" questioned Eric with a laugh.

Max gave his crooked smile. "I took a horse. I wanted to speak with Luc before we saw the king and queen."

As if on cue, the royals burst out through the front door. Tusta clasped his hands together, and Avery ran down the steps. The stunned guards stayed where they were positioned, watching.

"I cannot believe you are actually here!" exclaimed the queen, grasping her daughter tight.

Holding her mother, Kaitlyn let the tears of joy fall. "I have missed you," she whispered.

Avery pulled away, and grabbed Kaitlyn's hands. "Your brother is sleeping right now. He usually awakes for lunch. I cannot wait for you to meet him."

Kaitlyn kept the smile on her face, but inside, a strong sense of trepidation flowed. Something about her brother was not right.

Tusta moved to see his daughter and expressed his happiness with a tight hug. "I am certain you all are famished. Lunch will be served in an hour. The servants will escort you to your rooms. Hot baths are waiting."

Gillock let out a loud sigh of relief at the mention of food, and an even louder one with the bath. The sound caused Eric to laugh hard, and to motion Gillock to follow the servants waiting for them. With a quick smile to Kaitlyn, Eric followed as they were shown to the rooms.

Unlike last time, Eric and Gillock's rooms were much closer to the royal family and were across the hall from each other. The last room they stayed in were beautiful. These new ones put them to shame. Although he was a prince, and used to small luxuries, Eric was still amazed at what he saw. Eric moved in to find he had a sitting room, bedroom, small study, and a bathing area. As stated, hot water filled the tub. It took seconds for Eric to strip off his clothing and set himself in. Nothing helped tired, achy muscles like a hot bath.

Gillock was not in awe as much as Eric but was impressed. It was clear they were staying in the rooms meant for dignitaries and other nobility who happened to stay at the castle. The study had parchment, a quill and fresh ink, making Gillock wonder if anything had been discovered about Vernia. His thoughts wandered to the fight with Brin, and he worried. Moving into the bathing area, Gillock realised a hot bath would be a perfect way to relax and think.

It felt like only moments had passed when the soft rap to let him know lunch was ready, came. Not wishing to answer questions, Gillock got dressed quickly, and went to the dininghall. Eric was only steps behind. The smell of stew and fresh bread hit them as they entered the room. Cheese, meats, and vegetables were also on the table. Gillock's stomach grumbled, causing Eric to stifle a chuckle. Gillock shot the prince a glare, but it was lost on Eric. His eyes were on the king, queen, Kaitlyn, and a small boy. An old woman sat beside the boy, offering him bits of food to eat. Although the boy was eating, his eyes were glued to Eric. Eric knew Dominic was a year old now, but the intelligence and curiosity behind his eyes stunned the prince. Everyone was being shown their seat, and Eric took his. It was then Eric noticed Kaitlyn. Her eyes met his, and Eric knew she sensed something as well. Pushing the odd encounter aside, Eric turned his attention to the food before him.

There was only the royal family, the nanny, Gillock and Eric present for the luncheon. When Dominic was done, the nanny - Clayanne by name - took the boy back to the nursery, leaving only those interested in the upcoming events.

"Another quest," stated Tusta.

Gillock placed his glass of wine on the table. "Yes."

Tusta sat back, eyeing the wizard. "According to the message I received, it has nothing to do with the war, but more with something far darker."

With a shake of his head, Gillock sipped his wine. "Dark creatures were released into this world. Two of them have most likely gone home. They belong to the Shadows of Ruineh. One, has made things personal."

"What does that mean?" asked Avery, her concern clear.

Eric saw Gillock was struggling, and turned to Avery. "What it means, highness, is that the wizards of old imprisoned these creatures. One has decided to exact revenge on Gillock. It is not strong enough yet, but it will not be long."

The news bothered Tusta, and it was clear by his expression what he was going to ask next. "How does it gain strength?"

Before he could answer, an exasperated messenger came running in. "My apologies, highness, but this is of the utmost importance." He handed the note to Tusta, and immediately left the room, closing the door tight.

Tusta took the note, and his face fell. "Your creature likes to drain the life out of beings, leaving them dead." His matter-of-fact voice, followed by the note being thrown on the table, made it clear it was not a question. Eric picked up the note and felt sick to his stomach. "It has hit the Elbrien Forest."

Gillock covered his face with his hands in an attempt to clear his head. After a time, he lowered them, and looked to Eric. "We cannot wait to leave." His eyes turned to Tusta, whose anger was obvious. "I know this isn't the best time to travel on open water, but we have no choice. We must leave soon, or your entire realm may be in danger."

Tusta remained silent for a few moments, before sitting back in his seat. "The day after you left on your last quest, I had a new ship commissioned. She is called Serenity's Quest. Captain Goram's idea, and now I see why. She is at your disposal but will take at least a week to

supply."
"We understand highness, remarked Eric. "As with the last quest, only a small group is coming on this one. King Garelin wishes two of his elves to join us."
Tusta listened to Eric's words and came up with an idea of his own. "I would like Dorien to go as well. He has grown much in his abilities and would be my representative on this quest."
Gillock hesitated, and then agreed.

Tusta waved the servants over, and more wine was poured. The conversation turned to how the realm was faring, as well as to the new royal addition, but stayed away from what was occurring in Marlsman Keep. It wasn't long before Tusta had to excuse himself, leaving Avery to lead the group to a more comfortable room to continue their discussions. Here, they were joined by the Queen Mother, and Eric marvelled at how beautiful the woman was. His eyes went from her, to Kaitlyn, and the resemblance was uncanny. Eric wondered if in her youth, the Queen Mother had the same-coloured hair.

They talked until dinner was served, the conversation carried by Avery, Eldrina and Kaitlyn. Gillock's mind was on his daughter and Brin. Eric listened to mother and daughter talk and noticed that the conversation rarely turned to Dominic. All that was said was, he had a cold and slept a lot right now.

Dinner had far more people attending. Max, who had been briefed on what was occurring in the north, came in with Luc. Once again, Tusta was seen, and before the meal was served, told Eric that a notice had been sent, and the ship would begin supplying immediately. A few nobles were in attendance, and it was only due to Kaitlyn's return. They had no interest in the prince from another land. That is, until Tusta made an announcement.

Everyone was seated, and the wine poured, so the king stood, and raised his glass. "I have kept this from the land, until my daughter was home. This is my official word. Kaitlyn Malore, princess of the Realm of Lungast, is betrothed to Eric Traven, a prince and next in line to be king of the Central Lands."
Tusta watched the faces of the nobles and wasn't surprised this news was not a shock to all. Nor was he surprised to see they were all disgusted. Rumours were abound in the city, but no one thought the king would marry his daughter off to another land, especially one only recently discovered.

Suddenly, Eric became a more interesting subject. With a signal from the king, dinner was served. The nobility was seated far from Tusta, and Eric was grateful he was a royal guest, and that garnered him a seat close. By the glares he was receiving, Eric was all they were talking about. Kaitlyn, who was seated across from Eric, couldn't help but smile at his discomfort.

After much food, and even more wine, the socializing began. Some moved off to sit on plush couches which had been placed in front of the large hearth, others stayed at the table, heads bent close in discussion. Eric had moved to a chair beside Kaitlyn, and Avery had gone to see that Dominic was put to bed. With many spread out discussions happening, the dininghall carried a low murmur.

"I apologize for springing that on you two," began Tusta, who moved a chair to sit behind Eric and Kaitlyn. Both turned their bodies to look at him as he continued. "With all which is going on in the realm, I thought announcing it when you came home might offer a glimmer of light to these unusual times."

"I had thought it was already announced," remarked Kaitlyn. "That explains why no one had congratulated me," she added with a giggle.

Tusta smiled at his daughter, and at Eric. It was quite clear these two were in love, and it made him happy to know Kaitlyn would not be a trophy. He slapped Eric's knee, and kissed Kaitlyn's cheek, then stood. "I must make my obligatory rounds of the hall," he said, grabbing a glass of wine, moving off.

The night ran late, and in the wee morning hours, the castle became silent. Only two remained awake, and for very different reasons. Gillock, whose mind bounced between the war, and the quest, and neither was giving him a sense of peace. The other, Dominic. He was only a year old, and prone to waking in the night. However, unlike most children, he didn't cry out. A voice had spoken to him since he was a babe in his cradle. Now, it was familiar, and soothing. Dominic didn't quite understand what the voice in the shadows told him, but he enjoyed the emotion it showed when speaking. Dominic also couldn't tell if it was a man or woman speaking, for the voice was always just below a whisper. It went on about the greatness he was going to achieve, and as always, Dominic fell asleep to it.

Morning came, and with it an amazing headache for Eric. Splashing cold water on his face, Eric stared at his reflection, and shook his head. "I wish I had the magic to make me look more alive," he muttered to himself. When he came into the sitting room, a hot pot of tea, along with biscuits, was waiting. After having both, Eric began to feel much better. Throwing on his clothes, he left the room. There was nowhere in particular, he needed to go, so instead he wandered about the floor.

Eric had noticed some of the architecture in the castle at Keenley, however, it paled in comparison to what lay before him. Eric recalled when he was last here and smiled. His interest was more in Kaitlyn, than in paying attention to the details. He also didn't see this floor, which appeared far more lavish. Again, most likely due to the fact that important visitors stayed here. Each pillar was carved with intricate patterns, the walls adorned with paintings depicting battles, and scenery. Eric could only assume they were from actual events and places.

"This particular painting is of the mountain area where your dragon friends lay their eggs," came the voice of Luc.

Eric turned and accepted his outstretched hand, eagerly shaking it. He was going to speak, when raised voices came down the hallway. Gillock and Max were in an intense argument, and Max was looking quite angry.

"If you wouldn't mind, Prince Eric, I think we should go downstairs," suggested Luc.

Eric cast a last look at the two arguing and moved towards the stairwell with Luc. The voices grew quiet, and once they were heading down, Eric turned to Luc. "What was that about?"

Luc stopped on the step and glanced back. "Max received a letter today. Something about Vernia, and he thinks Gillock was aware of what it contained."

Hearing this news, a thought came to Eric. "Something about Vernia?" he remarked, and it was clear. "Yes, I think Max is right. Gillock has been keeping something from us since we were back in the Central Lands. Whatever was in that message must be what it was."

The two continued down, and as they began walking down the hallway, two pages approached, one stated their presence was requested by the king. The other asked if they knew the whereabouts of Gillock and Max. Eric pointed up the stairs, and the page was off. Following behind, the second page took them to the king's audience study. Tusta and Dorien were inside, along with two elves. Eric almost laughed. Of course, Garelin had sent his two representatives. After the attack in the forest, he was probably quite concerned for the well-being of those within Traybidon.

They took their seats, and a minute later a clearly agitated Max, and annoyed Gillock, entered.

Curiosity as to the nature of the argument was clear on Tusta's face, but he pushed it aside. "I have gathered you all because the elves have come with grave tidings. The creature has moved into the forest area outside the city. It is only a matter of time before it enters and begins feeding. I think the time for you to leave has come."

Eric's heart sank. Not only for those who might be killed by the dreadwraith, but also because he would be leaving Kaitlyn so soon. "Is it wise for us to travel by carriage if it is near?" he asked.

"We can't travel by conventional means," stated Gillock. "We must get out of the city unnoticed, but we must also draw the dreadwraith off."

"What do you suggest?" questioned Tusta.

Gillock looked at the faces before him. "It is here for me, so I must draw it away. Is there an area where few live nearby?"

"If you go north, across the river, there are few inhabitants. The ground can't be worked by farmers, and the forest has little animal life," replied Dorien.

"Then north I will go," said Gillock, who then disappeared before their eyes.

"Why did he go already?" asked Luc.

Dorien stared at the spot Gillock had been standing a moment ago. "He used magic on purpose, so the dreadwraith would sense him, and follow."

A worried look crossed Tusta's face. "What happens to your quest if he is killed?"

Eric turned and stared at Tusta. "It would be pointless. I have no knowledge of what I am looking for, let alone what to do with it."

"And without whatever it is you are to find, the dreadwraith will take over the land," added Dorien.

Moments of silence passed. "I will lead you down the secret tunnel which heads south. At the end you will find carriages to take you to Hucksley, and your ship," announced Max. "You have until tomorrow morning to prepare. That should be enough time for Gillock to do whatever it is he's planning."

Tusta eyed Max and nodded. "I agree." Turning to look each person in the face, he paused on the elves. "Do you still wish to join this quest?"

"Yes," they replied in unison.

Tusta stood, and motioned to the door. "Then may the gods speed you on your journey."

Eric sat on his bed, staring at his pack. He hadn't removed much, so it didn't take long to place the items back in. In fact, he was ready within a few minutes of returning to his room. Still, he sat and stared. Tomorrow, quite early, he would be on his way. This time, without Kaitlyn. The idea bothered him more than he thought it would. Here she is safe, out there, terrible things could happen, yet he wanted her by his side.

"One quest ends another begins. We do not get much time to relax," said Kaitlyn from his door.

Eric jumped up and grabbed her close to him. "This time you are not coming, and the idea bothers me."

Kaitlyn rested her head on his chest. "It is strange to know we will be apart, but I take comfort in the fact that when you return, we will be wed."

A page appeared in the entry, so the prince kissed the top of her head, and pulled away. "I suppose we should head down for lunch."

Drying her eyes, Kaitlyn nodded her agreement and the two headed down to eat.

Midday turned into night, and before they knew it, the knock to say it was time to leave came. Eric and Kaitlyn had said their goodbye's earlier in the evening, wanting it to be private, so she was not there when they all met up. No words were spoken, only hand signals to show the way, and once again, when they arrived at the end of the tunnel. Gillock still hadn't returned, but Eric expected they wouldn't see him until they were ready to head out onto the ocean. Max waved them forward, and the four were rushed into a carriage and off into the night.

Dawn arrived, and as with most winter days of late, it was gloomy. Clayanne, nanny to the royal family since Tusta was born, bundled up Dominic for their morning walk. The young prince was always up with the sun, and instead of bothering others in the castle, the nanny had taken him out for a walk each day. It wasn't chilly, and the wind calm, so the walk took them further through the garden than usual. Large pine trees covered in snow lined the walls of the castle, to try and create a sense of serenity. A break in the clouds brought a stream of sunlight, which reflected off the snowy trees. The beauty entranced Clayanne as she moved about the far side of the garden. Leaving Dominic in his carriage, the nanny moved to observe the beauty before her. Something rarely seen in the winter months. Dominic watched as his nanny moved away from him and turned his eyes to the shadows. He saw the creature hiding within, and the creature stared back. Dominic turned to see Clayanne moving closer to the shadows, raised his arm, and pointed to her. The dreadwraith hissed with glee, moving along the darkness towards the woman. Clayanne, sensing something was off, turned to head back to the prince. The young prince was standing in his carriage, pointing to her, with a strange look of elation on his face. A moment later, the dreadwraith attacked, and with her last thought, Clayanne realised Dominic was the reason for all the bad things occurring in the castle.

The dreadwraith finished its task and moved back into the shadows. It had sensed the wizard, and felt a spell to the north, but wanted to be certain he had truly left. The young boy also intrigued him. The wraith could easily take him as well, but something stopped him. Instead of moving off, the wraith remained, watching the boy. After a time, the cold was taking its toll, and the prince began to scream. It only took a moment for a guard to come running, and another more to see the dead nanny. Scooping up Dominic, the guard ran to the king's study, to hand over the prince and report what he had found.

CHAPTER TWENTY-ONE

Hucksley came into view, and Eric sat back, closing the curtain. The awe he held with the city had ebbed since his last visit. In fact, the entire idea of a quest was no longer something which held any interest to him. He remembered how a couple of years ago he wanted to go off on his own, put himself into the history books as a hero. Now, nothing sounded more inviting than to marry Kaitlyn, and be a boring prince, flitting about the land. A smirk crossed Eric's face. How many seventeen-year-olds have a quiet life, and dream of adventure. Eric made a mental note immediately, no more adventures. Staying close to home and helping with any issues in the Central Lands was going to be his life.

Having to use a carriage not fit with sleigh rails made their travel be slower than they wanted. Still, it took no time to arrive at the port city. The carriage bounced through the muddy streets, and they arrived at the same inn they stayed in last time. Without a word, Eric and Dorien left the carriage, and made their way inside. Smells of fresh bread and beef stew assaulted their senses. Although all the bouncing around as they travelled had upset their stomachs, the smell of food changed that. They sat down, and it wasn't long before the two elves, Tark and Simian, took seats beside them. Lunch was eaten in silence, and when finished, Eric took to his room. A bath, followed by a nap, was on his mind. Before he made it up the stairs, a familiar voice called his name. Turning, Eric was stunned to see Firadon Dey, and a stranger, coming towards him.

Running back down the stairs, Eric grabbed the big man by the hand. "Firadon! What are you doing here?"

Firadon turned to his companion, and back to Eric. "Perhaps we should discuss this in your room. It's complicated."

Dorien, and the two elves, came up behind Firadon and Aremeth. Eric waved them forward and pointed up the stairs. Once they moved, Eric looked at Firadon. "We are on a quest, and I assume what you have to say has something to do with this. They are my companions, and will sit in." Turning, Eric headed to his room, closely followed by Firadon and Aremeth.

With all huddled in the room, Eric told of the quest, and Aremeth told his tale. It was clear Aremeth's god wished him to partake. The why, was not clear. Eric knew the quest needed few people to move through the land across the ocean, but adding Firadon's strength, and their new companion, wouldn't cause an issue. Eric agreed to have them along and was interrupted by a rapping on the door. Opening it, Eric was shocked to see Gillock, looking quite haggard, on the other side. Moving into the already crowded room, Gillock took to the only chair. Tark poured a glass of water from the pitcher and handed it to Gillock. Gillock downed the water and took a deep breath.

"The dreadwraith is on its way. We don't have time to spare. I've already spoken to Captain Goram. Instead of staying the night, we are going to the ship now, and heading out before the sun sets." Gillock stood and took Eric by the shoulders. "The city is safe now, but we must go."

Eric nodded. "Our things are still on the carriage."

Firadon opened the door, and the entire group headed down the stairs. The carriage took whom it could, the rest finding another one to bring them. When the harbour came into sight, Eric's stomach tightened. There weren't as many ships as last time, which was expected due to the time of year. Serenity's Quest came into view, and it brought gasps from almost all. Still designed to carry the royal family, it had a few new features. More cannons were the first you noticed, but to Eric, second was the beauty. The wood was stained such a deep colour that it drew you into it. The mast now had a sister to match it, giving the vessel the ability to move quicker through the water. Portals sat on the side, and it was explained they were for oars, so a repeat of the last quest didn't occur.

Upon approach, Gillock noticed many men flying about the ship. He had forced their timetable ahead, and now things were being loaded as fast as the men could move. Captain Goram could be heard barking orders as he attempted to get the items stowed away safely, and as fast as possible.

Slipping up the gangplank, they approached the captain, who ordered a man to show them their quarters. "I expect you all to come back up and help load this stuff," he stated, before moving off.

As requested, each one came and assisted, with Firadon moving twice as much as the rest. Within an hour, they were settled onto the new ship, awaiting the start of this leg of the quest.

"I'm not liking this," declared Mena.

She was alone with her husband in the captain's cabin. They were slow moving, for the wind was ahead. Looking out a window, Mena watched as the harbour moved further away.

"I didn't expect you to like it," muttered Goram. "We belong to the king, and when he says we go, we go."
Arms crossed, Mena moved to a chaise, and flopped down. "Yes, but to head out over open water in winter is dangerous enough. This time, we are going to the maelstrom. No ships have ever made it."
Goram poured two glasses of wine and brought one to his wife. Taking a chair across from her, he sat down. "Look, we aren't going into the whirlpool. Even I'm not that daft. I have an idea of what to do."
Mena sat up and drank her wine. "Our last adventure was amazing. This, however, holds more danger."
"If the word we've been hearing is true, this is only the beginning," stated Goram.
Both fell silent, and allowed the rocking of the ship to calm their nerves.

Eric and Gillock were sharing a cabin this time, and neither could relax. It wasn't the constant motion of the ship. Both were used to it after an hour. Neither could explain it, but when they moved into the mess, it was clear no one was relaxing. Usually, the start of a quest is filled with fears and hopes. Feeling uneasy is part of it. This, however, felt quite different. Firadon and Aremeth were seated having an ale. The two elves were off to the side, drinking wine. Dorien was the only one not present, and that was because he had become ill within moments of the ship pulling away from the dock.

A soft murmur developed as some of the crew came down. It wasn't long until tales of winter travel circulated. Laughter went along with the stories of dangerous trips, and the mood on Serenity's Quest began to settle down into something positive. The bell signalling shift change echoed across the ship, and those who were now needed on deck went to perform their duties. Many hours had passed, and the guests began to feel tired. Leaving the mess, and the crazy stories from the crew, Eric, and his companions each had a smile on their face. Perils existed on this quest. Unknown dangers, and creatures, were waiting for them. That is, of course, if they were actually able to navigate to the maelstrom. The one thing which stuck with Eric was who was with him. He might still be naive about certain things in the world, but his companions were not. Each one brought something different to this quest, and the prince had a feeling every bit was going to be needed.

Gillock watched as Eric drifted off to sleep and was happy to see he was relaxing. The old wizard knew he wouldn't. Not even at the end of this quest would he be able to calm down. Eric was a War Wizard, and that alone weighed heavy on his heart. His daughter was missing, and very well could be turning to Brin's cause. Dreadwraiths, the Therin, all added to the weight. Gillock looked to the few stars he could see through the porthole. His time on this world was growing short. So much he needed to pass on to the world. If events played out, as he feared they could, the world might be without the last true wizard.

CHAPTER TWENTY-TWO

Sniffing the air, the dreadwraith followed the magic of the wizard. Although it entered the castle grounds to be certain the wizard had indeed left, it was closing in on his prey. Draining humans was giving him more strength with each attack, however, it was not ready yet. The dreadwraith new he was not at his full abilities, but he also knew the wizard was old, and the dreadwraith felt him to be a weak man. Coming up to a river, the creature sneered. Not even a river would slow him down for long. On the other side, was his prey. One of the dark magicians who destroyed its kind and banished he and the others to the realm without sunlight. True, a dreadwraith should keep out of the sun, but the shadows it casts hide his kind the best.

When the shadow of a tree stretched across the river, the dreadwraith made his way over. Again, he sniffed the air, and an evil grin crossed his face. The wizard was not far off.

Night fell, and a fire blazed through the trees. The wizard sat off to the side, but something was off. Sniffing the air, no other magic was present, but the dreadwraith had the feeling the wizard was not alone. Carefully shifting along the treeline, the creature observed the wizard, while checking every corner for a trap. When nothing presented itself, the dreadwraith moved into the small area in which the wizard had chosen to build his fire.

"You are quite brave to risk coming out of the woods," said Gillock.

His tone showed no fear, yet something still wasn't right. The wizard moved around the fire, coming closer to the dreadwraith. Magic flowed all around the two, and when Gillock raised his arm to cast a spell, the dreadwraith attacked. Instead of knocking the wizard to the ground, the creature found itself smashing down, alone. It was an illusion.

In a flurry of robes, Gillock moved from where he hid, and threw spells at the dreadwraith. It had grown much in the last few days, and easily dodged the strikes. Flying around the fire, the dreadwraith managed to get close, knocking the wizard to the ground. In an attempt to weaken Gillock, it attacked, clawing at the robes. Blood began to show on the wizard's robe, and the dreadwraith knew his strikes were true. Moving in to finish off the old man, Gillock stood with a strength which stunned the dreadwraith.

Pulling an orb from his robes, Gillock chanted into it. Once it was glowing, he threw it at the creature. At the last moment, the dreadwraith realised the trap. The orb absorbed it, then fell to the ground. Gillock scrambled over to where it sat. Using another spell, Gillock sent it further north.

Collapsing to the ground, Gillock pulled out a vial and drank the contents. It wouldn't stop the poison but would give him time to reach the temple of Narkomet. He could only hope they would have the means to slow the dreadwraiths poison down. Closing his eyes, Gillock called out to the temple. An answer came almost immediately. Using a spell, Gillock moved himself to the area in which the temple lay. Three healers were waiting and brought the injured wizard inside. The last thing Gillock remembered was being given a draught of some kind, and then everything went black.

With the dawn, Gillock opened his eyes to see a strange woman sitting near his bed.

"It's good to see your eyes open," she remarked.

Gillock looked about the room, then back to the woman. "How long have I been here?"

The woman stood and poured Gillock some water. "Only a day. We were able to administer an antidote which your body took to quickly."

Taking the glass, Gillock drank it all. Once finished, he stared at the woman. "What is it I'm not supposed to know?"

The woman placed the glass on a table and turned her gaze back to Gillock. "We were able to slow the poison down with the antidote, but the creature was too advanced for us to cure you."

Gillock swung his legs over the bed and stood. "I understand," he stated, and moved to get his robe.

"If you stay, we can give you herbs to help," she began, but Gillock stopped her.

"I have something to finish. Besides, the dreadwraith is not dead. I only moved it further away. Gives me time to get out of these lands," Gillock remarked.

The woman nodded, and left the room without another word.

Gillock thanked those he saw as he left the temple. A silent wish for those within to be safe was foremost on his mind. There was no telling if the dreadwraith would track Gillock to this point. Standing out in the snow, the wizard looked south. Once again calling on the transport spell, Gillock moved himself to outside the town of Hucksley. Only one thing mattered now, finishing this quest.

CHAPTER TWENTY-THREE

With slow, careful steps, Brin paced angrily across the floor in the great hall. Her pregnancy was coming to an end, and nothing but clear skies graced the area. Arket was back at the front lines, after practising the spell to freeze the river, to prepare. The spell wasn't too complicated, and he was strong enough to perform it alone. Still, Brin was frustrated.

News had come to her ears about unrest in the camp. The men weren't fond of the creatures roaming about the sand, and more than one had wandered into an area they were told to avoid, to come face to face with a dragonworm. They were getting restless, but with Arket back there now, hopefully word of his plan will spread through the camp, giving the men a new hope.

One of her general's commissioned catapults, and they would be arriving at the front in a day or two. Perfect as a distraction, Brin allowed herself a brief smile. Perhaps she won't need to perform the spell during her delivery. As if the child heard, the baby began to shift about. Brin rubbed her belly. "Do not fret little one. You will be the strongest of us all," she said, trying to soothe the child. The thoughts of the war finally turning in their favour brought a true smile to Brin. Instead of pacing in the large room, she decided to head back to her chambers, and relax.

Walking to her rooms took far longer these days, and it gave Brin a chance to admire the palace. Normally she moved with swift steps, not bothering to marvel at the architecture. Her thoughts were usually focused on running the kingdom and planning their next move. Columns carved by hand, but artisan the like Brin had never seen, adorned each doorway. Upon closer inspection, each one appeared to depict a scene of some kind. It was clear the previous occupants had designed the carvings. Each column depicted degradation, torture, and other dark scenes. The sight upset Brin. Boroten, who was her shadow on this day, cringed at what he was seeing.

"There's no happiness in this place," he remarked, and Brin didn't disagree.

Brin ran her hand over one of the columns, and scowled. "Boroten, find me someone who can fix these. I do not expect perfection but would like to see something a little more positive."

With a curt bow, Boroten left her side to head out into the city.

Moving off, Brin made her way to the eastern garden. With its clear view of the ocean, it was a place which usually improved Brin's mood. Finding a comfortable spot in the sun, Brin sat down and enjoyed the quiet. It was rare these days she was able to take comfort in the simple things. With the child arriving soon, things would be even more hectic.

The child moved about again, and another smile crossed her lips. A shadow crossed as a cloud moved in front of the sun, and she raised her head to watch. Instead of observing the cloud, her attention went to the window of the tower. In it, sat Vernia. Brin had almost forgotten about her captive. Vernia's cell was more a small room, made comfortable by Brin. Arket had found it odd the woman hadn't even attempted an escape, but Brin knew why. Vernia was trying to figure out why she was here, and what use they had for the candle she had stolen from her father's secret room.

From the side, Brin saw Boroten moving towards her. "Highness," he said, taking a knee beside her. "I have brought three of the top artisans. They have begun to fix the carvings. They have stated it should be only two weeks to make the changes. If you wish any particular scene, it may be longer."

Brin reached out and squeezed Boroten's hand. "I do not wish anything particular at this time. Tell them to create something positive and inspiring."

Boroten bowed his head, kissed Brin's hand, and moved off to speak with the carvers.

Attention once again drawn to the sea, some things crossed Brin's mind. Would Arket's spell work, and allow them to attack the enemy straight on? The child moved again, and Brin knew the answer. It would work, for a time, but in the end, she was going to have to perform the spell. Barely a cloud in the sky made her wonder if a storm would hit when she needed it.

Arket looked into the basin and smiled. Each time he practised the spell, it took hold immediately. The river would only take a few seconds to freeze, and with the men ready, it should be no problem surprising the enemy. Shouts came from outside the tent, and Arket pushed aside the spell, grabbed his sword, and ran out to see what was going on. Men were running about, and it wasn't long before Changru and a few guards threw four elves, and two humans, at Arket's feet.

"They are spies, highness," said Changru.
"How many were there?" asked Arket, annoyed.
"We are not certain. Some met the dragonworms, and the rest went back across the river. These were the last ones to leave the shore, and were easily captured," replied Changru.
Arket glowered at the captives. "You should feel honoured," he began. Shock registered on the elves faces, for Arket was speaking in their language. Seeing the confusion on the faces of the humans, he switched to the common tongue. "You all are going to witness how powerful this army truly is." Turning to Changru, he changed to his own language. "Get the men ready, at dawn we are going to strike."
Yanking the prisoners up from the ground, soldiers them dragged to the river's edge. Here, they were tied to poles. Arket wanted them to have a front view of the attack.

As the sun rose higher in the sky, Arket stood alone on the shoreline. Although he was supposed to wait until Brin cast her spell to throw their enemy off guard, he felt now was the time to attack. Arket could sense the enemy watching him. Most likely waiting to see if he was going to kill the prisoners. Closing his eyes, Arket focused on the sound of the water flowing past. His voice a whisper, the spell came from his lips. The chanting became a low murmur, and the spell began to take hold. When he could hear the water stop flowing, Arket opened his eyes, and a cruel smile crossed his lips. Changru yelled, and the generals took up the cry.

In no time the river was frozen solid, and in a blink, the army was rushing across. Calls could be heard running along the enemy line, and a few arrows took out some of the soldiers, but the enemy hadn't been expecting an attack like this. It was slippery, but the soldiers managed to make it to the far side, crashing through the bushes, and attacking. Arket finished the spell and drew his sword. The second wave would follow him, and he waited until Changru gave the signal, then was on the move.

The enemy ended up mobilizing faster than Arket had anticipated, but the element of surprise had allowed his army to catch many off guard. When he arrived, there were many enemy bodies littering the ground. With a cry akin to a growl, Arket engaged a soldier. He sensed they were pulling back, drawing them further into the woods. At first, he assumed it was due to the surprise, and that they were winning. It wasn't long before Arket realised reinforcements had come. Elves.

After forty-five minutes of fighting, the attack turned to the enemy's favour. A wave of arrows hit the men surrounding Arket, and he ordered the retreat. Moments later, the call came to let him know the spell was fading. Without a thought, the men ran back across the river. As spell ended, Arket was perturbed. There were far too many men still crossing the ice. A voice was heard on the wind, and Arket felt the energy of a spell being cast. The river raged and frothed, drowning some of his soldiers, carrying the rest down the river.

Changru placed his hand on the arm of the angry emperor. "We slaughtered many, my lord. This was not a defeat."

Arket sneered as he looked back across the river. "Brin has one more trick up her sleeve. For now, bring forward the catapults. Let us see how they react to having their men sent home."

The screams of the captives echoed through the area and brought a smile to Arket. He had ordered them dismembered, alive. The body parts were then placed into the catapult and shot across the river. Yells and curses came at them, along with another volley of arrows. None hit the men, for Arket had ordered them to move back from the shore. They hadn't pushed the enemy back, but they had done some damage. Now, he had to await the birth of his child to deal the final blow.

CHAPTER TWENTY-FOUR

Word came of the attack, and how they were pushed back, and Brin was annoyed. Arket stated before he left that he felt if the time was right, he should enact the spell. However, Brin disagreed. It was clear her husband felt they would deal a decent blow to the enemy, so he had used the spell, and attacked. Brin did not wish to belittle her husband's choice and kept her anger in check. Truly, with no storm clouds seen in the last few weeks, they had needed to do something. With a heavy sigh, Brin conceded that her husband had made the right choice.

Thinking on the spell, Brin knew it wasn't meant to last long. It was their hope to take out as many as possible before they needed to head back. Still, Brin was disappointed more of the enemy weren't killed. The war had been raging on for months, and spring was not far off. They had to do something before then, or they might end up losing.

"My queen, you must come to the window," said one of the servants.

Brin saw his eyes were lit up and wondered what could be causing his excitement. Moving to the window, she looked out over the sea. With a shout of glee, she danced about. "Get the midwife. I must speak with her," she shouted, and a page ran off.

Brin turned back to the open water, and to the dark clouds in the distance. It wasn't any storm showing on the horizon. From the look of it, a hurricane was brewing.

Shuffling of feet let her know the midwife was there. Turning from the window, Brin motioned her to sit. Pouring a cup of tea, Brin sat across. With a soft smile, Brin sipped her tea. "Teyla, it is almost time for my child to come. If I have not gone into labour before the storm hits, I wish to take the herb."

Teyla fiddled with her cup and looked up at Brin. "Majesty, you are far enough along that it will not harm the child, but I still don't recommend it. However, you are the one having the child, and I will do as you ask."

Brin took a few more sips of tea before commenting. "I do not want to force you, Teyla, but I have no choice. When the storm arrives, so shall my child."

The midwife finished her tea, and with Brin's permission, left to prepare. By the look of the clouds, the storm would hit land the following evening.

Alone once again, Brin took out a piece of parchment, and wrote a note to Arket. Using a spell, Brin sent it. Brin wished the army to pull back from the area. She had no idea if the storm would focus over the enemy or span a much larger area. No reply would come from Arket, because she requested no further communication until the child had arrived. Her focus now would be on preparing. Although the spell didn't appear complex, there was much focus required to do any kind of magic. Until the storm arrived, her plan was to read, and reread, the spell until she had it embedded in her soul.

Vernia sat in her window, watching the dark clouds move closer. People had begun running about the castle, and she assumed it meant they were preparing for a terrific storm to hit. She understood the urgency, but something else was going on. There were no clues, because no one ever came to see her, but Vernia still felt something happening. Magic was all about in this palace, so she tended not to focus on it. Today, Vernia decided to place out feeler spells, to see if she could detect anything that would help her figure out what was bothering her.

Many areas were blocked, so instead of probing, she moved to the next area. By the end of it, nothing new had become known. Moving back to the window, she studied the storm. Perhaps if she used magic outside of the palace, she might have better results. A sea bird squawked, and she had an idea. It had been many years since she saw through the eyes of a bird, and Vernia hoped she still remembered the spell.

Moving to a chair, Vernia made herself comfortable and began to focus. Attaching herself to the bird, Vernia concentrated on the spell. It wasn't long before she was fully connected. Soaring through the sky made her feel queasy at first, then she remembered to feel her surroundings, a way to remind her body she was still in her room. Up the bird flew until it came to what Vernia knew had to be the royal suites. The bird landed on the ledge of the balcony and stared intently into the room. Brin had her back to the window, so the bird moved to the window ledge in an attempt to view what she was doing. A ragged book laid out on the desk before her, and Brin was examining every word. Vernia knew it must be a spell and wondered what it was for. Brin shifted in her seat, and part of the spell could be seen. The only thing Vernia could make out were the words 'rubsidian candle'. Vernia released the bird from the spell and sat back in her seat hard. That was what she had taken from her father, and it was clear it was going to be used soon. Despair hit Vernia's heart, since it was clear the war was about to be turned in the favour of Brin, and there was nothing she could do to stop it.

Night turned into day, and still Brin studied the spell. The wind was beginning to rage, and rain had started to come down. It wouldn't be long before the storm was close enough to be used. Brin drank her tea and watched the lightning flash. Midday came, and the baby decided it was time. When the first contraction hit, Brin was surprised. A shout to Boroten, and the midwives were summoned. Teyla was the lead, but she was bringing two others to be safe. Brin's bedchamber became the birthing area, and she watched as the midwives brought in all they needed to help bring the child into the world.

Wind whipped against the windows, and Teyla ordered them shuddered. Brin had wanted to watch the storm strike but preventing glass shattering and harming her was more important. Many doorways leading from the balcony were shuttered as well, and stronger contractions hit. Brin ordered a table to remain at the bedside, with the candle on it. When the midwives were ready, Brin was moved to the bed, and was made comfortable. Steady contractions set in, and it was now just a waiting game.

With the storm raging all about, the baby came. Brin's blue eyes flashed with dangerous undertones as one of the midwives tried to push the table which held the candle away. Taking hold of the rubsidian candle, and gripping it tight, Brin ordered it lit. When the baby was ready to arrive, Brin focused all her might on the last push, and her voice screeched the spell. Thunder rumbled so loud a midwife fainted, while lightning flashed, filling the room with light. Wind whipped open the shuttered window, and the candle absorbed the storm's energy. Brin could feel the strength of the storm trying to fight containment within the candle. The entire experience exhilarated Brin.

"You have a son, my lady," said a midwife, lifting the baby for Brin to see.

Exhausted from the ordeal, Brin looked at her son. "His name will be Tomaz," she stated, tears of joy falling down her cheeks. The midwife moved off, and Brin's focus went back to the spell.

For a moment, Brin wondered if the spell had worked. However, a second after thought came into her mind, so did the rush of power. Pushing aside the two standing midwives, Brin hurdled herself at the open window. Raising the candle, Brin finished the spell. "With this gift of power from the gods, I send the wrath of this storm into the forest beyond!" she shrieked into the wind. The candle flame grew bright and high. Not even the gale force wind coming at them could blow it out.

The power within Brin and the candle hurled out over the land. An entire hurricane contained in a single cloud, begging for release. When the spell hit the forest hiding the enemy, they had no warning, and nowhere to hide. In a matter of minutes, half the forest trees were uprooted and flying about, taking the lives of many hiding within.

Vernia watched as the storm appeared to shrink into a single cloud, and rush to the north. Dark magic filled the palace, and for a moment, there was a break in the wards surrounding her. With a deep breath, Vernia cast the spell to transport her back to Keenley.

Arket watched in wonder as the dark cloud raced overhead. It came to a full halt over the forest and let loose its fury. It wasn't long before screams of death and terror came to his ears. Brin had warned him to be far away from the forest, but the emperor couldn't resist, and he was happy to bear witness.

Winds tore through the forest, knocking him down. Moving between some rocks for cover, Arket smiled when the lightning came. Strike after strike hit the forest, destroying those hiding in the trees. Once again, the winds raged through, ripping up trees, and throwing them into the river. More screams followed as the enemy were pulled from their hiding places and tossed aside. At that moment, Arket was happy they had moved their army miles away. They too would have lost many men. When the spell ran its course, the forest was unrecognizable. Arket laughed and headed to his army. They would wait a few days, and then return to the river's edge. This time, there would be no one to stop the rafts from crossing.

Elizanne watched in horror as Vernia hung suspended in the air. Many months back Elizanne had placed a spell on the castle. It was to prevent the enemy from showing up unexpectedly. Unfortunately, Vernia had attempted to appear within the castle walls. Now, Vernia was caught in the spell, her face held in a silent scream.

“Is there nothing you can do for her?” asked a guard.

Elizanne continued to stare, “I can end the spell, but she will fall into a sleep until her mind can fix what is being done to her.”

Raising her hands, Elizanne spoke the words to release Vernia. The woman fell in a heap, and as expected, was unresponsive. “Move Vernia into her room, and I want around the clock care for her,” ordered Elizanne, holding back tears.

A guard picked Vernia up, and a page ran to find healers while Elizanne moved over to a bench, falling down upon it. All she could think of was the horror’s Vernia must be facing, locked in her mind.

CHAPTER TWENTY-FIVE

Of all the soldiers and elves who went across the river, only five returned. Each one speaking of the horror they found once across the river. Large sand creatures, which resembled a worm, containing rows of razor-sharp teeth, had killed those on the first raft not long after they were on the shore. Most of the humans Jeremy had sent were on the first raft, along with two elves. Sorrow crept into the hearts of those listening.

Jeremy shook his head in disbelief. They had seen strange tracks along the sandy shoreline, and now they knew what caused them. The report continued, and the generals grew wary. Powerful magic could be felt coming from the far side of the river. Glomain knew a great spell was going to be cast, but the uncertainty as to what it would do bothered them. Shouts from outside the tent drew them all out. A scout reported seeing six who were captured, tied to stakes. Night fell, and nothing more happened across the river, but all knew it would only be a matter of time. When dawn came, their fears were realised.

Even with the information that a spell of great magnitude was going to be used, they were surprised. The river froze and as it did, the enemy flowed behind it. Shouts went up, and the army mobilized. General Chenkit and General Traug took up the charge, with the few remaining elves not far behind. The wave of enemy soldiers swept through their ranks, killing many. Jeremy was forced to the back of the forest for his safety and was quite annoyed to be dragged away from the fighting.

Screams came to Jeremy's ears, and despair filled his heart. A sound came from behind, and the few guards with him draw their weapons. A smile spread across Jeremy's lips when he saw it was more of Glavlin's elves arriving. He ordered them to the front, and followed behind, his guards protesting.

"My daughter is in the fight," shouted Jeremy. "I can do no less!"

No one argued, for his tone showed Jeremy was not in the mood. Instead, the guards followed in silence, hoping their king would survive the fight.

The elves moved in with arrows slinging at the enemy, then swords slashing them down. The leader of the enemy army turned his head as a signal was sounded. With a growl, and a sneer, the leader ordered his men back across the river. As they ran, the spell began to fade, giving Darly an idea. She moved to the shoreline, and placed her hand on the river, calling forth its fury. Many of the enemy crashed into the depths and were held under. Those who were able to rise to the surface were washed away as it suddenly turned into a raging river.

No cheer came to their lips, for although they pushed the enemy back across, many dead and wounded lay at their feet. Jeremy arrived close to the front as General Chenkit ordered the bodies to be removed, and the wounded tended to. Jeremy watched as Koral, and Glavlin, moved to speak with the new arrivals. Many elves had been lost, as well as his own men, this day.

"They will regroup quickly," stated Jeremy to Glavlin when he came over. Glavlin nodded his agreement. "We have no time to mourn our dead. We must be ready for another attack."

The dead were removed, and the wounded resting with the healers. A silence, which had dominated the camp, was broken when the screams of the prisoners came to their ears. Men moved to the bushes along the shore, and some turned to vomit. Across, those captured were being dismembered, alive. Tears flowed freely from the eyes of the elves bearing witness, and their moods quickly turned to anger. Catapults were moved to the edge, the parts placed inside, and the prisoners were sent back to their forest. Hearts and faith became lost on the men as the body parts flew into their ranks. The elves, however, were angered in a way no one had ever seen. Koral shouted curses across the river and launched arrows. None hit their mark. Disheartened, and angry, everyone but those on watch went back to the camp.

Dawn arrived and Jeremy, having barely slept, drank the tea brought to him. The elves had found certain plants, and when dried, made a tea which would rejuvenate you. Today, Jeremy had three cups, and still didn't feel any better. Something was nagging at the back of his mind, and he couldn't shake the feeling that the attack the day earlier was only the beginning.

Glavlin sat in the tallest tree along the shore, while Koral and Darly were in the bushes below. Something strange was occurring across the river. They had all thought more rafts would push across to continue the attack, but they were wrong, Instead, it looked as if the camp was packing up. Glavlin, with practised leaps, dropped down the tree and landed on the ground.

"Did you both see what I did?" he asked, crouching down between them. Darly's eyes stayed glued to the shore across. "Yes. But are they leaving,

or just pulling back to try a different tactic?"
"There is great magic in that army," stated Koral. "Whatever is going on, I fear we are not equipped to handle it."
Her two companions stayed silent, each knowing her words were correct. The catapults were the last thing to be pulled away, and after they began to move, Koral was up and running to her father's camp, to report.

Jeremy was perplexed at the information presented to him.
"Moving back makes no sense," he stated.
"I agree," remarked Olrond. "It doesn't seem a prudent course of action. We were weakened, and they knew that. Why leave?"
"There is only one explanation," said Glomain, moving to sit at the table. "They are planning a different kind of attack."
Ender stared at the makeshift map which lay on the table before them. "Pulling back into the open sand doesn't appear logical. If we ever found a way to come at them from the side, they wouldn't stand a chance."
"Unless they possess many of those sand creature's which attacked those who went across on their west side," grumbled Koral, who was growing frustrated.
Jeremy sensed his daughter's annoyance and placed his hand on hers. "Go back to the shore. See if anything new has been determined."
With only a curt nod, Koral left the tent.
"I believe we all understand her frustration," sighed Glomain.
Nothing was worse than knowing an attack was inevitable, but not having a clue as to where or what it would be. With no sign of any action across the river, or in either direction from their enemy's camp, Jeremy ordered everyone to get as much rest as they could. When the next attack did come, it might be a time before they would find rest.

On the second day after the attack happened, the elves were on edge. A strange and old magic could be felt on the breeze. Something dark and dangerous was coming. Glavlin and Koral were taking counsel with Jeremy and his two generals when they felt the strange magic increase.
"A foul voice is mixed in with the wind," whispered Koral. Looking about the tent, her eyes fell on her father. "We must leave!"
The force and fear in her voice momentarily stunned Jeremy. Within a breath, the storm hit.

Running from the tent, they witnessed a dark cloud move, and pause, over the forest. When the wind hit, Jeremy knew they were doomed. The hurricane dropped on the forest, and within seconds, many were dead.

Trees were ripped from their roots, tossing elves to their death. Lightning struck hard, killing any who were near instantly. The screams of those who were caught partially by a strike could be heard, as well as the moans and shouts of the people who were thrown about by the wind. When the storm dissipated, Jeremy looked about in horror. The camp was destroyed, as was most of the forest. Finding a page, who was one of the lucky few to escape without a scratch, he told him to find all who could work, and immediately get a tent set up for the wounded. With a curt bow, the page was off.

Where the healing tent had once stood, was emptiness. The entire tent had been ripped from the ground, and now rested far off, in a tattered ruin. The few men who had been inside had also been tossed about, their broken bodies lay in death along the edge of the camp. Finding some soldiers who were barely wounded, the page informed them of the king's order. Without hesitation, the men found some of the extra supplies, including another large tent, and put it up. It wasn't long before the many injured were being brought in. By luck, or design, another group of elves showed up. Glomain sent some off to the temple of Narkomet to get a few who may be able to help with the injured. By dawn the next day, four healers were there, tending to their wounded.

"How bad is he?" questioned Jeremy.

On the bed before him lay Ender. One of the uprooted trees had come down on him, but instead of crushing him, a branch pierced his side, pinning him to the ground. It had taken many hours to get him out, and by then he was unconscious from the loss of blood.

"I don't know," answered one of the healers. "If he survives the day, he might wake."

Jeremy nodded, and left the tent. Grave news was not uncommon these days. Already quite a few of the wounded had died.

Jeremy looked about at the ruins of the camp, and his eyes came to rest on Koral. Many elves were scouting in the trees when the wind hit, and most were dead, or unaccounted for. Darly was one of the missing. Jeremy walked over to Koral and sat down beside her on a fallen tree.

"This was magic far beyond what any mortal is capable of," she said absently.

Jeremy put his arm around Koral and held her tight. "We are not certain what her abilities are, however, I agree. That kind of power feels like something only a god could conjure."

Koral rested her head on her father's chest and stared down at the ground.

Darly was one of the missing, but she along with five others had been scouting to the west. It could be they were beyond the destruction but were having trouble navigating back. It was a slim hope, and Koral clung to it. A flicker of light caught her eye, and Koral realised it was from one of the few trees standing. With a light kiss on her father's cheek, Koral stood, and moved over, placing her hand on the tree. Once again, tears came to her eyes, and Jeremy got up.

"What is it?" he asked, concerned.

Koral sobbed lightly, and turned to face him. "This forest was quite old. They have no memory of such destruction ever occurring here. It is in pain."

Jeremy felt for his daughter. Feeling the nature around her was new to her, and clearly overwhelming. Koral turned back, and he watched as she lovingly stroked the bark. A moment later, she jumped back, and an odd look crossed her face. "I may be able to help somehow," she said, and her excitement shocked Jeremy.

Placing her hand on the tree again, Koral closed her eyes and began chanting. When she was finished, Koral took her hand off the tree, stepped back, and sighed deep. Another second passed, and Koral turned into the silver tree they had seen many times before. Glavlin came into camp as it happened and smiled to Jeremy as he approached her.

"Perhaps a way can be found to fix this disaster," Glavlin said.

Jeremy walked up to the strange tree, placing his hand on it. "Let us hope."

Koral opened her eyes, and saw she was in a familiar grove. Looking about, she noticed something odd. The grove, although vibrant and alive, appeared strange. Her eyes found a bush, and it was here Koral realised was the difference. While the rest of the area was blooming and bright, this bush appeared to be dying. Koral went over to it, and sat down, staring at the strange bush.

"That bush represents the forest you are in," stated the Earth Mother, appearing beside Koral.

Koral lightly touched a leaf, and watched it fall. "How is it my sister was able to perform such a spell?"

The Earth Mother waited until Koral was standing before answering. "She stole a small part of power from a god," she said, motioning to Koral that they should walk.

"Is there a way to fix the forest?" questioned Koral. "I have done so before," she added, recalling hiding the bodies of the soldiers and repairing

the forest outside of Keenley.
They arrived at a bench beside the river, and the Earth Mother sat down. "That forest is quite old, Koral. You cannot ever bring it back to what it once was. I do feel that you may be able to do something."
Koral sat beside her and waited for the Earth Mother to continue. As if gathering her thoughts, the Earth Mother took some time before continuing.
"Besides healing the forest, you must also figure out a way to push your enemy further back," she began, her eyes focused on the flowing river.
"That has been foremost on my mind for many months," sighed Koral.
"To help the forest, channel your energy into the tree, and ask the earth to reclaim its fallen. You and the other elves should be able to sing new trees into growth." The Earth Mother appeared to have more to say, so Koral stayed silent. "There is a way to widen the river, although I am not certain if you are strong enough to do it alone."
Koral jumped up, moving into the goddess's line of sight. "Please give me the chance to try," she pleaded.
The grey eyes of the Earth Mother stared hard into Koral. "Speak to the river. If help can be found, it will tell you."
A familiar feeling of floating ran through Koral, and she knew the Earth Mother was sending her back to the waking world.

Shimmering fluttered through the silver tree, and moments later Koral lay on the ground. Any of the elves not out searching for survivors, were guarding her until she returned. Glavlin helped Koral to stand, and she looked about. "Something is different," she stated.
Glavlin nodded. "You were gone for a week."
Koral allowed him to sit her on a stump, and she realised the entire area had been cleared of debris and the camp had been reset. "That long?"
"We wondered if you were ever coming back," remarked Glomain coming over to them. "Were you able to speak with the Earth Mother?"
"Yes," she replied, standing. "There is something I can do. It is not much, but it is a start."
Both elves looked at her curiously and watched as she wrapped her arms around the largest tree, rested her head on it, and began chanting. As she chanted, the ground began to rumble, and a strange glowing mist came from it. The mist crawled across the ground, and after it went by, all traces of the dead trees were removed. Behind it came bare earth, and the elves followed the mist, joined in with her chanting. Small sprouts popped up

from the ground, and within two hours, the elves had walked the damaged area, bringing new life to the forest. They were also able to find many of the missing elves, including Darly. A few were still alive, and with the damage done to their bodies, there was little hope the wounded would survive. Each one was carried to the healer's tent, and the clerics immediately went to work on them.

Koral finished her spell and was informed of what happened. Running to the healer's tent, Koral burst in and went to Darly's side. The elf was pale but breathing. Grabbing her hand, Koral kissed it and whispered in her ear to survive. One of the clerics asked Koral to go, and although she didn't want to, Darly needed their care and medicine. Exiting the tent, Koral decided it was time to speak with her father. He was expecting her, so food and drink were waiting in his tent.

"At this moment, I am grateful you and Eric opened up the area between us and Lungast," said Jeremy as Koral ate. "Without the clerics of Narkomet, I do not think most of the wounded would have survived."

Koral sipped her wine. "I heard about General Chenkit. He was a good man."

Jeremy's eyes closed slightly as he thought of Ender. "He would have rather died facing an enemy," he said.

"As would all soldiers," responded Koral, taking another bite of cheese. "At least we know Brin is not capable of using strong magic like that again."

Jeremy said nothing, instead, he looked at the map on the table beside him. So many places were vulnerable now, and he wondered if it mattered at all what Brin was capable of.

In the late hours, as the hearth burned low, a strange man, hidden behind his cowl, sat staring out the window. Soft footfalls came to his ears, and he watched as a figure moved into the shadows. Many a night he had seen this man hiding in the shadows as if waiting for something. The man entered the inn, taking a seat in front of the fire. A few moments passed, and another man, one whose steps were barely a whisper, sat across.

"It needs be done soon," stated the first man, pushing a pouch across.

The other took it, and hid it in his cloak. "May I ask why you wish the queen dead?"

"It be that witches fault me boys dead. If not fer her kind, he be alive!" The man hadn't meant to get so excited, but his son had been killed by the dreadwraith, and he wanted vengeance. "I be wantin your name," he added quietly.

Fox knew this would come up, it always did. In case of failure, the person hiring him always wanted someone to blame. "I am called Fox, and that is all you need to know."

Fox moved out of the inn with barely a sound, and the man quickly followed. Jervin moved from his hiding spot and was no longer certain if he had been noticed. Fox appeared to be a man who noticed everything and left nothing to chance. Not wishing to meet the man in an alley, Jervin made himself comfortable in a chair, staring once again out the window.

CHAPTER TWENTY-SIX

Bushes lined the shore still but gave little cover. Across, the army of the Saviour was returning. Three weeks had passed, and although they were lucky the enemy hadn't returned sooner, the soldiers were nowhere near healthy enough for another battle. Only a third of their army were able to fight.

"Koral, now would be a good time to follow the Earth Mother's words," whispered Glavlin.

Both headed away from their hiding spot, hoping not to be noticed. When they came back to camp, Koral had decided it was time. Kissing Glavlin deep, she ran off to the pool which once held the dryadshee. Through the pass, spring was taking hold in the Central Lands, and Koral knew it was only a matter of time before Brin came up with a new plan of attack, perhaps one from the sea. The pool came into view, and although she had no idea what to say, Koral moved into it, allowing her mind to focus on nothing more.

Nothing told of time's passage, so Koral had no idea how long she had been calling to the water before it was answered. A splash to her side drew her out of the trance and seated on a rock was an unusual creature. Her skin was a blue-green, as was her hair. Where legs should be was a tail, and the strange creature sat, eyeing Koral.

"I am Mirrah," she stated, and the words spoke depths.

"Y-o-u are the goddess of the under-sea," stuttered Koral. Many times, she spoke with the Earth Mother, but this was the first time one of the other gods had presented themselves.

Mirrah nodded and continued to stare at Koral. "You sent out a call, I answered."

Koral gulped, and noticed the water was giving her a chill. As if the goddess sensed it, the water warmed, and Mirrah moved back into it. "I wish to widen the river," stammered Koral. "Is it possible?"

Mirrah shifted in the water. "You possess magic not your own. It blends well with that which is truly yours. Do you wish my permission to do this feat?"

Koral didn't understand what Mirrah was meaning but decided she should answer. "I do seek your permission, as well as your help in achieving this."

After many minutes of contemplation, Mirrah nodded. "I grant you this," she replied. "However, I cannot help you with this task. Ask those who have strong abilities to assist you."

Relief crossed Koral's face. "What do I need to do?" she asked, happy to have Mirrah's permission, but not certain as what was needed to perform it.

Mirrah rose out of the water, and her voice became that of a god. "On the night with no moon, find the river's edge. All those who are helping the spell must cut their hand, releasing the blood into the flowing water. Speak to the river of what you wish to achieve. Concentrate, and channel the part of you linked to water. The rest will be shown to you."

Koral watched as Mirrah faded from sight and took a moment to compose herself before heading back to the camp.

"Has there been any word on Vernia's condition?" General Traug had joined Jeremy, Glomain and King Glavlin to report, and found them discussing Vernia.

"Elizanne's last note said there was no change, and she fears if Vernia does not wake soon, she never will," came Jeremy's solemn reply.

A shout, followed by Koral bursting into the tent, drew them from their conversation. Taking an empty seat, Koral sat down, reached for the bottle of wine, and poured herself some, drinking deep. Placing the glass down, she looked at the faces before her. "I can perform a spell which will help us with this fight," she began, and after a deep breath, continued. "I require help. Not just any help, I will need my mother. I also feel that I will need help from you Glavlin and you Glomain, and possibly Vernia."

Jeremy's face clouded. "She has yet to wake."

Koral turned her eyes to her father, and he saw hope within them. "I plan on waking her myself. I am leaving as soon as I eat. The roads are clear now, and the spring storms have yet to hit. I can run and be there within a few days."

"I will be going with you," came Darly's voice from the doorway. Instead of a white, half-dead elf, she was a fully healed one.

"How is it you healed so fast?" hollered Glavlin, rushing over to hug her close.

Darly pushed away and gave Glavlin a friendly glare. "Apparently, the spell Koral cast to rid the forest of the fallen trees also helped the elves who were wounded. The clerics only had to accentuate the magic."

Koral stood, and hugged Darly. "I will happily have you with me. We leave in thirty minutes."

Darly nodded and ran to prepare a pack.

Koral turned back to the room. "Keep them on their side of the river. Throw every arrow we have at them." With a quick smile to her father, Koral left the room and the remaining people in a stunned silence.

Three days after Vernia's return, word came of the devastating attack. Although her husband and daughter were fine, so many others weren't so lucky. The stress was beginning to wear on the queen, however, Elizanne knew she had to appear strong in front of others. "I thank you for bringing me this message. What is your name, so that I may remember you for future messages?"

The soldier smiled a crooked smile, "Names Emil Fawkes, my lady. Friends call me Fox."

Elizanne nodded. "Alright, Fox. Please take a night to rest before heading back to the front. I am certain they can do without you."

Fox bowed low, "Much obliged, milady."

Elizanne watched as the soldier followed the page for food and lodging, then headed to Vernia's room to check up on her.

Ditching his guide at the first possible moment, Fox backtracked his steps and followed the queen. Having magic of his own, the assassin sensed Elizanne had let her guard down. Clearly, the war, and running the kingdom, was taking its toll. Fox knew he would have only one chance against someone with her abilities. He watched as the queen ordered a page to bring her tea and shut the door tight behind her.

Having already spent many hours being shown the secret passageways of the castle by their spy, Fox knew a passage went from where he hid, to the closet in Vernia's room. With practised steps, he moved into the opening, and ran to the room. Inside, he could hear the queen conversing, as she always did, with the unconscious witch. Fox crept into the backside of the closet and moved through. He had left the door slightly ajar on a previous visit and was happy to see it was still so. Pulling his knife from its sheath, Fox waited.

A knock came, and a page brought in the tea. Fox watched as the same scenario unfolded as it had on the previous nights. It had been luck that he crossed paths with the soldier carrying the message for the queen. Unfortunate for the soldier, who was now lying dead in the sea.

Fox observed the queen as she poured her tea, and waited until she took to her usual seat, with her back turned to the closet. When the queen began talking, Fox made his move. Silence was one of the first things a Shadow is trained to accomplish and is also one of the most difficult. Elizanne reached forward to adjust Vernia's blanket, exposing the rib area. With a sneer, Fox lifted his knife, and thrust it forward into the queen.

Time appeared to slow. A gasp escaped Fox's lips, and he looked down to see a knife sticking out of his side. His knife, which he had thought struck true, was stuck in the side of the chair. Falling back onto the floor, Fox looked up to see a familiar face looming over him. "Bastle," he gasped. "You traitor!"

Bastle stood up and spat on Fox. "I knew it be you. Always wantin the royals."

Fox chuckled, and blood flowed from his lips. "She will not allow for this. Your head is next." His final words were followed by a spasm, and then the man who tried to assassinate the queen, died.

Elizanne looked at the man on the floor. "I must send a thank you to Jervin for his information." Her gaze moved to Bastle, "And to you for being here."

"First thing we be taught is to be silent. Second, be knowin when it's a trap," replied the old man as he bent down to retrieve his knife. "I be owin you and the king much. This be the least I could do."

Elizanne flopped into the chair and stared at Vernia. "This castle is not safe, my friend. Please wake up, so I may take counsel with you once again."

As always, the young woman remained asleep. Elizanne stood and walked out with Bastle close behind. She ordered guards placed in the secret passageway and wondered if even that would be enough to keep them safe.

The gates came into view, but the two elves kept their pace until they were at the castle. By the time they were scaling the steps, the entire castle knew. Elizanne was in the throne room, discussing things with Jervin and Morgan when the news came of their arrival. Elizanne gave orders, and within half an hour, Darly and Koral entered the room.

Elizanne motioned to two chairs, then turned her attention back to Morgan. "I will not accept anything but a yes on this matter."

Morgan's eyes narrowed in contemplation. "This is a lot to think about, majesty."

Jervin turned to the confused elves. "The queen has just informed Lady Macray that she wishes her to take the position of Grand Duchess. As to be expected, the lady wishes to run from this room screaming."

The remark caused Koral to chuckle, and Elizanne and Morgan to glare at the minstrel. Jervin laughed and shrugged. Morgan sighed, shaking her head, he wasn't wrong.

"The attack did one thing, it made it clear there are few I can trust, Morgan. I need you to do this," said Elizanne.

"What attack?" asked Koral, interrupting.

Elizanne looked at her daughter and took her hand. "Someone hired an assassin to attack me. Luckily, Jervin had observed the conversation, and Bastle came for a visit. Without them, things may have gone bad."

Jervin stood and made an exaggerated bow. "A loyal subject does what he can."

"Making light of this situation is unbecoming," scolded Morgan, standing as well. "But we should head out. Your highness, I will take your words under consideration, and give you an answer by morning."

Elizanne smiled. "I thank you for that. Until morning."

Jervin and Morgan left, leaving Elizanne with Darly and Koral. "Shall we move to a more comfortable room?" she questioned.

"Yes, mother. I wish to hear more about what went on here," muttered Koral.

Elizanne could hear the concern, and annoyance, in her daughter's voice. No words were spoken until they arrived at the library.

Two pages opened the grand doors, and Elizanne sent one to get some tea, and a light lunch. Elizanne moved in and took a deep breath. The queen often came here to think in front of the large hearth. A fire burned bright, bringing warmth to the chilly, wet spring day. Large, plush chairs circled the hearth, and each took one. Koral sunk into her chair and relaxed almost instantly.

"This library makes the one in Klayhern look like a bookshop," remarked Koral.

Elizanne looked about. "When I was a child, I wanted to read every book in here."

"A noble idea," said Darly, glancing at the enormous amount of books. The library went off in many directions, each leading away from the sitting area. Servants brought the tea and lunch, making Koral and Darly realise how long it had been since their last meal.

"So, what has been going on around here?" asked Koral, filling her plate with fruit and cheeses.

Elizanne sat back, and sipped her tea. "The dreadwraith killed more before it left to follow Gillock. Many blame magic users. One decided to hire someone to remove me, as I am the strongest in the city."

Koral eyed her mother. "Why did we not hear of this?"

"You and your father have far more important things to worry about," replied Elizanne, and her tone made it clear it was the end of the discussion.

Time passed, and they all enjoyed the small meal.

"What brings you two here?" asked Elizanne, as the servants removed the dishes.

Koral was going to reply but noticed one of the servants was taking their time leaving. Standing she said, "The assassin would have needed help. Someone familiar with the castle." One step, then another, and the servant realised Koral was moving closer. Throwing the tray at the elf, the young man ran from the room. Koral was going to pursue, but a shout from her mother stopped her.

"You are right, Koral, but we have always known whom. Now, he will leave the castle, and hopefully we will not have any more issues," stated Elizanne.

Koral returned to her seat. "Do you not wish to find out why they were here?"

Elizanne looked to her daughter. "Yes, and the passageways are all guarded. Hopefully, he will be caught."

Not impressed with being unable to go after the man, Koral decided to change the subject to why she is here. "You were told of the attack, and the many things which happened since," Koral started, taking a drink of wine to calm herself. "My time with the Earth Mother gave me insight. I spoke with the goddess Mirrah and have come up with a plan which may keep Brin on her side of the land."

Elizanne stared at her daughter. "You spoke with Mirrah? How extraordinary," she commented absently. "What is it you wish to do?"

Another long drink of wine, and the glass was empty. "I plan to create a wider gap by expanding the river. The goddess gave me her blessing but stated I would need the help of others. I require you, the elves, and Vernia."

At the mention of Vernia, Elizanne grew tense. "No one has been able to get to her," she remarked.

"I know that mother. I wish to try though," said Koral.

Silence followed, and Koral waited for her mother to reply, although her response would not change her mind.

"When we are finished here, I will take you to her. Perhaps where we have failed, you will succeed."

In the small chamber, Vernia slept. Koral looked down on the woman, then asked all to stay outside, and magically sealed the room to ensure they did. Since Koral had no idea what exactly was going to happen, she felt it better to contain the room in case things did not go as planned. Standing over her, Koral reached out, and placed one hand over Vernia's heart, the other on her forehead. Slowing her breathing down, Koral closed her eyes, and began to chant. The spell was one designed to give you entry into another mind, but not control it. The clerics of Narkomet told her of it, and how they would use it to try and help heal issues of the mind. Koral hoped it would work with Vernia.

Opening her eyes, Koral noticed she was no longer standing in the castle room. Around her was a forest, and not far away sat a lake. Vernia was standing near the lake, and she wasn't moving. Koral made her way over and saw a look of extreme terror on Vernia's face.

"I do not know what horrors are keeping you in this place, Vernia, but I need you to leave it," whispered Koral. "You need to fight your past issues and come back into the waking world."

Vernia didn't acknowledge Koral, so she kept repeating the words, turning them into a spell by placing a bit of elven magic to them. After what felt like hours, Vernia turned to face her. Koral saw recognition in her eyes, and a moment later, Vernia screamed. It was primal, filled with fear, and carrying powerful magic on it. A moment later, everything went dark.

"Princess, are you alright?" asked a voice.

Koral slowly opened her eyes to see Vernia looking at her, concern on her face. "I believe so." Koral had collapsed to the floor, so she brought herself into a sitting position.

Vernia was still in the bed but was now sitting up. "I don't know what you did, but I thank you."

Koral stood, and poured them both a glass of water. "Your dream was a beautiful place, yet it appeared to hold much darkness."

After drinking some water, Vernia shook her head. "I don't remember."

Koral eyed Vernia for a moment, then stood again to open the door. Elizanne entered and a look of joy crossed her face. The queen sat on the bedside, and hugged Vernia tight. "I am so sorry for whatever you went through."

Vernia was confused by the words but said nothing. Instead, she returned the embrace.

"How do you feel?" asked Elizanne.

"Hungry, but otherwise fine," replied Vernia with a smile.

"Well, how about you get dressed and come down to the library. I will have food waiting. We have much to tell you," stated Elizanne, standing.

Again, Vernia was confused by her words. "I only need a few moments, and I will be there."

Elizanne waved everyone out, leaving Vernia to her thoughts.

"How do you fare?" asked Darly.

Vernia had eaten two platefuls of meat and cheese, and was finishing a second glass of wine. "Finally satisfied," she said with a sigh.

Elizanne ordered the servants out, and once the door was shut, turned her attention to Vernia. "As I said, we have much to discuss. First, I wish to apologize about what happened. I did not realise my spell would harm you as it did. I should have had it focus on dark magic. You have lost weeks because of me." Elizanne noted the stunned looked on Vernia's face. It was apparent the woman did not realise how long she was in that state. "Now, I will leave the next explanation to my daughter."

Vernia turned to face Koral, and the princess began her tale.

Koral first spoke of the freezing of the river, and then of the hurricane dropped on them. She ended by telling Vernia of the plan. When she was finished, Vernia was shocked, and impressed with the idea. "A bold plan, with the blessing of a goddess. I don't see how we can fail."

Koral laughed at her forced optimism. "Will you come and help?"

For a moment, Vernia's attention was on her glass of wine. Spinning it back and forth in her hand. "I don't really have a choice. You will need as much magic as you can muster. When do we leave?"

Elizanne rang a bell, and two pages entered. "I wish to speak with Lady Macray, immediately."

Bowing low, the pages ran out the door.

Turning to her guests, she said, "I am appointing Morgan to Grand Duchess, whether she likes it or not. At dawn tomorrow, we will be riding back to your father's camp." Elizanne then stood and began to leave. "I will be making it official right now."

The three watched her move out of the library, and then turned back to each other.

"Well, I guess we sit and enjoy the fire," said Koral.

Darly shook her head, poured herself a glass of wine, and did exactly that. By nightfall, a Grand Duchess had been appointed, and was in charge of the city in the absence of the king and queen. When dawn arrived, they were off, riding hard, for there was no telling what had happened in the short time they were gone.

"Horses through the pass," came the shout, and guards surrounded the king's tent. Moments later, it was declared who was coming, and a sigh of relief went through the camp.

Elizanne leapt from her horse and ran into her husband's arms. After a long embrace, the two stood side by side, and Jeremy knew what was about to happen.

"Tomorrow is a night with no moon. Will you be performing the spell then?" asked Jeremy. He had hoped Koral's visit to the city would have taken longer, so she would have to wait a month. Jeremy, although trusting in his daughter, wasn't so certain if this was the best course of action.

Before she could answer, another shout of someone coming through the pass came, followed quickly by the notification that it was elves, carrying the banner of the elves of Almberson. Glomain rushed to the edge of the camp and was overjoyed to see the group was being led by General Destra.

"I had thought my son would have you assisting the dwarves," he remarked, reaching out his hand to Destra.

"The dwarves have their little skirmishes under control. He did send a garrison, but that is all," answered Destra.

The elves who came spread out along the outside of the camp. Two dozen elves, with an understanding of the art of war, and who had real life training behind them. Jeremy would have thought this to be too few, but they were elves, and he had seen firsthand what one was capable of.

Koral moved beside her father and leaned close to his ear. "I will be doing this tomorrow, but no one can be nearby. Only those I choose can come to the river's edge. It is a danger we must accept."

Jeremy turned, and pulled his daughter in. "I understand. Tomorrow, when night falls, you will take command. We will follow your orders to a man."

Koral took a step back and smiled at her father. Without a word, she turned and left the camp, heading into the woods, and to the river's edge, to see what the enemy was planning.

"Rafts," whispered Glavlin. "This time, we have nowhere to hide to send volleys of arrows across."

Darly looked about and saw Glavlin was right. They had taken to the trees, well out of the reach of the bows of men. Now, almost all of the tall trees were gone. To shoot from the bushes would make them a perfect target. Darly opened her pouch and pulled out a smooth black stone. "This will not do much, but I hope it will at least deter them for a few days." Darly whispered to the stone, then flung it at the river. A great stirring occurred in the water where it landed, and a large spiral of water shot up, throwing itself at the enemy. Two rafts were ripped apart by the force. Only a few men had been near them and were crushed under the water. "Let us hope Koral will achieve her goal tonight."

Night fell, enveloping the entire area in darkness. A few clouds floated above, covering some of the stars, hiding their light. Now was the time. Koral closed her eyes, and let her mind guide her to the perfect spot. Her companions followed in silence, not wishing to break her concentration. For an hour and a half, they walked. Koral turned abruptly through the bushes, and they came to a small inlet.

"We are upstream," remarked Vernia.

Koral moved into the shallows, and then turned to her companions. "Are you all certain you wish to do this?"

"Little late to back out now isn't it?" said Vernia.

The sarcasm in Vernia's voice was not lost on Koral, or anyone else.

"We all know what to do, Koral. You do what you need to," said Elizanne softly.

Koral nodded and pulled out a knife. "With this blood, we ask for the river to heed our wishes." Slicing her hand, she bent down and watched the blood spread towards the main flow. The others followed her lead. When their blood began to mingle, Koral spoke to the river, asking it to widen and separate the lands. Over and over, she repeated her words, and after many minutes, she received a reply. At first, she heard whispers, so low Koral couldn't make out the words. Then, a soft light shone in her face. It lifted from the water, and the whispers became clearer.

"Koral, what will you give to achieve this. Your dearest love? Your family? Your life?"

Koral was not expected this. As the words continued to repeat in her mind, they were followed by images of those she loved dying by the hand of their enemy. Only a whisper but meaning so much more. Taking a deep breath, she looked directly at the light before her. "I will give up whatever is necessary to achieve this. It is the only way to change this war."

"So be it. Princess, we take from you, one of the wizards given. Make no mistake, this will weaken your abilities. Do not give up the last lightly, for it may mean your demise."

The light withdrew, and Koral thought herself lucky that was all they wished from her. Then it happened. If the soul could be broken and ripped out in pieces, Koral imagined this was what it would be like. She winced as she felt the memories being pulled from her mind, and the magic being drained. It was over in a mere blink of an eye, and Koral was left with a hole, as if a part of who she was had been taken. The ordeal made her weak, and she collapsed into the water. Immediately, Glavlin and Glomain were at her side, pulling her ashore. Koral opened her eyes and looked to them. "We must move away. Quick!"

Rumbling began, and the small group moved inland as far as they could, and still see what was occurring. The river took on a savage grace. Churning and frothing as far as the eye could see. Then, it grew. Where there was an average river, now became a flowing, raging one. Slowly, the gap widened, and the six companions watched in awe as the land to the south crumbled into the intense river. It wasn't long before the far side was barely a speck, and a cheer came from Glomain. Koral smiled, happy it had worked, and collapsed again. This time, blackness took her.

CHAPTER TWENTY-SEVEN

After travelling for weeks, the mood on the ship was still dim. Eric stood on the deck, contemplating life, as he tended to do these days. The moon was only a sliver, but the sky was lit bright. Stars twinkled above, and Eric admired their beauty. The water was choppy, but he got his sea legs quick this time, and wanted to be on deck. His thoughts wandered to Kaitlyn often, but he was more focused on what lay ahead. Another trip into an uncharted land. Another quest where Gillock knew much and was telling little. Eric found himself questioning if that was the way of the wizard order, or if something else guided Gillock.

Scuffling feet drew his eyes from the stars, and he saw Dorien coming up. He was rubbing the sleep from his eyes, and Eric wondered what drew him up on deck in the middle of the night. With a yawn, the young wizard made his way over to Eric.

"What brings you here?" asked Eric.

"You," he replied with another yawn. "Your thoughts were projected. You worry about Kaitlyn, and this new quest."

Eric took a step back and eyed the wizard dangerously. "How..." he began, but Dorien put up his hand and silenced him.

"I'm connected to strong magic, Eric. It's a gift, or curse, depending on how you look at it. You are strong, and as such, my mind sought yours out."

A confused look crossed Eric's face, and he shook his head. "So, whenever I am pondering life, you come along for the ride?"

Dorien chuckled at the remark. "Essentially."

Patting Dorien on the shoulder, Eric again shook his head. "I guess it is time for bed." With a smile, Eric headed down, with Dorien not far behind. Something new discovered, and Eric wasn't certain he liked it.

A week of stormy waters passed. Travel was wearing on the crew, and the small group. Gillock noticed his companions were sticking more to the galley, than on deck. Conversations were the usual. Family and life before the quest. Eric had been shocked to learn the two elves were cousins of Alyarra, and grandchildren of Ender, the king's advisor. Firadon refused to answer any questions about family, and Aremeth was only too happy to explain his people, and their way of life. When Aremeth told them of the disappearance of his village, and the hope he may see them again, Eric became annoyed. Brin was behind it all, and he couldn't be there to fight for them. No one spoke of the Saviour being Eric's sister, although the prince wasn't certain if any beside Gillock even knew. Eric wanted to speak to Aremeth alone on the matter but knew it would need to wait until they were off the ship.

On deck, things were tense. The usually talkative Goram was rarely seen, and Mena's temper flared often. Eric worried something had happened to the two after they left Keenley but kept his concerns to himself. Gillock quietly muttered searching spells, to see if the two were truly who they appeared to be and found nothing. Dorien and the two elves, inexperienced with these people, thought it was how a ship ran in bad weather. When the waters finally calmed, Goram requested Eric in his ready room.

Eric arrived, and noticed he was alone with the captain. "Is something amiss?"

Goram studied the prince a while before answering. "When word came about this voyage, I was ready. Somehow, I knew we'd be heading on a quest. What bothers me is the fact that we are dropping you off, and heading home after."

Finally, reality hit Eric. The crew was upset because they were just a transport. "We have to keep the group small. If we are caught, many could die."

Goram leaned forward on the table and stared hard at Eric. "I'm aware, I just don't like it."

A flicker of the captain Eric knew crossed Goram's face. "The maelstrom alone is going to be dangerous, captain. Good chance we will not survive past it," stated Eric, hoping it would help the situation.

Goram slammed his hand down on the table and let out a hearty laugh. "Yeah, heard we had to sneak past that. No ship has ever made it, so I know we won't. Means we need to ask for help. A small island sits near the maelstrom. It's said to be frequented by merfolk. Mena hopes we will be able to speak with Mirrah and ask for help." Goram stood and moved over to where a bottle of wine sat and poured the two glasses. Placing one before Eric, he sat down again. "Do you think the goddess will help us?"

Eric sipped his wine, considering the question. "I do not know. Has any of the crew seen a mermaid about of late?"

Goram sighed, placing his glass down. "No."

Eric finished his wine and stood. "I am going on deck and putting out a

magical call to them. Perhaps there is a reason none follow this ship."
Goram gave a low chuckle. "There is, we are cursed." Then waved Eric out.
Eric ignored the remark and left the captain.

Moving onto the deck, Eric noticed Gillock and Dorien standing at the railing, looking out. Firadon and Aremeth were not on deck, but the elves were, practising their swordplay.
"We must call to the merfolk," he stated, approaching Gillock and Dorien.
Dorien turned to face Eric. "We did."
Eric followed Gillock's gaze. "No reply?"
"Not yet, but something is amiss," replied Gillock.
With a heavy sigh, Eric slid down onto the deck, resting his head on the side. Without the help of the Mirrah, or at the very least, merfolk, they were doomed.

The next day, the small island was in view, with the maelstrom swirling in the distance. Coming around to a small cove, Eric's heart leapt. On the rocks sat two mermaids, and it appeared as if they were waiting for them. The captain manoeuvred the ship closer to the rocks, and Eric, taking a rope, lowered himself down beside them.

"We have been expecting you, Prince Eric," said one.
"Do you know what it is I must ask of you?" he questioned.
"Yes," replied the other. "At the moment, your sister is performing a very dangerous spell, and our goddess must watch. She instructed us to show you the one safe passage around the swirling water."
Eric wanted to ask what his sister was up to now but thought better of it. He had to stay focused on this quest.
"Your ship cannot pass beyond this island," came the voice of the first mermaid. "You, and those who are to accompany you, must travel under the water." The woman disappeared below the surface and returned moments later with what looked like seaweed. "You must eat this and lower yourself over the side into the water. Take only what is necessary, for anything more could drop you too low in the water, and you will drown."
Eric was shocked. "Travel below?" Accepting the seaweed, Eric said no more, and climbed back up to explain what had to be done to his companions.

As he expected, no one was open to the idea, but there was no choice. Strange winds occur all about, and no ship could survive. No one wanted to risk the ship attempting to get them to shore. As ordered, they packed only a change of clothing, and weapons. Goram stated that the ship would remain in this cove for a few days in case they needed assistance. With short goodbye's, they ate their seaweed, gagging at the taste, and jumped over the side.

Landing in the water, and sinking quick, put Eric, Firadon, and Dorien into a panic. The two mermaids were before them, telling them to breathe in slowly. Inhaling the water caused Dorien to panic more, but only a moment passed before he noticed his lungs were accepting it. Eric pointed to his neck, and the young wizard realised Eric had grown gills. With a smile, Dorien relaxed. They had no knowledge as to the length this special seaweed would last and could only hope it would be long enough.

"It is a fair ways to travel," said one, and Eric noticed her voice sounded deeper under the water.

The other swam up and pointed. "We have brought dolphins to help speed things along."

Seven dolphins swam in circles around the group. One of the mermaids motioned for them to grab onto the dorsal fin, and once they did, the dolphins were off, with the mermaids keeping pace.

The underside of the island gave way to a different world. Coral and underwater plants could be seen everywhere, along with many schools of fish. Moving away, only the deep blue water waited. Quick movements had them going at a great speed, but once they drew near the swirling water, their pace slowed. Eric and the others marvelled at the magnificence of the water. Far above them, it swirled with unbelievable speed. Their travel had taken them lower down, and what was in front of them was the centre, where many sailors perished. It spun far down into the ocean, and all felt trepidation at the sight.

Tark turned his green eyes to the closer mermaid. "How are we to get past that? The water swirls at a great rate."

The woman placed a reassuring hand on the elf. "The dolphins traverse it often. It is not without danger, but if we go slow, and follow the right current, we will make it to the other side."

The expression on Tark's face showed he wasn't so certain but said nothing. They had no other choice, so ahead they went.

Eyes darting about, as if checking every inch of water, the dolphins kept their pace slow. Firadon followed the eyes of his dolphin and knew the look. Something other than swirling water was out there. Even the mermaids appeared to be on edge. They were now going single file. One mermaid in front, the other in back. Both had the small knives they kept on a belt, drawn. Gillock, who was behind the first mermaid, noticed that where they were headed, the current was different. When the elven wizards of old created this maelstrom, they went against the wished of Mirrah. Clearly, to appease the goddess, they made a way for her followers and creatures to get around it.

Manoeuvring into the current, all felt odd when it grabbed them, rushing them along. It wasn't long before the other side could be seen. Eric couldn't believe their luck, and was going to comment when Simian, who was in front of him, was dragged downwards. His dolphin companion screeched in anger, and Eric looked to see an enormous tentacle wrapped around Simian's waist. Far below, a creature out of a sailor's nightmare sat. Black, conniving eyes stared up at them. Before anyone could react, Gillock release a bolt of magic, hitting the tentacle. The dolphin dove down, and Simian gripped its fin tight. With amazing speed, the dolphins swam, adding their movements to the current until they were on the other side of the maelstrom. They continued until the water became shallow, and the mermaids told the men to release the dolphins. Scrambling up, each one broke the surface, and took a deep breath. Not far off was the shore, so they headed for it.

Dragging themselves out of the water, everyone fell to their knees on the sand. Simian, holding his side, lay down. Aremeth moved to the elf and noticed a wound.

"That creature had claws," gasped Simian.

Aremeth moved his hands, and lifted the bit of tunic surrounding the area. "It appears to have been toxic as well."

Gillock sat down beside Aremeth, viewing the wound. "If this isn't treated, it may kill you." Turning to Dorien, he added. "Bring me my pack."

Dorien jumped up and rushed the bag over to Gillock. Out came a small bowl, spoon, and many small vials. After mixing up the ingredients, a strange smell wafted from the bowl.

"This will sting, and burn," said Gillock, looking into Simian's eyes.

The elf nodded and set his head back on the sand. Gillock applied the salve, and Simian cried out. Tark, who had been standing back, cringed at his brother's cries. Eric got up and surveyed the area. Simian was going to need a day to rest, and he wanted to be certain that could happen.

Splashing in the water drew his attention, and one of the mermaids

sat just offshore.
“There is a village a few hours in. You might be able to take a boat from there,” she said.
“I thank you for all you have done,” replied Eric, and before he could ask about his sister, the creature was gone. With a shake of his head, Eric moved up the sand to see what was ahead.

A small cropping of trees sat a few hundred yards away, and after walking just inside, Eric figured it would be a good place as any to stay the night. Running back to his companions, Eric saw Simian was asleep. He informed them of the forest, and how it was a good place to stay until the elf felt good enough to move. All agreed, and with careful hands, they carried the wounded elf. Once Simian was settled, a fire was made, and food brought out. The journey had just begun, but all were hoping their luck would continue.

CHAPTER TWENTY-EIGHT

Hands over his face, Jessup tried to maintain his calm. More attacks from the group of people unhappy to be under the rule of King Jeremy. They had been granted land to the north. The forest there was perfect for them to hunt, with many streams to fish, but it wasn't enough. They wanted it all. The town they set up held many, but the rest began roaming about the Central Lands. They had become gypsies and bandits. Taking what they want, whenever they wanted. The new nobility settling into Hope's Light Keep were demanding the heads of these bandits. Many were former leaders in the area and welcomed the chance to have a say in their land.

"If they are caught, they will be dealt with in the same manner as thieves," grumbled Jessup. "I will not set out to hunt them down."

"And what of the property damaged? Or items stolen? Will we get them back?" asked Tiana. Her family had settled outside the Keep. Having been taught farming, they had taken to it quickly. Their farm was the latest one attacked.

Jessup sighed. "It is doubtful we will find the few cows stolen. If they are, they will be returned to you. As for the burnt barn, I will supply the wood, but nothing more."

Tiana's eyes narrowed in anger, but she held her tongue. With a curt bow, she exited the room.

"I think you handled that well," remarked Malya with a giggle.

Jessup turned, "There really wasn't anything I could do. Your people aren't happy, but this is going too far."

Malya took her seat beside him. "Yes. Destroying property is a bit much."

Silence followed as both contemplated their rule.

"We should have some food," said Malya after a time. Standing, she motioned for Jessup to come.

Jessup stood and followed her to the sunroom. Her only request in their home was an area to enjoy the sun, regardless of the time of year. It was her favourite place to take afternoon meals. Food was already set out on a table, and Malya filled a plate the moment they walked in. When Jessup sat down across from her, Malya placed her plate down.

"I've been meaning to tell you something," she began. Eyes which were turned down, lifted to look into his. "I am with child."

Lifting a fork to his mouth, Jessup paused and stared at his wife. "With child?"

Malya was nervous about revealing this new, especially with the king at war, and the problems they were having. "Yes. It is expected in the fall."

Jessup stood, walked over to his wife, and knelt before her. Looking into her eyes, he placed his hand on her belly. "This is the best news I could ever receive."

Tears filled Malya's eyes, and she embraced her husband. "I'm happy to hear that."

They were only able to enjoy the moment for a short time before a page appeared and informed Jessup of an issue with part of the wall being built. It was a daily occurrence, and with a kiss to Malya, he left the sunroom to go out into the city.

Clouds graced the sky, and it was clear a rain was coming. Jessup moved along the makeshift walkway towards the far side of the keep. Men arguing appeared before him, and they quieted once they saw him coming.

"What is it now?" asked Jessup, anger clear in his voice.

Jack, leader of the stonemason's shifted uneasily. "Sorry, sire, but things were taken again. At this rate, we won't finish this wall anytime soon."

Jessup turned to Ezra, the other man on the wall. "You two were disagreeing about something."

Ezra lowered his eyes. "We know it's those gypsies. No one else wants to slow this construction down."

"I see," said Jessup, understanding the men. "You didn't want to say anything to me because of my wife."

Both men nodded.

"My wife and I don't like these thieves any more than you do. However, we cannot jump to conclusions," stated Jessup. "Now, as always, I will pay for the replacements. Please just do what you can until they arrive."

Both men nodded again and moved off down the platform.

Jessup moved passed the platform, and onto the actual wall. His path was towards the harbour. His rooms had an amazing view of the Sea of Arran, but he wanted to see the waters. The wind grew stronger as Jessup approached, and he could smell a storm in the air. Out in the harbour, many vessels could be seen. Some larger ships, bringing supplies between Keenley and the keep, were moored at the docks. Smaller fishing vessels were coming back in, and with how low they were sitting, Jessup assumed they were laden with large catches. Fish was something they weren't worried about running out of. Not yet. Hunters and trappers were a different story. A few had moved into the area, teaching anyone who wanted to learn. Game was beginning to frequent the area, but not enough to exist on. Many farms were what was feeding the people, and at the moment, there were no poor or hungry.

Sadness crept into Jessup's heart as he turned back towards the growing city. Yes, it was thriving. Most were happy with how it was coming along. It wouldn't be long, though, before others came. Once the city was done, people wanting a change would seek their fortune in a new area. Some will succeed, but most will fail. Thieves had already arrived. Most wanted to blame the gypsies, but Jessup knew the missing supplies weren't being taken by them. He had noticed people hiding in the shadows, trying hard to go unnoticed. Most didn't know he was once captain of the guard for the king. They thought him to be naive to such things. However, he paid attention to everything, and wasn't happy to see that side of a large city already existing in his. Pushing the thoughts aside, Jessup made his way back to the keep. An announcement needed to be made.

Within a few hours of the notice going through the city, notes of congratulations began to arrive. A courier was sent to Keenley to ensure the king and queen didn't hear through rumour. Malya was amazed at how many people supported them. She knew it would take time to adjust to this new life, but each day something new happened.

Court life was something different here in the Keep. Some nobility came from Keenley and were appalled at how lax they were in protocol. Jessup had to remind them repeatedly that they were creating a new city, and those sorts of things would come later. This lead to a few sending letters to the king, who of course was at war and wouldn't see them for quite some time.

Artisans came in, excited to be a part of something new. Sculptures already were coming into being, making the main courtyard of the city something magical. Gardeners, happy spring was beginning, were attempting to bring flowers from all over the Central Lands into Hope's Light Keep. Malya marvelled at everything being created in the city, and for them personally. So much beauty surrounding her once again brought a tear to her eye. Not for a moment had she thought her life would be this wonderful.

Gracing the front entry were portraits of the royal family. If Elizanne hadn't been kidnapped, and Koral sent to rescue her, Malya's life would have stayed that of a slave on the run. A large smile graced her face, as it often did when she gazed at the portrait. With a silent thank you, she stroked her stomach. Making her way about the Keep, Malya felt that her life was beyond perfect.

CHAPTER TWENTY-NINE

Goosebumps ran over Arket's arm, and a moment later, he sensed strong magic brewing. To the west of their camp, and on the far side of the river, a slight glow emanated. Immediately Arket knew something amiss, and it felt dangerous. Without hesitating, he turned to the camp, and screamed at his men to flee. His words came too late.

Soldiers curious as to why the river was acting up were caught in the spell. In a blink, the river surged, and the land around them changed. Soldiers ran with all their might to escape the changing landscape. Screams came to the ears of those fleeing, and no one stopped. The ground beneath their feet shook and began to split. For quite some time, the mild earthquake continued, with pieces of land falling into the growing river. Panic set in, and if anyone fell, they were left behind. A few men who tripped, never got up again, for the fleeing soldiers stomped them into the desert sand. Arket couldn't believe the chaos this spell was causing, or that such fear had crept into the hearts of these seasoned soldiers. Something foul was mixed in with the shaking land, causing the havoc.

When the shaking stopped, Arket ordered the remaining men back to the city. Calm came over the soldiers as their emperor stated his wishes. No one hesitated this time, but they also weren't in a panicked run. Arket wasn't certain if they regretted their panic, or if they even realised it happened. Either way, a defeated army made their way back home.

Once those who survived were moving away from the strange occurrence, Arket went back to the river. What once was a short distance, now was at least two dragons wide. The waters were deep, and a strong current could be seen. His eyes attempted to scan the far side, but to no avail. There was no way his army would be returning to this spot. They had dealt the enemy a hard blow, and the enemy retaliated in turn. Walking away from the river Arket had a scowl on his face. Once he felt no eyes from the far side could glimpse him, Arket cast the spell to bring him back to the palace.

The hour was late, and once in his room, Arket gazed upon his sleeping wife, and their son. Although he was angry at their defeat, Arket didn't want to wake Brin, so instead he moved over to a couch, and lay down. In the morning, he would let her know what had transpired.

Sun shining in his face brought Arket awake. Sitting up, he turned to the bed, and saw Tomaz facing him, eyes wide open. Arket stood, and the baby began to cry, waking Brin. Upon seeing her husband, she motioned him over.

"Tomaz is just hungry," she said with a smile, taking the baby into her arms.

Arket was awed at how quickly the child grew silent, and after feeding, he was finally able to hold his son. Once the nanny came to take Tomaz away, Arket felt it was time to inform his wife of the events of yesterday.

Breakfast was served in the sitting area, and it was here he told her. "The enemy has cast a spell of its own." Arket went on to explain what had happened, and Brin stayed silent.

"That took great magic," she said, picking at the food.

"What are we to do?" asked Arket.

Brin stood and moved out onto the balcony. "We know they have ships built. We must put ours on alert. Their next move might be to hit us here."

Arket joined her. "The army will be back outside the city in a few weeks. It will take them at least that long to get the ships ready to sail. We will be ready should they decide to attack by sea."

Brin walked along the balcony, wondering what the future held. Did the enemy know her son was here? Would they try to take him? The more she thought, the more Brin became worried about Tomaz. Now wasn't the time to speak of it to her husband. Once she had an idea in place to make him safe, she would bring it up.

"I would like to see the river," said Brin later that day.

Arket eyed his wife with concern. "I do not advise that. The enemy might still be there."

"I am not concerned about them. The spell took much magic. I doubt whoever cast it is capable of doing any more damage," she replied, curtly. Not wanting to argue, Arket agreed.

Standing on the shore, Brin was amazed at the new size of the river. A strong current could be seen flowing, and she realised Arket's decision was a sound one. No one would be attacking this way. The enemies next move would most certainly be to hit them from the sea.

Back in the Temple City, the two contemplated what would be next. Taking carriages to the harbour was their first task. Each ship was well made, created for the soul purpose of attacking. Decades ago, they were captained by pirates. Those men still ran the ships but were now under the control of the Saviour.

Brin walked along the dock, staring out at the ships. Dark, with cannons aimed, they were ready for the enemy. Arket went to the harbourmaster. Ensuring the safety of the city was apparent, so the emperor gave the order for constant patrols, and to be alert for enemy vessels. By morning, each ship would be given a patrol schedule. Satisfied that their wishes would be followed without question, the rulers made their way into the city. It was rare that they ventured into the part of town near the water, but with the events of late, Arket wished to seek out all points which could be taken advantage of.

The carriage driver moved the horses slowly down the streets. The outer wall extended right into the sea itself and was patrolled regularly. They came to the main gates, which held two sets of doors to prevent enemies from entering the city. No army had ever taken the city, and Brin felt none ever would. Arket didn't agree. The enemy to the north wasn't like any army this city had faced in the past. In fact, the emperor was certain if the Central Lands had pushed themselves into his realm earlier, King Jeremy would have succeeded.

They rolled to the west wall, and the darkness took over. Hours had gone by, and no weaknesses were apparent in their defences. Arket still worried he was missing something. Something simple, that would bring about the downfall of the city. With a heavy sigh, Arket and Brin went back to their palace. Now all they could do was plan a defence and wait for the enemy to find their way to the Temple City.

CHAPTER THIRTY

Looking across the river, Jeremy was amazed. The river was too large for rafts to cross without being noticed, and it appeared as if the enemy was in retreat. Walking back to their camp, Jeremy realised the war was now changing. By the time he had arrived, his mind was made up. Signalling to the pages to gather all those needed, Jeremy went into his tent, and waited.

"I have gathered you all here to tell you about my plans," began Jeremy, making certain all eyes were on him. "We are moving the army back to Keenley. It is time we took this fight to Brin's door."

Everyone looked at each other, but it was Glomain who spoke. "I agree with this course of action. I do recommend that you leave scouts behind, to ensure the enemy is not going to come across the river."

Koral stood and moved to her father. "I also agree, however, I believe you need to lay claim to this area. No longer is this forest part of the southern area. It is now part of the Central Lands."

Pondering the idea, Jeremy smiled at Koral. "Yes. When we get back to the city, I will make that declaration."

"When do we leave?" asked Elizanne.

"Now," replied Jeremy. "We must stock the ships and send them down the coast. It will be a few weeks before we are ready, and the trip down the coast will be at least another. The sooner we end this war, the better."

Pages were signalled, and immediately the camp was taken down. Within a few hours, the entire army was heading back to Keenley, with a new outlook. No longer would the battle be back and forth, with neither side gaining ground. Now, the Central Lands were on the offensive, and it was clear Jeremy wasn't going to back down.

A few days of hard riding, and they were home. The barracks outside the city were cleaned and ready for the men, but this night, they were allowed to stay in their own beds. Those without families took to their small rooms within the barracks inside the city walls, and to a night without worry.

Jeremy ordered everyone to have a hot bath, and then to come down to the dininghall for a hearty evening meal. Before he headed upstairs, he took Morgan aside.

"I thank you, milady. I hope you did not have too much trouble," said

Jeremy, handing her a glass of wine.

Rolling her eyes, Morgan accepted the glass. "Highness, it was a nightmare. The nobles are so petty. I had forgotten how terrible they could be."

Jeremy laughed at the comment. "I wish you and Jervin to be present at dinner tonight."

"Of course," she replied, and finished her wine. "Until tonight, majesty." With a bow, Morgan left to see to her home.

Jeremy watched her go and signalled two guards to accompany her. He knew Morgan would be upset at the extra guards, however, Jeremy felt it necessary. After the attack on his wife, he wanted to ensure all those close to the royal family were taken care of.

Heading to his room, Jeremy's steps were slow. The castle looked different to him now. Perhaps living in the forest for the last seven months had changed him somehow. Arriving, Jeremy moved inside to see Elizanne sitting on a chair near the window. When he entered, she went to him, and held him tight.

"I fear many things," she started. Pulling away, Elizanne once again sat in the chair.

Jeremy took a chair across from her. "Tell me about them."

Elizanne stared out at the ocean. "Our daughter wants to destroy us. Outside sources want to destroy us. So many enemies, and I worry about who we can trust."

Outside the window was a planting box, with tulips in full bloom. Jeremy grabbed her hand and pointed to them. "Spring is here. Renewal is all around us. Do not fret, my love. We have many enemies, but our friends are many as well."

Turning to her husband, Elizanne offered a weak smile. "You always find the best in situations."

Jeremy stood and brushed her cheek. "We should bathe and get ready. I think we all need to relax."

Elizanne watched her husband go into his bathing chamber, then turned her attention back outside. Jeremy was always looking for the bright side of everything. Elizanne wondered what would happen if one day, there wasn't one. A servant announced that her own bath water was ready, and Elizanne moved into her bath chamber. Perhaps a long soak would help calm her fears.

The dininghall was filled with talking and laughter when the king and queen arrived. It eased the pain on Elizanne's heart and brought a smile to Jeremy. The elves from Almberson were sitting off to the side, conversing with Glomain. Their musical voices always created a lively atmosphere which was enjoyed by all. Glavlin and Koral sat at the table, their heads bent in close. To Elizanne, the conversation appeared intimate. When people began to notice they had arrived, it grew quiet. Taking Elizanne's hand, Jeremy proceeded to the head of the table. Everyone moved to stand behind their chair, and once seated, the food was served.

The conversation stayed light, until a page handed a note to the king. After reading it, he handed it to Elizanne, who squealed and hugged her husband. Those seated became quiet, and stared at the two, curious as to what information the note held.

"It appears that the royal bloodline is continuing. Duchess Malya is pregnant," stated Jeremy, who then raised his glass, and everyone followed suit.

The talk remained jovial for the rest of the meal, which eased the tension Jeremy was feeling.

Once the table was clear, conversations turned to what lay ahead. The elves from both lands agreed to accompany the soldiers on the ships. No one knew the lay of the land to the south, but elves always fared better in situations like this. The ships would be in the harbour within two days, then another week or so to prepare them. Everyone needed to be ready. Morgan was relieved to hear the king and queen would not be going, not yet anyway. Koral, who had been unusually quiet the entire dinner, excused herself, and left to go to her room. Elizanne's eyes followed her daughter, and she wished she could go and speak to Koral. However, her place, for now, was here.

Koral wandered the halls for a time. Eventually she realised where she was. As she stood outside Gillock's room, Koral could feel the power within.

"I hope Brin never uses me like that again," said Vernia, coming up beside Koral.

Koral understood her fear. "You know the feel of the magic now. I do not think anyone will be able to make you do anything like that again."

Vernia hoped Koral was right but didn't agree. "I can only hope."

Koral moved towards her room, and Vernia followed. "You are different, princess," commented Vernia.

Koral sighed. "The price to expand the river was not what I expected. I feel weak, like part of me is missing. It will take some getting used to."

Not knowing how to reply, Vernia told her good night, turned down a hall, and went to her room. Koral continued to hers and was happy to be inside. Right now, she wanted to be alone.

As she left the dining hall, she had asked for tea to be waiting. Upon entering her room, she noticed a pot sitting on the table, and after she changed into her nightgown, Koral poured herself a cup. Grabbing a blanket, Koral curled up on the lounger in front of the fireplace. Too many months had passed since she had known the comforts of the castle, and although she enjoyed the woods, nothing felt as good as being able to sit alone in a room, in front of a fire, and think.

Dark were her thoughts of late. She was going south on a ship, but with her power weakened, Koral wondered if she would be as much help as she once was. Glavlin had told her she was still powerful, and she did feel strong, but something was missing. Taking a drink of her tea, the warmth flowing through made her feel better. Koral placed her glass down and focused on the fire. Perhaps an answer would show itself.

The dinner party continued. Most topics were on the city, and how it was faring. Some brought up the new land, and the issues Jessup was having, others focused on the ships, and the coming offensive they will be undertaking. Glavlin had moved off by himself and was now standing near the hearth.

"You look like someone who wishes to speak," stated Elizanne approaching the elf king.

Glavlin smiled and accepted the glass of wine she handed him. "Yes, actually, I do." A sip of wine, and Glavlin turned to Elizanne. "It is not the time, but I wish to ask permission to marry Koral."

Although Elizanne expected this news one day, she was stunned to hear it now. "I believe the king and I support this. However, it is Koral you should ask first."

"In my culture, you first live together, then decide if marriage is appropriate," he stated. "We have already made the first step, although with the war happening, we have not had any time to spend together, alone."

Elizanne motioned to two chairs, and both took one. "I understand," she remarked, offering a smile. "Perhaps on this trip, you should bunk together. It might help. Besides, Koral is still reeling from the spell, and I am certain she would benefit from the closeness."

Glavlin nodded. “Yes. I think I will go to her now. She appeared lost today.”

Elizanne placed her hand on his arm. “Then go, King Glavlin.”

He stood, said farewell, and made his way to Koral’s room.

With only servants about the hallways, getting to the room was easy. Now Glavlin stood outside the door, wondering if this was the right move. With a deep breath, he knocked. A quiet ‘Enter’ came from the other side, so he did. Koral lay on a couch, staring into the fire. When she saw it was Glavlin who knocked, she sat up, and motioned to a chair beside her. He took it and stared at Koral.

“I know you are troubled by the loss of some power, but it will pass,” he said softly.

“I know,” she replied, with a heavy sigh. “It will just take some getting used to.”

A fresh pot of tea had been brought up, so Koral offered some to Glavlin. He accepted and glanced about the room.

“I believe your room is nicer than mine. Perhaps I will stay here tonight,” he remarked, then took a drink of his tea.

Koral looked at Glavlin, and realised he was serious. The idea was just what she needed to hear. “We do share chambers at home, so here only makes sense.”

Glavlin took her hand and kissed it lightly. He had hoped the thought of them being close tonight might ease some of her apprehension. The slight smile Koral had as she sipped her tea proved it was exactly what she needed.

Time flew by, and a sunrise came which saw a fleet of newly built war ships sitting in the harbour. Jeremy marvelled at the sight. Not long ago, the only vessels to grace this harbour were fishing, and pleasure crafts. The war ships, built from designs sent by King Tusta, were magnificent and terrible to view. Cannons, strange devices which hurled large iron balls at enemy ships, poked out from the side.

“We lost so much being hidden from the rest of Melarandra,” Jeremy thought to himself.

It took a few hours to load up the soldiers, but by midday, they signalled, and left. The last ship held the elves who would be dropped off on the shore down a bit from the city, in an attempt to sneak in. Jeremy stood long after they left his sight, wishing he could have gone. Vernia, Olrond, and Glomain were in charge, and Jeremy could only hope it would be enough.

Herbs were passed to most of the soldiers to help with seasickness. Vernia was grateful Elizanne was able to find enough for each one. Luck also had many sailors from Lungast come join the crews and teach the fishermen of Keenley what the open sea was really like. Olrond wondered if this attack would have been possible without King Tusta's help.

Three days out, a storm hit. It wasn't severe, but enough to make some of the soldiers worry. Olrond made certain to be about, to comfort those who might view this as a dark omen. His eyes were drawn to the vessels following behind. The elves would take care of those on their ship, but there were three others, and Olrond hoped they would be able to weather this storm. By nightfall, the storm had ebbed, bringing a soft breeze. It was a welcome feeling and appeared to calm the soldiers.

After a second week passed, the vessel carrying the main bulk of elves turned off and headed to shore. Glomain and the two dozen elves, along with Koral and Glavlin, grabbed their packs, and jumped on shore. No hesitation could be had, for they had no time. With a wave to the vessel, the entire group ran south.

Olrond watched as the ship moved towards shore and said a silent prayer for them. Many dark creatures lurked in the sands, and he hoped most, if not all, of the elves would make it to the city.

By the third week, those aboard the ships knew they were drawing close. An enormous city lurked in the distance, and that meant the many ships Brin had in her possession, would be nearby. There in lay the problem. They had no idea how many she actually had.

A few more days passed, and the bell chimed; they had arrived. All vessels stopped and surveyed the water before them. Fifteen ships sat between them and the city. Fifteen, to their four. More were being commissioned, but they would not be ready in time for this. With a heavy sigh, Olrond sent up the flag to signal all to be ready. Movement near the bow caught his attention, and he noticed Vernia had finally come on deck. Raising her arms, Vernia chanted. A flicker of light surrounded each ship, protecting them from magical attacks. Olrond knew the men were breathing a sigh of relief upon seeing this, and he wasn't about to dash their hopes with realism. Any hope would benefit the soldiers.

Once Vernia had the spell in place, they were hit by magic. The strikes bounced off the front ship, and relief was clear on each soldier's face. Vernia turned her eyes to the looming palace. The magic had come from the topmost area, and she knew it was either Brin or Arket. From her time in the palace, Vernia realised only those two possessed strong magic. Although they were powerful, with the distraction the elves were going to provide, Vernia felt in her heart that they would win this fight.

Olrond had been right to worry. Strange prints in the sand drew caution from the elves. As they drew nearer to their target, nothing unusual came for them. In fact, even the army itself was nowhere to be seen. At least, not from this area. The elves were well versed in the art of war and this tactic had them confused. Glomain knew they had no time to waste. Ignoring the strange lack of protection, he pushed his band onward.

Glomain signalled Glavlin. A day after being dropped off, the band of elves which had come ashore now sat in a rock cropping outside a city gate. An alarm sounded on the shoreline, and it was clear Jeremy's ships were sighted. It would be at least a day before battle on the sea was engaged. Although not all eyes were on the water, now was a good time to enter. Coming up to the wall, Glavlin pointed out footprints. Clearly, many soldiers patrolled the space outside the wall, however, none was anywhere to be seen. A scout, keeping to the shadows, went out to see why, and found the main camp away from where they were. The scout suggested perhaps widening the river made them leery about water. Koral smiled at the thought.

The elves hope was to take out the soldiers, get through the gate, and start a panic within the city. As the sun began to set, they made their move. A volley of arrows, hidden in the setting sun, took the soldiers. Moments later, they were at the gate. Guards stood on the wall above, so a few well-placed arrows dropped them. Moving with speed, they were through the gate, and keeping to the shadows, made their way into the city. They were in an alley a few blocks from where they entered when another alarm sounded. Unsure if the bodies were discovered, or if this represented the ships at sea, they move quickly and with stealth. All knew to be caught meant death. Finding a tall building, they scaled from an alley to the top, hoping they weren't seen.

CHAPTER THIRTY-ONE

When the sun began to rise, another alarm sounded. People emerged from their homes, and word spread throughout the city. The hiding elves heard inhabitants nearby say the alarm was announcing the enemy was within the city walls. The bodies of the guards were discovered by their replacements, and a panic hit the city.

People scattered in fear, nearly toppling over one another to hide. Not long after, a carriage was observed rolling through the city. The rulers were showing no fear. Although it was expected, Koral was still surprised to see her sister outside the palace. They kept to the rooftops, but their elf ears heard all. The inhabitants were concerned for their safety, but more questions were asked about a child. Brin and Arket had a son, and when the elves heard that news, an odd look crossed Glomain's face. No words were spoken, but it was clear the old elf was worried about something. Hours crept by, with the elves remaining on the rooftop. It would be another day before the ships were in position, and they needed to be certain their plan for the city would go off without a hitch.

From the high vantage point, Koral eyed the palace, which sat in the distance. Although it was beautiful, the size of it made it appear cold, and heartless. Perhaps it was the fact the rulers were evil and heartless themselves, which made Koral feel that way. Alternatively, the fact that Koral had promised to finish what Brin had begun could also be a factor. One thing was certain, somewhere inside Brin was planning. The carriage had rolled its way around but made certain not to stray too far from the gates. Their attempt to show the inhabitants they were not afraid, had worked on the city dwellers, but not on the elves. Glomain saw it for a ruse. The rulers were worried.

After a time, it was decided they should leave their hiding spot. With ease, the elves bounced from rooftop to rooftop until they were in the centre of the city. Here, they sat on the highest building, able to see in all directions. Each elf scanned the area, but Koral's gaze focussed on the sea. In the morning, her father's ships should be engaged with the southern ones. It was decided before they entered the city that Koral and Glavlin were to move closer to the water. Should it appear Jeremy's fleet was faltering, they would try to help using the sea itself. Should this fail, an attempt on the palace would be made. All they could do was hope Brin and

Arket wouldn't try anything to aid their ships.

At sunset, the city was shutting down. They noticed the previous night how the people appeared to leave the streets with the setting sun, something the elves found interesting. It cooled some at night, but not a lot. Normally those who lived in these conditions finished tasks at this time. Clearly, the breeze coming off the Sea of Arran gave enough comfort to these people to allow them to work all day long. Summer had begun, and the small band knew the days would only be more intense. They had little time to end this war, so working fast was a necessity.

An eerie silence moved into the city. Wondering if it was due to their presence, or something more, Glavlin informed his father that he, along with Koral, was going to go wander the streets. Glomain wasn't fond of the idea but gave his blessing. Dropping down into an alleyway, both hid in the shadows until they made certain no one was near. Motioning to Koral, Glavlin took the lead, and headed out into the city.

Voices could be heard, and the two elves made their way towards them. A small tavern wedged between other businesses had a small crowd gathered outside. Hiding in an alley, they noticed a few tables were set up. Apparently, when night fell, people enjoyed their drinks outside.

"I like that idea," remarked Koral.

Glavlin shook his head. "I am not certain it is a good idea. Thieves flourish in environments such as these."

Koral understood his thoughts. Many thieves frequented inns and taverns in Keenley. With people outside, it would be even easier for them to grab something and run.

The patrons outside appeared to not be concerned about the idea the enemy was within the city. In fact, most acted as if it weren't true. Others made comments about the entire situation not being their concern. The two elves marvelled at the humans. Apparently, because they weren't military, the war was not their problem. It was up to the Saviour to deal with these situations and keep them safe.

Glavlin pointed back to the darkness, and they went off again. The stillness of the night unnerved the two. A city this large shouldn't be so quiet. Seeing a light on in a dwelling, the two elves moved to a window, hoping to get an idea of what was going on. Inside sat two men, and a young child. Their voices were low, but their conversation could be heard by the elves. Since the war was announced, those with children hid in fear. In the past, children were sacrificed to bring luck to the battle. Although the Saviour hadn't requested it from her followers, there was still worry. Talk changed to the fact that sacrificing your child was an honour. The two men, if asked, would not have given up their child. Others, however, offered theirs regularly. This was why it was quiet. They weren't worried about the Saviour coming for the children, they were concerned about their neighbours stealing, and sacrificing, them.

Disgust, and anger, registered on Koral's face. Glavlin's matched. Both were appalled and disgusted. The two had kept their weapons in check since leaving the rooftop. Now, small knives were held in their hand. Should they come across someone wishing to steal a child, the person would be dealt with.

Barely registering a footprint, the two headed back to their companions. Climbing back up, they still felt an ache in their heart for the children of this land. Glavlin reported what they learned and noticed the anger on every face. Children weren't common for the elves, so each one was cherished as a gift. Glomain motioned to all it was time for rest. It was more to calm the elves than for actual rest. Glomain knew to be riled up now could jeopardize their plans for the following day. With no argument, everyone found a spot, and went to sleep.

As the sun once again crept into the sky, the elves were blessed with a small amount of cloud cover. In the distance, cannon fire came to their ears, and they knew it was time. Koral and Glavlin set off at once, while Glomain took the rest towards the west wall.

Dancing along the rooftops, the elves moved swiftly to the west. Once close, the tall buildings ended, and gave way to smaller ones. Climbing down to the street was their only option. Luck was in their favour, for the inhabitants were curious, and most were making their way to the shore. The eyes of the guards were looking towards the sea, although some still patrolled, scanning everywhere for enemies. Glomain signalled, and two by two, they moved through the shadows, with scouts spreading out to search the area. One of the scouts appeared and pointed to the south. A building of importance lay just beyond the small dwellings they were hiding behind. Glomain signalled for the rest to continue on, while he and the scout went to look.

The building itself appeared odd, sitting off from the rest of the dwellings. Although it was roughly the same size as the buildings around, it had no windows, and a larger door. It was clear why the scout signalled to check it out. Arriving at the building, Glomain noticed the lock was old, and found it easy to break. What was inside brought a crooked grin to the old elf. Before him sat crates of arrows, with bows hanging on the wall. The two made their way to where the band waited and informed them of the find. Again, going two by two, the elves moved to the storage locker, and removed all they could carry. Glomain went last, and once he knew they had all they needed, poured some of the strange smelling oil he and his companions all carried, and ran off. Soon the city would be in a panic, and the elves couldn't wait to engage the enemy. Now, they just needed to wait for the signal.

Crouching behind some rocks, Glavlin and Koral watched as the ships fired on each other. The king's fleet was outnumbered, but Vernia's spell was holding. A low hit took out one of the enemy ships, but there were still fourteen left.

Koral winced as one of their vessels was struck by a cannonball. "Vernia will weaken soon."

"Yes," remarked Glavlin. "Are you ready?"

Koral nodded, and with a deep breath, moved down to the water. Glancing about, she was happy to see the bottom was deeper than normal at the shore. Plunging in, so only her head was visible, Koral waited.

Glavlin watched as Koral submerged herself, then he moved back into the city. A large house sat inside a small glade, and this was his target. Two arrows hit the house, both carrying pouches of oil. When he could see it running, Glavlin lit the rag on his third arrow, and fired it. Only seconds passed before the oil ignited, and the home burst into flames. People scattered from within, and shouts of fire began to float through the streets. Almost nothing could put out the oil, and with his task complete, Glavlin moved back to the rocks, to watch Koral.

The sun was high in the sky when the fire began. A scout gave a whistle, signalling it was time, and Glomain replied. Quick strikes took out the nearest guards on the wall. Scrambling up the stairs, the elves drew their swords and swiftly dealt with any who came near. Once the wall was secured, lit rags flew through the sky, hitting the rooftops nearby. Each roof they had run across had a trail of oil on it. It was a special elven blend, and water would not put it out. Soon, the city would be burning, and the efforts to put it out, would help it spread.

Alarms sounded, and more guards came at them. When some were near the armoury shed, they lit it aflame. On either side of the elves, the stairs were on fire. The elves knew how to contain, and extinguish, the flames, so they were not threatened by it. Soldiers from the far side of the wall began to move towards the city. Each one was struck down as they entered the elves range. Even though the arrows were human made, the elves would be able to hold this area for quite some time. Arrows, along with some elven spells, would help. Glomain only hoped it would be enough.

When the alarms sounded, Koral knew it was time. Channelling the last elf wizard, she called upon a water spell. She had not asked Mirrah for permission this time and hoped the goddess would allow her to complete this task. The water grew tight around Koral, and she sent the spell out. Small whirlpools began to form near the enemy ships. No attention was paid to the strange water, until they began to grow. Sounds of retreat echoed onto the shore, but Koral heard none of it. Enthralled with the spell, all she could feel was the wizard's glee in being able to use this magic. It intoxicated her, and if Glavlin hadn't been watching, there was a good chance she would have become lost in the spell and drown. Seeing that Koral was sinking, and not responding, caused Glavlin to move from his position. Without a thought, he jumped into the water, and pulled her onto the rocks.

Hours passed by, and the screams of those caught in the flames, along with those on the ships, were all anyone could hear. Night began to take hold, and the elves on the city wall, saw nothing but bodies below. No counter spells worked, and without arrows to fire on the elves, the enemy was no match. No one on the wall celebrated, for the fight was far from over.

While most of the elves were looking for moving soldiers, Glomain's eyes were on the sand outside the wall. Standing in the fading sunlight was a creature he thought long dead. Without a word, he leapt from the wall. Landing on the soft sand, Glomain took off running. All but one of the creatures were retreating to the south, but it was this one Glomain wanted to see. As he neared, his worst fears were realised. Standing ten feet away was Tralax.

"You and your kind should be dead," hissed Tralax.

Glomain studied the lazzard. "It was my thought your kind as well."

Tralax turned to the south. "One day, Glomain elf king, we will be avenged."

Glomain watched as the group of lazzards ran off, and wondered how they could be alive, and what it meant for his kind. The tale was not one sung by the elves. It was something Glomain had dealt with when he first took the mantle of king. A battle which lasted almost a year, and a large explosion between the two armies, with nothing but a crater left, made him believe the lazzards were destroyed. Now, he worried about what the future held.

CHAPTER THIRTY-TWO

Kaitlyn sat on the window ledge, watching the city below. The sun was setting, and the lamplighters were plying their trade. Flickers in windows popped up below her, and she sighed. An hour earlier, the city was alive. Every street filled with people flitting about. Now, it was in hiding. The dark creature which had taken a few lives, had moved off weeks ago, but the inhabitants were still wary.

Summer was here, and with the warmer nights, Kaitlyn hoped the people would once again grace the streets. Her eyes scanned all below her. The dreadwraith had indeed followed Gillock away, but something was about, and it unnerved her. Perhaps it was because she knew her darling baby brother was not what he appeared to be. Kaitlyn wanted so hard to tell her parents of the darkness she dreamt about nightly but couldn't. Who was going to believe a child only one year old contained a source of evil? With another glance at the city, Kaitlyn decided to turn in for the night, and moved back into her room. All she could do was hope her dreams about Dominic were wrong.

Her room was quiet, and lonely. Kaitlyn hadn't realised how much she was going to miss Eric. Months had passed, and Kaitlyn still felt emptiness in her heart. If only she could have gone, but her place was here. With the city worrying about dark shadows, and other unusual events taking place, she needed to be by her parents' side. One place experiencing strange occurrences was her uncle's area of Lungast. Kaitlyn didn't want to think about it, however, fate made the choice for her. Usually, her premonitions came in dreams. This one hit at that moment. Standing at the edge of her bed, Kaitlyn was locked in a waking dream.

Floating above the Border Wall, she saw a wave of darkness approaching. The sun was shaded, and the world below was difficult to see. Although she couldn't see, her other senses could feel. What she sensed, was hatred like she had never felt before. A brutal rumbling came, and she watched as one section of the wall crumbled. The wave turned into dark creatures she had only read about. The image flipped, and now the Keep was in flames, surrounded by strange looking elves: Therin.

Kaitlyn came back to her room, and tears flowed. She grabbed herself a glass of water, and once done, ran to find her father.

"You must stay here," said Tusta, and his tone showed he wasn't

changing his mind.
"You are king, but I am still your mother," stated Eldrina, not impressed with her son's view.
"Mother, Beluse wishes you to remain here. Something is going to happen, and he wants only soldiers with him," sighed Tusta.
Before his mother could offer a rebuttal, the door burst open, and Kaitlyn flew in. The look on her face gave both pause. She looked as if death wanted to take her. Tusta jumped up, and Kaitlyn grabbed him tight.

"I have seen a great darkness," she whispered.
Tusta moved her over to a couch and sat beside her. Eldrina took a chair across, concern clear on her face. "What is it child?"
Kaitlyn looked to her grandmother. "It is terrible. The Border Wall is going to be broken, the Keep set aflame. Darkness will flow in, led by strange elves. They are the Therin. King Garelin told us about them. Elves with dark souls, who worship an evil god. Their goal is to destroy the elves and enslave all others."
Tears sprung from her eyes, and Tusta again held her close. His gaze went to his mother, and her face showed her feelings. "Beluse, and the elves, must be warned," said Eldrina softly.
Tusta nodded, and she left to send the messages. It was clear Tusta would be busy for a little while longer, and time was of the essence.

Eldrina stood before Temmess. "You are the only one I trust with this."
Temmess stared at the two pieces of parchment in the queen mother's hand. "I can boost the eagle's flight, so it gets there quickly. As for the elves, I will deliver it personally."
"Thank you Temmess," whispered Eldrina before heading back to the castle.

Once out of sight, Temmess went back into her home. She was half the age of the queen mother, but their bond was that of a mother and daughter. In truth, they were aunt and niece. Eldrina's sister, Marla, died in childbirth, a fact no one cared about for the woman was a lady of the night. Pregnant by a customer, and because she wanted to keep the child, she was tossed out of her dwelling. Marla, confused and scared, approached Eldrina, in hopes her sister would help. Eldrina ignored her pleas, and when word of her death was brought to her, something inside Eldrina broke. Taking the child and having her raised among the wizards was the only thing she could do. Temmess was grateful Eldrina had cared that much for her, although she was certain it was a guilty conscious that drove her aunt.

Again, Temmess glanced at the parchments. War was inevitable now. An idea came then. Instead of sending an eagle to Marlsman Keep, she would go herself, and use an eagle to deliver the message to the elves. Although Temmess had never been to the Keep, she had spent much time in a village only two hours away. The transport spell was dangerous for one who didn't have strong abilities, but Temmess didn't care. Time was of the essence.

Beluse paced, as he did every day. The silence was gone, but the strange hum coming from the forest was more unnerving. Far back, fires could be seen at night. All in the fortress knew an army was out there, but they had yet to move closer. Beluse had ordered all but the soldiers to leave. All small villages which lay nearby were evacuated. Beluse had no cause, only the gut feeling something terrible was about to occur. The townsfolk had fought to stay, citing how the wall would never fall. Most soldiers were of the same frame of mind, but Beluse didn't share that thought. No army ever attempted to attack the wall, not one anyone had written about anyway. Now, a very real threat sat outside the wall. It was only a matter of time before they attacked.

A hard knock on the door brought the duke's thoughts back to his study. The person who entered was no stranger, but a truth only the royal family knew about. Held in her hand, was a parchment carrying his mother's seal.

"Thank you for delivering this personally," he said after reading the message contained within.

"I wish to offer my services as well," stated Temmess.

Beluse eyed the woman. Her voice showed worry, but it was most likely for his response, not the task. "My wizards were murdered in a way we still have not figured out. Your life could be in danger."

Temmess stood tall. "I'm not afraid, sire."

Beluse nodded. "Very well. I could use the counsel of a wizard. You may stay."

A servant brought Temmess to the room she would be occupying, and for once in the woman's life, she finally felt like she was going to help her family.

For days, Kaitlyn could barely sleep. Repeatedly, the scene played.

Not once did anything change, and it worried Kaitlyn. With her mother taken ill, and everyone else preparing for an attack from the north, Kaitlyn felt alone, and scared.

Within the village was a small shop, which dealt in herbs and was run by followers of Narkomet. It was here Kaitlyn was headed this day. Being unable to sleep was wearing on the princess, and she knew the shop would contain a powder she could mix into a tea to help her fall asleep. Perhaps, it would even make certain she didn't dream. The shop was colourful, and it brightened Kaitlyn's mood. Beautiful blooms sat in planter boxes out front, and they smelled divine. Inside were two elderly women, and their smiles were infectious. By the time Kaitlyn was making her way back to the castle, she felt certain this night, sleep would finally come.

After gazing down at the city, as she loved to do when the sun was setting, Kaitlyn made her tea. It wasn't long before she began to feel drowsy, so the princess lay down in her bed. Fate once again decided there was something she needed to witness, and with horror, she watched a new scene play before her eyes.

Smoke covered everything, and it took a moment to see why. Fire everywhere. Trees, buildings; nothing was safe. Above, flying around the sky, were dragons. Kaitlyn could feel their dark hearts. It felt the same as those of the Therin. Looking around, Kaitlyn realised she was in Traybidon. The castle was nothing but a crumbling mess.

The scene changed, and she was now on top of a mountain. The dragons still graced the sky, throwing flames at everything. A figure stood above her, so she turned her eyes to the ground. Down below, everything was dead, or chained up. Kaitlyn was shocked to see many of the bodies were Therin. When the vision had begun, Kaitlyn assumed it was another of the coming war. This was further in the future. Whoever was responsible, wanted nothing more than to rule the world, and didn't care who was destroyed to do it. Immediately her thoughts went to Dominic, and she turned her eyes to the figure on top of the mountain. Tears flowed, and she screamed in horror. The figure was not that of her brother, but of Eric.

Kaitlyn awoke, and continued to scream. Servants and guards flowed into her room, but nothing could stop the horror from staying before her eyes. Eric was destined to destroy the world.

CHAPTER THIRTY-THREE

For the second time in as many days, alarms echoed through the city. Brin ordered the nanny to take Tomaz and hide in the room she had set aside for this reason. Arket left before the sun was up and was speaking to the generals outside the main palace door. His plan was to discuss where the best areas to place the men outside the wall. This was interrupted when the second alarm signalled. Brin moved to the balcony and looked down. Her city was going into a panic. Citizens were rushing about, attempting to either leave, or hide. It was too late to set up a defence outside the walls. The enemy was already in the city. Changing into a light pair of leggings, and a thin tunic, Brin decided it was time to end this war.

"We haven't found them yet, sire," growled Changru. "It must be a small group. Most likely they are heading to get to you and the empress." Arket couldn't disagree with Changru, so he changed the focus. "Soldiers will be no match for whomever it is they have sent. We must focus on what we can defend, the sea. Ships are almost here. We cannot allow them to make land."

"My men will keep you both safe," stated Changru.

Anger was clear on the emperor's face. He was not at all happy with the new developments. "Yes, we will need you. However, I wish Boroten to go out, and assess the city situation. You two," he remarked, pointing to Changru and Testra, "along with Morley, will be by our side."

Changru waved for Boroten to leave, and a look of satisfaction crossed his face. For some time, Changru had been getting upset at the lack of protection the two rulers had taken with them. Yes, they were strong with magic, but some things can still get through. He was quite happy to hear the emperor state he was now considering protection.

Coming outside, with Morley close behind, came Brin. "Tomaz is safely hidden," she said, moving around to Arket.

Pulling her close, he whispered, "They will not get to him, I promise."

Turning her head up to see his eyes, Brin saw no fear. "The ships are a half a day away at most. I know the men are adept at fighting on the sea, but I still worry." It was then Arket realised Brin was dressed in travel gear.

Noticing his look, Brin placed a hand on his. "I am going out into the city. The people need to see we are not going to hide from this."

At first, Arket wanted to protest, but she was right. To keep the people on

their side, they had to show no fear. “I will come with you.”
Brin nodded her agreement, and headed to the carriage, the bodyguards, and Arket in tow.

Travel was slow, as many people were out in the streets, wondering what was going on. Changru, Morley, and Testra walked beside the carriage, but allowed the people to move close enough to speak. All questions were the same. What was going on, and who was attacking? Brin on one side, Arket on the other, both answered as many questions as they could. It wasn’t long before the people themselves were spreading the news. Enemies from the north are coming by ship, and some were already in the city. Report anything, or one, who appeared strange. It took many hours, but the city was informed. The enemy within had to see they were out, and not afraid. A thought that amused the rulers. As the sun was setting, they arrived back at the palace. Exhausted, and angry, both headed straight to the war room. Servants brought them food, and both ate out of necessity, but their focus was on planning their next move.

Arket spread out a map of the city, and placed pieces, which represented vessels, on the water. “We have fifteen ships lined up, ready to engage.”
Brin viewed the scene he was displaying and sat back. “I believe we will win the sea battle it is these infiltrators which bother me.”
“They will be found,” remarked Arket absently.
Although Brin didn’t share his comment, she changed the subject. “Should we bring the soldiers inside the walls?”
Arket picked at his plate of food and surveyed where the men were set up. “Not yet. We want the enemy inside to think we are being lax in our efforts. Perhaps Changru is right, and it is just a small band of men. No real threat, just difficult to capture.”
Knowing it would bring on her husband’s ire, Brin stated, “The guards found dead were shot down by a single arrow. It isn’t men in the city, it is elves.”
His wife’s comments did annoy Arket, but he brushed them off. “Men, elves, it means nothing. All will die.”
Time went by, and finally the rulers headed to bed. Both knew they needed to be well rested by morning. Even though the enemy would arrive this night, it was most likely that the ships wouldn’t be engaged until sunrise.

Clouds covered the sun, but another hot day was to come. Cannon fire rang through the city and came to the ears of the rulers. Both were awake and watching intently from their balcony. Bursts of flame came from the cannons, and although more were from the southern fleet, it didn't appear that much damage was occurring to their enemy. An angry look crossed Brin's face, and Arket felt the same. With a wave of her hands, Brin sent a spell towards the enemy fleet. As expected, it bounced aside. Irritation was clear on Brin's face. "Vernia is doing this," she growled.

Arket put his arm around his wife. "We knew magic would be a part of this battle. We need to come up with another plan of attack."

Brin pushed away and stormed inside. "We cannot affect the sea itself. I already tried and felt a strong warning to not attempt it again."

Following his wife inside, Arket sat down in a chair need the patio door. "Mirrah does not take kindly to those trying to change the sea. I must say I am impressed that her brother, Tampest, did not punish you for stealing his hurricane."

Brin stopped her pacing and stared at Arket. "I believe it was his spell, given to someone to use only when necessary. He cannot very well strike down one who uses it."

A chuckle came from her husband, and he shook his head. "Since when do gods ever show kindness or mercy to anyone? He must have been impressed with your power to perform the spell otherwise I do not think this city would still be standing."

Pouring herself a glass of wine, Brin took a chair across from her husband. "There must be a way to break the barriers surrounding those ships."

A soft knock interrupted their discussion. Upon beckoning, Changru entered. "The ships show no sign of gaining ground."

"We know," grumbled Arket, who then waved Changru out. The door had barely closed before another alarm sounded. "The city is on fire," exclaimed the emperor, jumping to his feet.

Anger and shock crossed both of their faces as they ran onto the far balcony to see what was happening.

"The entire west side is in flames," cried Brin in anguish.

Arket turned and stormed to the door, with Brin a step behind. Ripping it open, he ordered the page to send out every guard into the city to fight the blaze and find the ones who set it.

Another page came up, this one stating that the sea was doing something strange and taking their ships down. Instead of looking from their balcony, the two decided to head to the shore. The only way they would be able to stop the enemy from landing was to use whatever magic they could. Arriving at the gate, two carriages waited.

"You need to take care of the fires," Arket stated, pointing west. "I will deal with the enemy on the water."

Brin wanted to be with her husband, but knew he was right. "Of course," she said, hopping into the carriage, and ordering it to where the fires burned strongest.

Arket moved passed the second carriage, and went to the stable. Mounting , the emperor rode to the south barracks. All four generals were outside the city, controlling the soldiers. Those remaining in the barracks were left in case the enemy made it to shore. Arket was happy to see the men were already armed and awaiting instructions. "Follow me to the sea," he shouted, and the soldiers let out a cheer.

It took no time to reach the water, for the city streets were empty. People were either fleeing the city or fighting the fires. The order to evacuate was sent as he and Brin were leaving the palace. It wasn't something they wanted to do, but most city dwellers were a hindrance to a fight.

Arriving, Arket ordered the men to spread out, and watch the ships. Already some of the enemy vessels had turned and were heading in. Scanning the water, Arket was annoyed when he could find no sign of his ships. Allowing his anger to take hold, Arket brought his magic to bear, gripped his sword tight, and awaited the enemy.

CHAPTER THIRTY-FOUR

"The first ships have made shore," hollered a soldier to Arket. Scanning down the lines, the emperor drew a breath, and ordered them to attack. A wave of soldiers, swords drawn and desperate for the blood of the enemy, ran with all their might, and failed. Before they could even come close to engaging the enemy, well placed arrows flew from the ships, killing all within range. Hidden on the vessels, were more elves. All reports had stated only humans were on board. A ruse Arket should have seen through.

Arrows took the first line, making it easier for the ships to get close to land. Gangplanks extended to the shallow waters, and soldiers, poured onto the shore. Arket heard a shout, as more of his soldiers came to his aid. The lead man informed the emperor how they were ordered to come to his side. All he could do was nod and point towards the enemy. His anger only grew when the elves once again sent a volley of arrows towards the shore. The sword fight had moved further inland, so not as many men were taken down. Commotion on the lead vessel attracted Arket's attention, and he watched as the elves threw down their bows and drew swords. Fresh arms, which were much quicker, came at Arket's soldiers.

More soldiers, who came from battling fires, joined the ranks. For a moment, the south army had the upper hand. Sounds of metal clashing rang down the shore for quite some time, but the men, already weakened from fighting the city blaze, were no match for the fresh soldiers of the enemy.

Enemy soldiers swarmed onto the shore, engaging Arket which was preventing him from using magic. Many years had passed since he last felt the joy of actually fighting an enemy. Battle lust raged through his veins, but Arket was frustrated. Magic would have brought these invaders to their knees.

Fighting from his horse gave him a slight advantage but put a target on him. Elven arrows flew at Arket from the water's edge, but none hit the mark, and Arket wondered if they were actually meant to. There was no way he would be able to bring his power to bear while dodging arrows. A simple tactic and one which enraged him more.

Watching soldier after soldier fall to the enemy, Arket could tell the men were beginning to get discouraged. Arket was about to order another wave of soldiers forward, when a woman with white hair appeared in a flash of light in front of him. Before Arket knew what was happening, Vernia blasted him with a spell. Arket gasped as the magic hit. Falling from his horse, Arket gripped his heart. The spell stole a part of his magic, but also a part of his soul. When that was done, another spell hit, burning his skin. The last thought Arket Tzam had before the blackness took him, was wondering the fate of his wife and son.

Volley after volley of arrows poured down into the city from the wall. The guards, try as they might, couldn't get close enough to take out any of the elves. Boroten knew there was little hope. The elves had taken most of the arrows and burned what they couldn't carry. Swords were all the men had left, and they were useless against elven aim. When another volley landed nearby, he ordered a retreat. A page, hiding far from the line of fire, came to Boroten, and informed him of Arket heading for the water. Another approached, and stated the empress had arrived, and was wanting a report. Boroten ordered half the men to the shore, and the rest to Brin's side.

Fires ravaged almost half of the city and were still burning in some areas. The elves had used a type of oil which was quite difficult to put out. Brin ran from street to street, trying to find a way by. Their only chance was if she could blast the elves with magic. A page approached her and informed the queen of the lazzards running to the south, leaving the outer walls defenceless, and of the reports of what happened to their ships. Rage took over Brin, but she kept it in check. The lazzards had agreed to fight for her, came to the city outskirts to train, intimidate, and kill many of her men, yet hadn't raised a claw to assist. It was clear to her now they had never intended to help. For them, it was a scouting mission. What better way to ascertain your prey, then to work along side them? The idea ate at her, and she wished to scream in frustration for being so naive.

Her thoughts went to the fight at sea. Her ships were destroyed, and she knew Koral was the only person who could have achieved such a spell. No one else could control water without having Mirrah punish them. Her gaze turned east, and her thoughts went to her husband. Brin knew her place was here, as they had agreed. One day, she would strike at Koral. This time, making certain she was dead.

People ran passed, and shouts from soldiers could be heard

echoing along the streets. Brin made her way along the rubble, towards the commotion. It wasn't long before Boroten and a handful of soldiers, found her.

"Highness, you shouldn't be here," he said, coming to her side.

Brin pointed to the wall, and looked to her bodyguard. "Is it lost?"

Boroten lowered his head. "Yes, majesty. The elves destroyed all our arrows, and the fires they lit can't be extinguished."

Keeping her temper in check, Brin turned to the faces before her. "Get all inside immediately. The only way to put out those fires is with sand."

The men nodded and ran off. Few remained, so the area was clear within no time. Moving to be in sight of the elves, Brin began chanting. The enemy on the walls stopped firing their arrow and watched. Raising her hands to the sky, Brin created a small sandstorm, lifted it over the wall, and sprinkled the flames. Many moments passed, but eventually the fires were out. By the time the smoke cleared, the elves on the wall were gone. Bodies lay everywhere, and it brought a brief moment of sorrow. Maintaining her composure, Brin ordered the clean-up of the bodies, and city. With that underway, Brin returned to her carriage, and ordered it to the docks.

Fires still licked through the few houses near the water. Brin noticed only a few homes were destroyed, and by the look of it, the fires were controlled. The enemy successfully divided their resources, making the entire city easy prey. A dark scowl crossed her face. She might not have the military background to run an army, but her generals were experienced. There was no way her father, a man who had barely seen war, should have achieved this. As the carriage bounced along, her anger grew worse. Arriving at where the fighting was supposed to be taking place, changed that.

Climbing out of the carriage, Brin allowed tears to fall. Some in anger, but most for her husband. Laying not too far away, was Arket. With a scream, Brin rushed over, and dropped beside him. Taking him into her arms, she sobbed. His body was badly burned, and she thought him dead. Arket gave a slight gasp, and Brin hollered for help. A few soldiers heard her cry, and quickly came to her aid.

"Find something to carry him with," she ordered, and the soldiers scattered.

Within an hour, the emperor was in his bed, surrounded by healers. Brin sat in the throne room, dictating how she wished to proceed to those who stood before her. The people were proud of their empress and vowed to make the city great again.

The captains manoeuvred the ships in close, and the elves kept down along the rail.

"A few more yards, and they will be in range," whispered Olrond.

All heard, and nodded.

A man sat upon a horse, and Olrond knew it was the emperor. He was large, and would have towered over his men, even if he wasn't on a horse. Soldiers lined up along either side of him, and as the vessels came in, he hollered to attack. Olrond ordered the gangplanks down, and the soldiers awaited the order to attack. As the enemy approached, the elves stood, and arrows flew at the front line. Olrond looked to the enemy leader, and saw his face grow red. It brought a smile to the general. He hadn't been certain their ruse would work, but it was clear the enemy hadn't seen any elves on board. With a holler, Olrond sent the soldiers onto the shore.

With the first wave taken down by arrows, the enemy line was leery of approaching. Olrond had anticipated this and knew they would have to meet the enemy further away from the shore, thus making it difficult for the elves to fire arrows. The enemy came down to meet them but instead of driving them back to the water, they were backing up towards the city. Again, Olrond expected this tactic. A second wave of enemy soldiers came up and engaged. For a moment, the enemy appeared to be gaining ground, then the elves, realising their arrows were useless, drew swords. A few remained on board to protect the vessels, and crew, but the rest ran out, striking down the enemy with quick swipes. Finally, they were winning the fight.

Vernia stood on deck, watching the battle unfold. Her eyes found Arket, and never left him. Should he be able to use magic, they would lose this fight. Fortunately, the elves were keeping him occupied with random arrow shots near. Vernia wondered why they weren't hitting the mark, and realised the horse most likely had a protection spell around it, causing the arrows to veer off. The fight shifted in their favour, but it was still taking a toll on the men. Understanding what was needed Vernia called upon her magic, moving herself to stand before the emperor. As expected, she sensed a token around the horse, so her focus became that of the emperor himself. With a few words, she attached herself to his magic, draining it. It was something she had done often to those who refused to join the Order of Maget. Along with draining their magic, came a part of their soul. This man's soul was dark, and Vernia hoped she wouldn't get lost. Using all of her power, Vernia broke the connection, and blasted him with fire. Vernia's goal was to end Arket. She never had the chance, for General Traug ordered everyone back to the ships. The fight was won, and a hasty retreat before more soldiers arrived was warranted.

Back on board, everyone watched as smoke continued to rise from the city. The wind was on their side, and so the captain's pointed the bow to the north and left the Saviour's Empire to wallow in defeat.

CHAPTER THIRTY-FIVE

Sitting up on the ridge, Gillock's gaze was to the north. Finally, he was understanding so much, and it must be kept a secret. Koral and Eric returning magic weakened the elven spells on this land. The wizard didn't know what it meant, but he knew it wasn't something that would benefit humans, or elves. The group began to stir, so he made his way back to camp. Time was not on their side.

"There is a small village, as the mermaid stated," remarked Firadon, coming up from the forest. "They have some smaller vessels used for travelling. The people appear very quaint. I don't think speaking to them is a good idea."

Eric stopped packing up his belongings and looked to the big man. "Are you suggesting we steal one?"

Aremeth chuckled. "Already done," he said, pointing to the river.

Eric shook his head, as everyone gathered their things. Once done, they followed the two to a small inlet, surrounded by reeds. Hiding within, was a boat big enough to fit them all.

"Well, we aren't getting anywhere standing here," hollered Firadon, pointing to the vessel.

"There are only two oars," pointed out Simian.

"The river only flows west," stated Gillock, pointing to the water.

As odd as it was, his words were true. The ocean was only a short way off, yet the water flowed away. Placing their packs in the centre, everyone climbed in, and they were off.

From shore, the river appeared to flow fast, but once out in it, the small boat needed to be rowed. This fact wouldn't have bothered Gillock had they still been in friendly territory, however, something was off, and the wizard was bothered by a nagging feeling.

"What unusual water this is," remarked Simian.

Tark agreed, and reached over the side to feel it. The moment his fingers graced the water, it changed, and Gillock realised what was wrong.

"Remove your hand!" he shouted, although Tark already had.

"What is it?" asked Eric.

Gillock looked down, and dread took him. "This river was placed here to keep the dark elves within. It can't tell the difference between one of dark, and one of light. Now, it's going to stop us."

His last words hung in the air, and the truth was shown. The relatively calm river now began to surge. Rapids developed all around the small vessel and it wasn't long before they were being tossed about.
"Use the oars and try to head to the other side," hollered Firadon, grabbing one.
Aremeth grabbed the other, and both pushed with all their might. Slight headway was made, but the river wasn't finished. Stronger churning came, and when they were more than halfway across, the boat capsized, tossing everyone, and their belongings, into the frothing waters. Gillock knew the target would be the two elves, so once his head was above the water, he began chanting a spell. Water splashed his face as he tried to cast, but his determination was strong. The two elves broke the surface, and rose above the river, as if an invisible hand plucked them up. Moving them swiftly over the water, Gillock hurdled them at the far shore. More waves splashed over his face, and all Gillock could do was hope he had succeeded. Now, his focus needed to be on himself, and the others. It wasn't an issue, though, for only a few seconds after the elves were out of sight, the water began to calm. Not wanting to take any chances, everyone made their way to the shore.

"We managed to keep a few of the packs," said Firadon, dropping the wet supply packs on the shore.
Eric built a small fire, and hoped things wouldn't take too long to dry out.
Firadon patted Eric on the back. "It's summer, kid. Shouldn't take more than a couple of hours for everyone to dry."
Gillock sat down and looked to the elves. "I should have realised that would happen. This land was designed to keep elves in."
Tark glared at the wizard. "Not elves, Therin."
Gillock locked eyes with Tark and didn't waver. "Your wizards apparently didn't see fit to have the spells differentiate between your two races."
Anger and silence hung heavy within the group, and Eric hoped it was only temporary. He couldn't afford for anyone to go rogue on this mission.

By midday, they were again on their way. This time following the shore. The area was marshlands, and once they travelled for a bit, a path presented itself. After many minutes of discussion, they agreed it would be safer to move inland than to travel along a river bent on killing elves.

As the sun began to set, the bugs came out. Firadon pulled out his special salve, passing it to everyone. "Don't have much, so here's hoping this is the only day we need it."

Their steps were careful on the marsh trail. Water oozed up with each footfall, but it was firm enough to allow passage. Noises of crickets and other marsh creatures followed them for a time, then stopped. Once silence was all about them, trepidation set in, and weapons came to bear. Gillock and Dorien brought their magic forth should they be attacked. No words were spoken as they continued down the trail, although each one had their guard up. Something was nearby, and the silence could only mean one thing: danger.

Simian, still recovering from his injury, took the lead, and it was his undoing. Coming around a bend then saw a strange being, which appeared female, standing on the trail. Covered in marsh grass, as if it were a dress, the woman stepped towards them. Before the Simian could ask what she wanted, a blast of magic came from her, tossing the elf into the marsh. Simian's dead eyes stared up at the group, before sinking into the murky water. Although Dorien and Gillock had spells on their lips, both found they were unable to speak. Instead of panicking, each one tried to break down the dampening spell the strange woman was projecting. It wasn't long before Dorien felt it weakening, and a smile crossed his young lips.

"You dare trespass in my marsh," hissed the creature.
Raising her arm again, she released another blast. Dorien, although unable to perform a strong spell, was able to do a basic one. As soon as she released her magic, Dorien placed a shield around them. This time, her magic hit the shield, which turned the spell back on her. With a screech, the creature vanished into the marsh. For many seconds her screams could be heard, and then once again, there was silence.

Although Tark wanted to find the body of his brother, he knew to tarry would be their deaths. The marsh witch was wounded by her own magic, but once healed would most likely come after them again. Taking the lead, the elf ran the rest of the trail, with the companions close behind. For another hour they ran, until the marsh trail became hard. Not long after, a forest sat before them. Still, they ran, until they came upon a glade. Here, Tark stopped, allowing them to finally catch their breath.
"We can make camp here," he said, then left to scout the area.

The trees were tall and the brush around them thick. Eric was impressed at how much this area looked like home. Although the shock of losing Simian was still fresh in their hearts, everyone knew rest and food were necessary to continue in this strange land. A fire was made, to warm their bodies, and to cook over. Not much was left for food in the packs, so Aremeth and Firadon went to see if they could catch something. It wasn't long before they returned with two rabbits. The meal was bland, but filling. Something they all needed. Barely any words were spoken, and after deciding watch detail, the rest went to sleep.

Dawn approached, and Aremeth, last one on watch, heard a familiar sound in the distance. The sun was creeping up, so he woke his companions. Once they had a meagre breakfast, and were packed, Aremeth spoke of what he heard.

"Are you certain?" asked Gillock.

"I know horses, Gillock. There is a herd just beyond the trees, I'm positive," replied Aremeth.

Firadon faced the direction Aremeth had pointed to. "Horses you say. Maybe we should take a look."

Gillock wanted to argue but held his tongue. This was a foreign land and investigating anything at could mean danger. However, horses could make their trip go much quicker. With a wave of his arm, he motioned them off towards the horses.

It took nearly an hour to traverse the thick woods, but once free, a great plain lay before them. Shouting could be heard, so they moved back into the tree line. To be seen by whoever was with the horses could mean death. Time passed and began to try their patience. Eric was about to say as much when the sound of galloping hooves came to their ears. Around a bend of trees came six, but they weren't horses. Sniffing the air, and glancing about, were six enormous centaurs. Everyone stiffened at the sight, and Firadon motioned them to move carefully into the forest. Aremeth agreed to stay, to ensure the centaurs didn't follow, but it was for not. As they turned to move further in, another four centaurs stood waiting. The centaurs were angry, and the spears they had aimed at the four made their intent clear. They were now prisoners.

Firadon raised his arms to show he meant no harm, but it was for not. One of the centaurs drew a pouch. Reaching in, he pulled powder from within. With a puff, the creature blew the powder into their faces, causing all to fall unconscious. Scooping up the bodies, the centaurs let out a holler, and ran back onto the plain. Tark, hiding in a tree, and Aremeth, hiding just below, watched the ordeal with despair.

Tark jumped down, landing quietly beside Aremeth. "We must follow, but at a distance. Their sense of smell is keen."

Aremeth agreed, and the two headed out, with the hopes of rescuing their friends foremost on their mind.

CHAPTER THIRTY-SIX

After weeks of travel, the ships were pulling into the Keenley harbour. They had lost one ship on the trek home. It was damaged in the fight and couldn't handle the storms they traversed through. With the remaining ships being tossed about, none could offer aid. All hands were lost, and it made Vernia angry. They won their fight, but lost men to a ridiculous storm. Standing on deck as they made their way to the dock, Vernia stared at the castle. Home, but would it ever truly feel that way to her?

Finally off the ships, the soldiers made their way to their homes. The war was over, and now, they could relax with their families. Koral and Glavlin said their goodbye's to Glomain upon exiting their vessel. Koral wanted to see her parents, but Glavlin had already been away for far longer than he wanted to. His home needed its king. Darly agreed to stay and give a report to King Jeremy and watched as the two headed into the city.

Seated in the throne room, Queen Elizanne and King Jeremy looked to those before them. General Traug, Glomain, and Darly each gave their report. The loss of those on the one vessel brought a heaviness to their tales. They had won the war, and it would be some time before Brin would consider attacking the north again. No one present thought it was over with the young woman. One day, she would threaten their livelihood again, and the kingdom needed to be ready.

Jeremy motioned for the three to take their leave and turned to Elizanne. "The fight was won, but I fear more is to come."

Elizanne placed her hand on his and smiled. "We will be ready."

Another month passed, and fall was full on. Jeremy announced the new patrol towers, and how ferry travel down the newly formed River Divide connected the Central Lands to Lungast. A new village was set up to house soldiers, as well as give another landing area to those transporting goods. Another village came into being, and sat between the boundary, and library. The area was expanding, and it occurred to Jeremy that perhaps it was time to give the Central Lands a new name.

"Any ideas?" Jeremy asked those before him.

Elizanne smirked, as all had a blank stare.

"It is a grand idea, father," said Koral. She and Glavlin had just returned from checking on their land. Koral knew her father had plans, but this was

not something she had anticipated.
Glomain stepped forward. "If I may, highness. As you know, the Cyprian Forest elves have named their city Eldarson. In the ancient elven language, it means reborn ones. Perhaps, you should come up with something which reflects what you see the future of your lands to be."
All agreed it was a good idea, but that didn't help with a name. Jeremy dismissed them all but asked for suggestions by the evening meal.

The day dragged on, and Jeremy dealt with the many issues brought before him. Some nobility were questioning the details of the night's feast. Rolling his eyes after reading the third message requesting ridiculous things at the feast tonight, Jeremy threw it in the pile. More matters were brought up, and the king wondered if the day would ever end. When everything was finally done, Jeremy left the throne room. His thoughts were of his own chamber, and the relaxing bath which awaited him.

Hoping for a moment's rest, Jeremy locked the door, and settled into the tub. Sipping wine, and reflecting on the day, the name came to him. With a smile spanning from ear to ear, King Jeremy finally relaxed.

With the setting sun, guests began to arrive. Cross looks were apparent on the faces of the nobles who specified their seating, and other ridiculous things. When the king moved to the head of the table, silence enveloped the room. Everyone settled into their seats, and all noticed the look of glee on Jeremy's face.

Jeremy beckoned for silence. "Before we feast, I would like to announce the new name for the Central Lands. From this day forth, these lands will be known as Free-Realm."
It took a moment for the nobility, and guests, to register the name. This was immediately followed by a cheer, and clapping. It was a perfect name for a land which was once held under a cloud of fear. Now, it was clear. All who lived in the land would know acceptance.

The meal was a grand affair, with delicacies from the Realm of Lungast at its centre. Excitement at the new prospects, and villages popping up. The land was beginning to heal from the years of fear, and flourishing. It was stated that one day soon, the king and queen of Lungast would be present at a feast, a thought which intrigued the greedy nobility.

Announcements began, and they started with the Duke and Duchess of Hope's Light Keep having a daughter, Mahnay. With the ending of the war, came new beginnings, so Koral and Glavlin announced their engagement. Glomain decided to speak as well, informing all that a son had been born to King Garelin and Queen Alyarra, and they named him Gitson. Toast after toast occurred and the wine makers rejoiced.

The party ran well into the night, and although the royal family wondered how Eric was faring, they allowed themselves this one night of merriment. Tomorrow they would worry about Eric and Gillock. The morning would bring announcements sent to all areas of Free-Realm, as well as notices to Traybidon. The days following would be filled with wonder. Tonight, they celebrated.

EPILOGUE

Brin looked from her balcony to the city below. They were lucky the fires left the palace alone. Tomaz was never in any danger, and Brin was quite thankful for that. The fires were all out, and the citizens rebuilding. Brin knew the importance of keeping their loyalty, so she personally went to each home, giving funds to help rebuild, and condolences to those who lost loved ones. It took her weeks to see every soul, but felt it was worth it.

Moving back inside, she took the chair set up beside the bed, and took her husband's hand. Arket was alive but had a long way to go before he would be out of the woods. "My love, you were right. It was wrong of me to go after the north, especially with such an inexperienced army. I promise this, you're wounding, and the destruction, will be avenged. One day, we will push to the north, and take it all. For now, we will be a family, and rebuild our city to its glory." Holding his hand to her lips, she kissed it softly. Brin stood, closed the curtains, and then left the room.

The four loyal bodyguards stood in the hall and followed Brin. When she arrived at the war room, the man she had requested stood within. "You are the greatest shipbuilder I have. Build me another fleet. One which can travel great distances."

The man bowed low. "It shall be done, highness."

Brin smiled, and left, her guards following close behind. Brin kept walking until she was outside, taking a deep breath, she turned to her men. "I need soldiers. When the ships are built, I wish each of you to captain one. Take them to every corner they can reach. Bring me back ones who wish to fight, and slaves. We will need both in the coming years." The four bowed, and Brin smiled a dark cruel smile. "It may take years, but we will have our revenge."

They didn't reply and didn't have to. They were on board for whatever the rulers of Kaijitsa-Mur wished.

****

Deep in the heart of what the Realm of Lungast refers to as the Unforgiving Wilderness, live the Therin. If they were seen by a human from the realm, they would wonder at the sight. The Therin are elves, but ones whose hearts and souls are dark. Blood and sacrifice rule their world. Their skin is so pale it almost appears translucent. Their hair, black as coal. The only variation in their look is the eyes. The colours range.

For centuries, they had been waiting for a sign. A sign which would signal the start of a prophecy. One which told of how they would rule the world. They had no idea what existed outside of their land. Most rarely even left the fortress, having wiped out all the races which had lived nearby decades ago. Most of the time, if they left the fortress, it was to scout, and hunt. No one had dared try to attack them for centuries. The fortress was a giant wall and backed onto a great mountain. The mountain dipped down and created a formation that when the moon was right, appeared cradled in it.

Tonight, the entire Therin community was gathered below this point. The high priest was chanting. The prophecy said that their rule would start with the coming of winged demons, whose fire would burn anything in its path. Two years earlier, this had come to pass. Now, all eyes were to the sky. The moon was full, and the night clear. It was time to send out the army. Time to destroy the wall; the magical barrier keeping them in this land. It had been weakened, and now it was time to take it down.

*****

Taint still stained the grove, and the Earth Mother knew there was no cure for it. Tem-Pater, the Time Father, was to blame. This was the name he went by now. One given to him by the followers she lost. Standing in the area which represented the mate she once had, brought a heaviness to her heart. Eons had passed, yet the truth remained. Melarandra had been wild and untamed, and she along with it. He was no better. Light took her, dark he. Balance must always be maintained, but he was a bitter soul. Love once joined them, and in a way, it still existed.

The Earth Mother reached for a leaf, brown and dying. Not all leaves on his tree were this way, and she knew it meant he was once again a strong power. Tears came then, for she understood what it meant, and it was her fault. Koral had done everything asked, and it brought a prophecy to being. One no one in their lands knew about. Dragons were again about, and two went west. The sign to the Therin it was time to move against the east, against their cousins, who cast them out, and bound them to the Unforgiving Wilderness. Soon, the elves would know an enemy the like they have never seen. Blood would flow in Almberson, and the humans of Lungast would be caught in the middle. Dropping to her knees, the Earth Mother wept.

www.ingramcontent.com/pod-product-compliance
Ingram Content Group UK Ltd.
Pitfield, Milton Keynes, MK11 3LW, UK
UKHW041855190726
13854UKWH00002B/922

9 781544 730486